WITH A TWIST

New York Times and USA Today Bestselling Author

Sawyer Bennett

ISBN: 978-1-940883-26-7

Find Sawyer on the web!
www.sawyerbennett.com
www.twitter.com/bennettbooks
www.facebook.com/bennettbooks

Table of Contents

Prologue	1
Chapter 1	7
Chapter 2	20
Chapter 3	36
Chapter 4	46
Chapter 5	59
Chapter 6	72
Chapter 7	85
Chapter 8	99
Chapter 9	110
Chapter 10	122
Chapter 11	134
Chapter 12	146
Chapter 13	159
Chapter 14	171
Chapter 15	185
Chapter 16	198
Chapter 17	210
Chapter 18	222
Chapter 19	235
Chapter 20	247
Chapter 21	260
Chapter 22	272
Chapter 23	282
Chapter 24	293
Epilogue	306

Acknowledgments

To my fabulous cousin, GM… FBI agent extraordinaire, best trout fisherman ever and all around amazing human being.

PROLOGUE

Wyatt

I LOOK AROUND at all my friends gathered here to wish me well... to tell me goodbye. Fuck, I'm going to miss them. The whole crazy lot of them. I have no clue when I'll be able to return.

The back deck of Gavin and Savannah's beach mansion in Duck, North Carolina is monstrous, large enough to hold our ever-growing crew, plus about two hundred others. They're hosting my farewell party because let's face it... who doesn't want to party at a mega mansion on the beach?

For early April, it turned out to be a relatively warm day... as long as the wind doesn't kick up. Every once in a while, a westerly breeze comes off the Atlantic, causing the women to huddle in closer to their men to ward off the spring chill.

Almost everyone in our group has fallen to that miraculous emotion known as love. First, it was Hunter, my best friend in the world. We've known each other our entire lives and I knew when he finally

1

fell, he'd go crashing hard. It just happened to be with Gabby, his little sister's best friend, and I honestly didn't think that would happen. Gabby had some misplaced rage toward Hunter for the longest time, but he finally wore her down. Now she wears his engagement ring on a necklace around her neck, because she works in construction and doesn't want to damage it. I wonder when they'll get married, but they don't seem to be in a rush. Hunter owns a bar— The Last Call—and Gabby is a general contractor. Both of them are so focused on their careers, I doubt I'll be hearing the wedding bells anytime soon. In fact, I wouldn't be surprised if they just trotted off to the local judge on their lunch hour or something to get the deed done.

Just as Hunter's identical twin brother, Brody, had done when he married Alyssa.

Brody and Hunter got engaged at the same time while vacationing with their girls together, and I suppose that's a twin thing. I just assumed they'd have a joint wedding ceremony, but Alyssa put a kink in that plan by getting knocked up. It wasn't planned, but the baby was no less wanted at that time. Brody just hauled Alyssa off to the courthouse and got married, proclaiming they could have a ceremony after the birth if she still wanted to.

Looking at her now, with Brody's arm around her back as she cuddles their son, Trey, I don't think a ceremony will be forthcoming. I'd say they have everything they need right there.

Another baby cries, and my eyes slide over to Gavin and Savannah. Their daughter Clare was born almost a month ago, exactly ten days before Trey was born. There's apparently already talk of betrothing the two of them or something.

Gavin takes Clare from Savannah's arms, rocking her back and forth. She immediately quiets, and I hope that when I have a child one day, I'm as good with him or her as my friends are with theirs. Gavin and Savannah have yet to get married. Have yet to get engaged for that matter, but it doesn't seem to bother them. I asked Gavin about it when we had a guys' night out, and he said he wanted to marry her like yesterday, but that they always seemed to get caught up in life and raising a baby. It's coming though... I guarantee it.

"You nursing mothers are putting a serious crimp in my ability to party with my girls," Casey complains as she reaches a finger out to stroke along Clare's tiny nose.

My lips quirk upward as I look at the stunningly beautiful Casey Markham. She's Hunter and Brody's little sister, and by little, I mean she's four years younger than we are yet larger than life at the tender age of twenty-five. In addition to me, she remains single.

But she is unlike me in that she likes it that way. She burns through rich and sophisticated men the

3

way my grandma used to burn through copper at the penny slots in Atlantic City.

I'm definitely different from Casey.

I'm ready to settle down.

I've never seen Hunter and Brody look more peaceful or happy in their lives. I've only come to know Gavin over the past year, but I watched a self-proclaimed prick turn into a mushy teddy bear because of his woman.

Yeah, I want that shit too.

But it doesn't look like it's going to come soon. Not with me leaving and all.

"Going to miss you, dude," Hunter says as he steps over to me and leans against the deck railing.

I hold my bottle of Sam Adams up, and he clinks his beer against mine. "Going to miss you too, man."

"So you really have no idea how long it will be?" he asks genially as we look out over the ocean.

"Nah... they've told me to be prepared for several months probably. I'm going in cold to an established operation, and it's going to take a while to build trust."

"And you can't tell me a hint of where you're going or what you'll be doing?" he asks with a grin, nudging my shoulder with his. "Come on... I'm your best friend, for Christ sake."

"Dude... you know that's not how it works. You've seen me do this before, and you know I can't tell you."

"Fine," Hunter says as he raises his hands up in capitulation, and then swigs down the rest of his beer. "Just don't get your ass shot and you better fucking come back in one piece."

Reaching out, I give him a playful punch in his stomach, which causes him to issue a slight *oomph*, and I tip my bottle up to finish my beer as well. I need to head out. I have to get an early start tomorrow, and the last thing I need is a hangover.

This is my second time going undercover as a cop. I used to work in narcotics back when I first started with the Nags Head PD, and I went undercover to bust up a small trafficking ring here on the island. It was a short operation because the ring was minor, and that's testament to the fact that we're a fairly small community.

This is different though.

I'm being loaned out to a joint task force of the Raleigh Police Department and the FBI. What they have planned for me is much bigger. I haven't been given many details, but I do know that it involves a suspected sex-slave ring that covers the entire southeastern region of the United States and it happens to be based in Raleigh. The FBI is involved because it crossed state lines when one of the victims escaped and was found in Denver, but was originally abducted in Raleigh.

Tomorrow, I start a new life. I'll be debriefed for a few days and immersed in my new identity. Then begins the work of getting my foot in the door.

It could take months… maybe a year, who knows. It's all about gaining trust and building a case from the inside.

My life is going to be put on hold, and that warm and fuzzy desire I get when I look at my friends in love is going to have to chill out for a while. I volunteered for this, knowing that a successful bust will pretty much make my career going forward. It was too good of a chance to pass up, but until then… love is just going to have to wait for me.

CHAPTER 1
Wyatt

"RAZE... THERE'S A drunk douche up in VIP Room Number Two who won't take no for an answer. Not sure why Misty is telling him 'no' but go get a handle on it," Lance Portman says as he grips my shoulder to help get my attention over the thumping music. Luckily, the name Raze comes completely natural to me now, and I think if someone actually called me Wyatt, I wouldn't react very quickly.

That's merely a product of being deep undercover for the past three months, living as Charles "Razor" Hawkins... Raze to my friends, criminal acquaintances, and coworkers. I've completely assumed this new identity and outside of the disgust over working in a sleazy strip joint called The Platinum Club, everything else has been going well on this operation.

I nod at Lance, who is second in command here, and turn away, heading for the staircase. Out of the corner of my eye, I see Leisha crawling across the stage toward a patron who is waving a fifty-dollar bill at her, her huge double Ds swinging back and forth. Catching Leon's eye, I jerk my head upward so he knows I'm heading upstairs and to keep an eye on the stage. More than once, a fight had broken out when Leisha started jiggling her tits in front of the patrons, and Leon is one of the more reliable bouncers in here. I don't hesitate to remove myself from the main floor as long as he's around. His huge, ham-sized biceps are enough to handle even the rowdiest of customers while I'm gone.

My job here as the general manager is multi-faceted. On the legal side of things, I oversee the management of all the dancers and supporting staff of bartenders and bouncers, and I handle inventory and cash the registers out each night for deposit. I manage schedules, and I'm on duty every night to make sure things go off without a hitch. General business management stuff.

On the not-so-legal side of things, I oversee quite a bit too. Once I was brought into the circle of trust, one of my first criminal acts was to start vetting customers that wanted more than just a lap dance.

Yeah, I essentially became an in-house pimp and made sure that horny men with the right amount of cash could get a blow job or a fuck from one of the dancers if they passed muster.

Which is why I'm heading up to VIP Two now. Misty has two gentlemen—and I use that term loosely—in there with her. They are repeat customers, big spenders, and Simon would want them well cared for. Despite the oily feeling it gives me, I need to get Misty back on board with what she's promised them or else it's my ass Simon will be all over... because this little prostitution side business is how I first entered the circle of trust with him.

Simon Keyes is my main target—my objective in this sting.

He owns The Platinum Club, along with a variety of other semi-legitimate businesses. A pawnshop that actually fronts stolen goods, a Western Union franchise that cashes forged welfare checks for a cut of the proceeds, and a bakery that fronts as a meth operation. None of those businesses interests me, the Raleigh PD, or the FBI though.

No, the business we have our eye on is one that is very covert and has taken me quite some time to inch my way in on. That's because if Simon is ever busted for what I'm looking at him for, he's going away forever, and so, he's very picky as to who he brings into his circle of trust.

Simon Keyes is in the sex-slave trade. He came upon the FBI's radar about two years ago when they investigated a woman's claim from out in Denver, who showed up at the police station. Her name is Laney Tellar, and her story was that she had been abducted and sold into sexual slavery. She had no clue where she was being held, stating that it was on a private estate in a nondescript neighborhood. She was never out of chains for the entire time of her captivity, so she never even knew what state she was in. However, her owner—Master as she was told to call him—apparently couldn't be separated from her and insisted she go on a business trip with him to Denver. He kept her in chains there too, drugged and gagged when he was away, right in the posh hotel room he had booked for three days.

His mistake was in leaving the key to the cuffs on the nightstand while he went to take a shower one evening, and she made a quick break for it. By the time the police had gotten her statement and sent units to the hotel, the man was long gone. He had, of course, checked in under an alias and no trace of him could be found. Laney reported it took them approximately six hours to reach Denver by stretch limo from wherever she was being held, so the geographical radius of her prison could be ascertained but not much else.

The one thing Laney did know, however, was that she was abducted from Raleigh, North Carolina, where she had been living since dropping out of college at the age of nineteen. By age twenty, she had been dancing at The Platinum Club and was hooked on cocaine. Her last clear memories of North Carolina were going to bed at night in her little dingy apartment on Cowell Street in downtown. She woke up gagged with her hands and feet tied, rolling around the back of a cargo van.

She met her Master two days after that, enduring nearly two months of almost daily rapes before she was able to escape.

There was nothing to tie The Platinum Club or Simon Keyes to the abduction. He was known to the police and had done a few stints in prison for his various crimes, but other than his shady past, there wasn't one solid lead to tie Simon to the abduction. The only thing that kept the FBI's eye on him was the fact that over the past two years, numerous dancers who worked there would mysteriously go missing. They just wouldn't show up for work and turnover was abnormally high for this industry, which usually provided these women with more money than they could ever dream of. Down-on-their-luck women just didn't walk away from that type of cash.

The police and FBI knew the turnover was high because they had a man on the inside. He was just a bouncer and never stood a chance to make it into the circle of trust, because that wasn't his job. He was instructed to just watch and report, and that is what he did for almost eighteen months, alerting the investigators to the abnormally large amount of women that just never showed up for work as scheduled. The police would surreptitiously move in for follow up, trying to track down the women, but they could never be found. Their apartments were as if they had just left for a walk around the neighborhood. All of their clothes and personal effects were still there, including their wallets and identification. They had clearly been kidnapped. Even in the three months I've been here, two more of the dancers have gone missing. The sad part is that there's never anyone to claim them as missing. No family... no friends. The women had clearly been targeted as members of society that no one will ever miss.

Based on industry averages, of which the FBI has a statistic for about everything you could ever want to know, and the fact that when these women simply vanished, they had become convinced that the strip club, and more importantly, Simon Keyes, was very much involved in something nefarious.

The hypothesis was the sex-slave trade, and they needed solid proof tying him to it. They needed someone on the inside to bring it down and save these women.

My journey into the circle of trust was rocky. Getting the job was easy enough. The FBI provided me with a rock-solid alias as Charles "Razor" Hawkins. I was a man that had served time in the pen for drug dealing, getting the name "Razor" for my handiwork with...well... you guessed it, a razor. I came to Simon Keyes highly recommended by an FBI informant who was still active in the criminal underworld and did favors for the government in exchange for certain favors they would bestow upon him. Said informant knew Simon Keyes well and had some minor ties to the mafia, so his word was pretty solid.

Simon hired me on the spot after an impromptu interview, while we sat at the edge of the main stage one afternoon and watched tits and ass gyrating all over the place.

Starting as a bouncer, I soon proved my worth. I constantly accepted small "assignments" from Simon that I'm sure were illegal, but he didn't trust me enough to tell me the details. It may have been "picking up a package" from an associate to "delivering a briefcase full of money" to another associate. I never asked questions, did my job well, and proved to Simon that I was loyal and could keep my mouth shut. Within two months, I was promoted to General Manager.

My first major breakthrough in gaining Simon's criminal trust had to do with the prostitution that was rampant within the club. I had been told ahead of time during my debriefing that the club had been busted a time or two for it. It was small potatoes and nothing that could bring Simon Keyes down. But it gave me an in with him. It didn't take me very long to figure out it was pervasive and that most of the women were in on it. Watching footage of the cameras that were installed in the VIP rooms confirmed it for me.

So I made my move.

"Simon... got a minute?" I had asked as I

knocked on his office door one night after closing.

Despite the fact that this guy was a complete scum, you'd never know it by outward appearances. He was a good-looking guy at age forty-two with stylish, dark hair, thousand-dollar suits, and a cultured air of civility about him.

"Sure... come on in, Raze," he told me as he closed a ledger book on his desk and then stood up from his chair. I walked in, shut the door, and watched as he opened up a safe behind his desk. After he stowed the ledger in there and shut the door, he turned around and sat back down, directing me with a sweep of his hand to take a chair opposite his desk.

"What's up?" he asked as he steepled his hands in front of his face.

"Listen... I've been watching things carefully, and I think you got a problem. The girls are fucking the customers for extra money in the VIP rooms."

I watched him carefully for his reaction, but I really didn't need it to confirm what I already knew. That Simon Keyes was very much aware that this was going on in his club. The man never missed a thing and because he got a portion of the girl's tips each night, he knew exactly where they were making that type of dough.

"Oh, really?" he said neutrally. "That's not good."

"It's not good the way it's going down," I told him, watching him cock a curious eyebrow at me. I pressed on. "There's no reason why you shouldn't be getting a cut of that business. Those girls are working on your clock. Any money they make... well, that's only because you give them the opportunity to dance here."

I paused and waited for his reaction. I saw it... just the tiniest of uplift to the corners of his mouth and deep interest in his eyes.

Still... he was cautious with me, because I was not in the circle of trust yet. "But prostitution is illegal. I don't need that kind of heat."

I snorted hard... for dramatic effect, and leaned forward in my chair. "Don't matter if you don't get caught," I told him smugly. "I just hope you're getting a fair cut off that action for yourself."

Simon's eyes narrowed for an instant, and then he opened the door for me, giving me my first glimpse inside his circle. There were only two people there that I knew of so far. Simon Keyes and his right-hand man, Lance Portman.

"I already know the girls are fucking for money, and I get a cut," he said, while flicking off imaginary lint from the corner of his suit coat. His gaze was intent, gauging me for weakness.

I expected no different, and my answer was ready. I wanted to show him I was ready to be in the circle.

"Not really surprised," I said with praise, stroking his already over-inflated ego. "You're a savvy businessman after all. But I can make you more money."

He looked at me thoughtfully and leaned forward on his desk. "How's that?"

"I've got some experience in this. Right now, you've got a handful of regular customers that partake. I'm betting I could vet out additional potential customers, set a price menu... charge big because these fuckers will pay for it, and then you split the net with the girls fifty-fifty. Plus, I can smell an undercover cop a mile away."

This was true since I was a cop myself, but that was something Simon would never know. I needed to get word to my handler that the local police needed to lay off Simon for a while... let this little prostitution scheme play out so I could use it as a platform to get Simon to trust me further.

"And what do you want out of this? For your troubles?" he asked with a hard glint in his eye.

I leaned forward and looked at him confidently. "Ten percent off the top. I'll increase the business, keep the girls safe, and make sure you never get busted by the cops."

Simon's eyes gleamed with greed, and I knew it was a done deal.

Although the thought of being a john caused my stomach to roll, at least I was now inside the circle of trust.

Of course, my ten-percent take goes straight into evidence, to add onto the other charges I hope to layer on top of this guy until he's buried.

I reach the top of the stairs, turn right, and make my way down a narrow hallway that houses three of the VIP rooms. Each one is furnished with couches, plush chairs, and a private stripper pole. Each room also has a large, tinted glass wall that overlooks the interior of the club, so the VIP patrons can watch the private show or watch what's going on down on the stage.

I open the door to VIP Two and find Misty sitting on the couch, one leg crossed over the other, filing her nails in bored fashion. She's wearing a red corset trimmed in black lace, a thong, and black platform heels. Her blonde hair is up in her trademark long ponytail. She once confided in me that she wears it that way so her hair doesn't get in the way when she's sucking a guy off.

Classy, that one is.

Two of our repeat customers who take advantage of the VIP rooms a few times a week stand over in the corner. The one, who I know goes by Scott, marches up to me angrily.

"We've paid the bitch, and now she won't put out," he says, spittle flying everywhere.

I calmly wipe a spot from under my eye and look over at Misty. "That true?"

She looks up at me, her dark eyes wide and innocent. "He wants double penetration, and I don't take it up the ass for a measly five hundred. If that's all they can pay, one can have my pussy and the other my mouth."

I fight hard not to grimace with distaste but turn back to the men. "It's a thousand for what you guys want. If five hundred is all you have, then you get some mouth/pussy action but that's it."

The guys grumble but pull out their wallets, pulling out an extra five-hundred dollars. Scott counts through it quickly and then hands it to Misty, muttering curse words. She calmly takes the money, stuffs it in the garter around her leg, and then proceeds to start removing her corset.

I turn around to leave, knowing my work is done.

"You should stay and watch." I hear Misty, and my head swivels back her way. "Scotty-boy here is pretty drunk, and I'm not feeling exactly safe with them. You should stay... you know, to make sure things don't get out of hand."

I can't help myself. This time, my nose crinkles up in disgust. "You'll be safe," I assure her with confidence, and then pin the men with a direct stare. "These guys will be extra gentle, right?"

They both nod quickly, although their eyes are immediately pinned to Misty's ginormous boobs that pop free from the corset.

"Good then. You guys have a fun time," I say, turning away once more.

"That's too bad," Misty says in a mocking tone. "I know you'd enjoy watching me work, Raze."

"Not my thing," I say without even looking back

over my shoulder. Walking out of the door, I shut it softly behind me.

God, I fucking hate this part of the operation. Peddling ass to sleazy men that are here cheating on their wives in order to ride the next big thrill. It's fucking abysmal, so I keep reminding myself that the end goal will save numerous women.

When this sting is over, I know I'm probably going to bath in Clorox just to get the slime off me. I also know that after this, my undercover days are over.

CHAPTER 2

Andrea

I WIPE MY sweaty palms on my slacks, thankful the black material won't show the wet trail I'm leaving behind. Taking a deep breath, I knock on the SAC's door and let it out slowly while I wait for admittance.

"It's open," I hear the gruff voice say from within. Squaring my shoulders, I turn the knob and push the door inward.

FBI Special Agent in Charge, Dale Lambert sits behind his desk, which is covered with stacks of files and empty, paper coffee cups. His silver hair, though, is sharply styled and his dark, charcoal-gray suit is pressed to perfection.

He looks up and gives me a blank look. "What can I do for you, Somerville?"

"You wanted to see me, sir?" I ask as I clasp my hands behind my back, legs slightly parted to stand at attention.

"Right," he says distractedly and starts digging through the stacks of files on his desk. "Take a seat.

There's something I want to discuss with you."

My heart starts racing, and I try to maintain my rigid posture as I stride around one of the chairs that sits opposite of his desk. I sit down, perched on the edge, with my back ramrod straight. I clasp my sweaty hands in my lap and pray that he has the news that I've been dreaming of getting.

Four months ago, I applied to the Behavioral Research and Instruction Unit of the FBI or, because the FBI loves its abbreviations, the BRIU. I asked my SAC, Dale Lambert, for his recommendation, and he gladly gave it although he said he'd hate to lose me in the Pittsburgh field office where I've been assigned to him for the past two years. I've been through the interview process with the BRIU—three to be exact—and while I know it's a long shot—I can't help but keep my hopes up. I've never let anything stand in the way of my goals before.

Even at the cost of sacrificing something very important.

The reason it's a long shot for me to get accepted is because I've only been a special agent with the FBI for going on two years now. I've worked in the Criminal Investigative Division at the Pittsburgh field office since then and while I've done some pretty boring shit like background checks for new federal hires, I've also been a part of some interesting investigations ranging from violent to white-collar crimes.

Lambert pulls a file out, flips through it briefly, and then hands it to me. "The Raleigh field office is doing a joint investigation with the local police of a potential sex slavery ring. They need a female agent to go undercover."

I take the file from his hands even as dejection courses through me. Definitely not what I had wanted to hear. Not that this couldn't be a great opportunity, but I was really hoping he was going to tell me I was on the way to Quantico instead.

"There's been no word from the BRIU so get that forlorn look of despondency off your face," he growls at me.

My eyes snap to his, and I smooth out my facial features. I don't address his most recent statement, asking instead, "Don't they have an agent in Raleigh that can do this?"

The question isn't inappropriate. I'm merely curious because our field offices are usually well staffed. It's rare to have to go out on loaner when agents abound.

"Not one as qualified as you," he says with a sheepish smile.

"As qualified as me?"

"The head of this ring is Simon Keyes. He's a mid-level criminal, done some time. But he's smart and slick, and they don't have any hard evidence tying him to the traffic. We believe he uses a strip club he owns as the front and is pulling his stock from the dancers."

I nod in immediate and clear understanding, dropping my gaze back down to the file. "Of course I'm qualified then," I say softly, with absolutely no embarrassment whatsoever.

"Look kid," Dale says gruffly. "You're not the only special agent who worked a stripper pole in her life. You just happen to be the only female one in the FBI right now that's not immersed in another case at the moment. Plus, you have a southern accent and your cover will be as a local girl on the down and out."

I snicker and start flipping through the file. It's true enough… I know how to work a pole and work it good. I paid my way through undergrad and law school just dancing part time. It's not something I'm overly proud of, but it sure as hell isn't something I'm ashamed of either. I came out of school with two impressive degrees and not a dime of debt to my name. Of course, the FBI knows all about my "prior career," as I truthfully disclosed that information on my application. This was not a deterrent to getting in, because unlike most dancers, I actually reported my wages and tips and paid the appropriate taxes on my income. It was a legitimate job, and while I was grilled hard about it during my interview process before getting into the Academy, it was ultimately something the FBI didn't really care about.

Until now.

"What do they want me to do?" I ask with interest, my stomach now starting to fill with butterflies of excitement over the case. While I really, really want to get into the BRIU and do crime analysis, I get super charged up over helping to bring down any type of crime ring.

"Undercover. They already have a local cop on the inside, and he's well entrenched. He's ready to help coordinate a sting, and they don't want to put a civilian at risk. They need an agent to pose as a dancer. Be bait, so to speak."

"That I can do," I say solemnly as I flip through the file, looking at the color photographs of the women believed to have been abducted and sold.

So many of them.

"Knew you'd be up for this. And listen... you know the BRIU is selective. Your lack of experience hurts, but if you complete a successful undercover mission that brings down a slave ring, you know your chances of getting accepted increase tenfold."

My face tilts up to his, and I can't hide the smile of opportunity from my face. "You know that's my dream, sir, so rest assured... I'll put all of my effort into busting this ring."

"Make me proud, Somerville. I want you on a plane first thing in the morning. Head home and get packed up."

Walking out of Lambert's office, I head back to my desk down in the bullpen. I take a few moments to respond to some emails and set an auto responder that I'll be out indefinitely. Transferring a few files to some coworkers, I send the rest back to Lambert to reassign, and then jump online to Delta to make a plane reservation to Raleigh, North Carolina.

When that's all complete, I log off my computer and shut off my desk lamp. I take a look around the bullpen and shutter the smile on my face.

It's time to go undercover.

When I get home, I immediately crawl up into my small, dusty attic where I have a few boxes stored. Even though my dancer days are long over, I know I kept some of the costumes I had accumulated. Nostalgia, I guess, and maybe to remind myself that there is always a way to reach your goal, even if you have to swallow your pride a bit.

It doesn't take me long to find the box labeled "Law School" next to one labeled "Dad". I push the law school box aside for a moment, knowing it contains old textbooks, crib notes, and sparkly bras with tassels on them. Sitting back on the dusty floor, I open the one that simply says "Dad" and rummage through.

I flip through the old photographs of him and Mom, chronicling their love affair, their wedding, and then the arrival of my brother, Kyle. A few more years of memories, and there I am... being held by my father in a dark blue blanket with the U.S. Naval Academy crest on it in deep yellow. I run my finger over the picture... particularly the seal, which has a hand holding a three-pronged trident at the top and a galley ship in the middle. Below that sits an open book with the motto "Ex scientia tridens," which means, "From knowledge, seapower". Yeah... my dad was a Navy man for a brief time and while I very much wanted to be like him, that did not include any desire to follow in his footsteps to Annapolis. Instead, I did my undergrad and law school at the University of Virginia before applying to the Academy.

There aren't many photos of us together, because he died when I was just six months old.

Dropping the photos to the floor, I reach into the box, pull out the leather bound wallet, and flip it open.

Special Agent James Somerville.

I smooth my thumb over his picture, proud of the strong resemblance I have to him. Same golden-blond hair and crooked smile with a dimple in the right cheek but not the left. Kyle looks just the same.

My father became an FBI agent after he completed six years in the Navy after graduating from Annapolis. He was killed in the line of duty when he and the rest of his team closed in on a suspected serial killer who went out in a spray of bullets. He was a member of the BRIU, although it was called the Behavioral Science Unit at that time.

I place the mementos back in the box and issue up

a silent prayer to my dad. "Watch over me, Daddy. Shit's about to get real."

Dusting my pants off, I rummage through my law school box and grab up the pile of sequined bras and thongs, as well as my only pair of hooker heels that may be a bit outdated but would work well toward my cover. If I'm supposed to be a girl down and out on her luck who has to resort to stripping, the clothing I show up with has to look secondhand.

As I walk back over to the folding staircase, a small, stray shoebox sitting just to the side of it catches my eye. It's not labeled, but I know what's in it. I reach down, pick it up, and bring it with me.

In the kitchen, I set the box and clothing on the counter and make myself a sandwich. I eat it with swift efficiency while standing at my Formica kitchen counter, looking out of the front window of my little bungalow house. I don't make much money as an FBI agent but enough that I was able to buy this little abode. Besides, it's not like I have anything else to spend my money on. I'm without close friends because I work all the time, so there's no drink budget for girls' nights out. Dating is out of the question because my heart is still too bruised since David broke up with me almost three weeks ago. And, even if I was ready to get back into the game, I have found most men's egos can't handle the fact I'm an FBI agent, so no need to spend my money on pretty clothes and silky lingerie. I don't even have a dog to keep me company because I'm never home, so there's no kibble or bones to buy. I have a modest clothing budget that keeps me in black dress slacks, French blue dress shirts, and fitted, black blazers. Add in professional yet sensible black shoes, and you have the standard FBI uniform.

Rinsing my plate off and grabbing a beer from the fridge, I grab the stripper gear and box, heading into my bedroom. I pull my small suitcase from the closet and throw it on the bed. Dale told me this operation will be for an indefinite period of time and to pack lots of clothes. Sadly, what I have won't fill my large suitcase so it takes me no time whatsoever to get packed, and then I have nothing to do but wait for the next day to arrive.

I take a quick shower in my tiny bathroom, noticing a small area of rust at the base of the faucet. Fingering it lightly, I add a mental note to get that fixed when I get back. So many plans to update this house, yet I keep putting it off. I suppose that's because of my continued hope I'll get transferred to the BRIU, and that I'll be buying another house in Quantico, Virginia.

After donning a clean pair of underwear and an old Old Miss Law School t-shirt—a product of a short but failed love affair with a fellow FBI agent who also had graduated from law school there—I park myself on my faded brown couch with my beer and pull up the Contact list on my iPhone. A tap of my thumb to the screen and I'm dialing Kyle's cell.

"What's up, LPA?" Kyle says gruffly into the phone after the second ring.

LPA stands for Little Pain in the Ass. A bigger brother's prerogative, I guess.

"Not much, BPA," I say with a grin as I kick my bare feet up on the coffee table. And yeah... that stands for Big Pain in the Ass.

Kyle and I are fairly close, despite the physical distance that separates us. Strangely, I haven't told Kyle yet that David and I are no longer together. Maybe I'm hoping David will have a change of mind, or maybe I'm scared that the minute I tell Kyle, it will be real. Regardless, I have more important things with him to discuss right now, so my broken engagement will have to remain on the back burner.

"Catch any bad guys today?" he asks. I can hear ESPN's Sports Center on in the background, and I can envision Kyle sitting on his couch with a beer in his hand as well, booted feet kicked up on the coffee table, alone in his bachelor pad. He's three years older than me at age thirty and in many ways, we are eerily similar.

In other ways, not so much.

Kyle works as a mechanic for a motorcycle shop in Cheyenne, Wyoming. He moved out there from our small town of Little River, Alabama when he graduated from high school. We had moved to Little River from Washington, D.C. after Dad died to be nearer to my mom's family, and it's all I ever really knew. I loved it and missed it, but Kyle? Not so much. He never looked back after he left. He's a biker through and through and belongs to a pretty tight-knit motorcycle club out there, and the way he tells it, they are just as much his family as I am.

Regardless of his close connections out in Wyoming, Kyle would never turn his back on me and would come running if he was needed. Just three weeks prior to my graduation, my mother died from a brain aneurysm and I was left all alone. That is, until my BPA came home and stayed with me for a few weeks, nursing me through my heartache and bitterness at being left fully parentless. I obviously don't remember my father, and neither does Kyle for that matter, but both of us were extremely close to our mom. Kyle's visits back home may have been infrequent and brief, but he talked to Mom and me every week on the phone.

After I graduated high school, Kyle took back off to Wyoming and I puttered around my mom's house all summer until college started for me in the fall. We still stayed in close contact although we didn't see each other often. Kyle had his life and I had mine, and my goals were set. I was going to be an FBI agent like my dad and the first step was to graduate college. The second was to graduate law school. Third was to become a special agent.

I accomplished those goals but not without tremendously hard work. With mom dead and unable to help with my tuition, I started dancing halfway through my freshman year of college at UVA. I had to brave lecherous touching from drunk men who wanted to put dollar bills in my panties and knowing smirks from some of my classmates who ventured into the strip club where I worked, stunned to see me on stage. Didn't matter to me though. I looked right through their judgment, turned my nose up at their requests for dates, and kept repeating my goals.

College.

Law School.

FBI.

"Sis… you there?" Kyle says into the phone, and I blink my eyes.

"Yeah… sorry… went down memory lane for a moment," I tell him sheepishly.

"Thinking about Mom?" he asks gently, and I smile to myself. Kyle is a big dude… has long hair, tats, and most people think he's pretty scary. I think he's a big teddy bear.

"Yeah… just thinking about how you came back home after Mom died so I wouldn't be alone."

"Stop being such an LPA," he fake sneers into the phone. "You're going to make me cry."

"Dork," I tell him fondly.

"So why did you call?" he asks. "I just talked to you day before yesterday."

Absently fingering a lock of my blonde hair, I tell

him, "I'm going to North Carolina on an assignment. It's undercover, and we won't be able to contact each other. If anything happens and you need to get word to me, you need to contact my SAC, Dale Lambert. I'll text you his info."

"What's the case about?"

"You know I can't tell you that," I admonish gently.

"Then why you? Why are they sending an agent from Pittsburgh to North Carolina?"

It's classified information but even if I could tell him, I wouldn't. I'm not about to divulge to my older brother that I stripped my way to a higher education, therefore I'm the perfect candidate. He'd never understand and then feel guilty as shit that he couldn't help contribute to my education.

"Top secret," I tell him.

He sighs in frustration, and I can just imagine him running his hand through his own long, blond hair. "For how long?"

"I have no clue but if you get worried because you haven't heard from me, just call Dale. He can give you reassurances."

Kyle is quiet a moment and I hear him expel a deep breath into the phone. "Are you going to be in danger?"

Probably.

"Of course not," I lie baldly. "It's an easy operation. We'll laugh about it over beers when it's finished, I promise."

"You're a terrible liar, Andrea," he murmurs into the phone. "Your voice gets shaky when you fib, so you best get that under control before you go undercover."

"Don't worry about me, Kyle. I'll be fine and careful, and when it's all done... I'll be a hero and you can worship at my feet."

"I already worship at your feet, brat. Have since the day you were born."

But now only from afar, I think to myself before shaking my head. I can't be bitter over the fact that Kyle leads his life and I lead mine. The important thing is that he's there for me when I need him.

"I know," I tell him with love in my soul and tears threatening to form in my eyes. "Listen... I need to get going. Packing and other stuff to do. You'll be the first call I make as soon as this is over, okay? Maybe I'll even come out for a visit."

"Before you go," he says softly. "Are you going to tell me why you want me to call your SAC rather than David if I need information?"

Shit.

I close my eyes, rub the bridge of my nose, and take in a deep breath.

Kyle continues. "And are you going to tell me why you haven't mentioned David at all in the last few weeks?"

"Kyle... now's not the time—"

"Spill it, sis," he orders me gruffly, and I recognize that tone. It means he's not going to let up on me.

Sighing, I slide my finger over the shoebox sitting beside me. Flipping the top off, I see several photographs inside of David and me, along with a black velvet jewelry box. "David broke off the engagement three weeks ago."

"That fucking shit," Kyle explodes into the phone. "What the fuck did he do that for?"

I grit my teeth, because even as sad as I am that David and I are no more, I'm also still really pissed at him. "He doesn't want to move from Pittsburgh if I get transferred. He wanted me to pull my application from the BRIU. I refused, and he broke off the engagement."

"What a bastard," Kyle grumbles. "Let me guess... he couldn't stand to give up his precious season tickets to the Steelers."

"He couldn't give up any of it," I clarify. "His job, his family... he is Pittsburgh through and through. It's all he's knows, and he doesn't want to know anything else."

"I'm sorry, Andrea. He's a fucking pussy, and you deserve better," Kyle says, and my heart swells for love over how indignant he is. I want to be totally indignant too, but I succumb to moments of utter self-pity that the man I love doesn't love me enough to let me pursue my dreams.

"Look... I really need to get going so I can finish

getting ready to fly out tomorrow."

"Yeah, okay," he says sadly. "We'll talk more about this when you get done with this operation. Stay safe. Love you."

"Love you too," I whisper and hang up.

I tilt my beer back and take another healthy swig. That was the hardest part about going undercover… telling Kyle and knowing he's going to worry. But I have to put that aside now and start mentally preparing for this job. Because while I'm confident we're going to take these scumbags down, there's a possibility things could go to hell and I could find myself abducted and sold into sexual slavery.

And that certainly is not on my list of goals.

CHAPTER 3

Wyatt

SITTING AT THE main bar that runs perpendicular to the dance stage, I pour over the inventory spreadsheet before me, actually relishing over this rare opportunity to actually do non-criminal work for Simon. I take note of the current stock of beer, wine, and liquor laid out in neat columns, mentally calculate what will be needed for the week, especially given it's a payday weekend, and then handwrite out on a small pad of paper what I'll need to order.

I'm immersed deep in my work so much that I don't notice Lance take a seat next to me at the bar. It's quiet in here… just after ten in the morning, and we're the only ones here. The bartenders and dancers won't be in for another hour for our noontime opening.

"Need you to audition some fresh talent," Lance says beside me, and I give a slight jerk before turning my head toward him.

"Fuck, man… gave me a heart attack," I grumble

good-naturedly.

Lance snorts out a laugh, his eyes crinkling at the corners. Oddly, I've become sort of friends with Lance. Well, my alter-ego Raze has become friends with him. He's a morally depleted criminal who helps his boss sell women as slaves for a living, and yet, while immersed deep in the role as a criminal myself, I've found that we've forged a tentative sort of friendship. He's sharp, witty, and loyal, which makes it easy to find something in common I can hold on to. He's also coldhearted, dangerous, and my enemy... something I never let myself forget.

"What kind of talent are you looking for?" I ask as I swivel my bar stool to face him. Even though we're the only ones here, I keep my voice low.

"Need at least two... no preference on coloring. And most important, they need to be expendable. Simon's getting buyers lined up."

I nod sagely at him. By expendable, he means no one will miss them if they go missing. "Two in one month?"

"Nah... we'll unload one within a few weeks and then hold onto the other for a month or so. At the price they're generating, we don't have to move as much stock as we did before."

"Heard that," I quip as I stand up from the stool. "Give me a few days and I'll have them for you."

Lance holds his fist out, and I bump it with mine. "You're the man," he says with a grin.

"You the man," I joke back while pointing at him.

I gather my spreadsheet and tablet, making my way back toward the small office that I use. It's really nothing more than a large broom closet, but when I was promoted to General Manager, Simon seemed to think I needed my own place to do my work.

It has a metal desk with peeling, brown faux wood on top and a rickety old chair behind it. And that's pretty much all there is to my office besides a Playboy calendar hanging on my wall with a thumbtack, which I thought would lend credence to my overall scumbag cover.

Closing the door behind me, I sit down and let my shoulders sag with the weight that rests upon them. I just held a thirty-second conversation with a man about selling women to sex slavers, and for all Lance cares about this business, you would have thought we were discussing cattle. My stomach seems to be constantly pitching and turning from the sickness of my involvement and how deeply I've become immersed in this darkness.

Yeah… my full-fledged membership in the circle of trust came fortuitously last week, and by a sheer stroke of luck. Despite having worked at The Platinum Club for almost three and a half months, I still had not been able to find one piece of evidence tying Simon to the dancers' disappearances. It was frustrating, and I was wondering at what point the task force was going to continue with this operation.

I had just begun to think that maybe we were barking up the wrong tree, when one night, just as we were closing the doors and shutting off the lights, two Alcohol Law Enforcement agents showed up. Flashing their credentials, they demanded entrance and then audience with the owner.

I walked back toward Simon's office and gave a quick knock on his door before opening it up. It had become my habit to do that since he brought me in on his prostitution scheme, and rather than waiting for him to invite me in, I walked in boldly and with the hope I'd catch him doing something he shouldn't.

It was my lucky night when I walked in.

Lance was holding Carla—one of the dancers who had just come off duty—in his arms while Simon was pulling a needle out of one of her veins. Carla's eyes rolled back and her head lolled to the side.

Simon's head whipped toward me, and his eyes seethed with anger. "Get the fuck out," he barked.

"Sorry, Boss," I hastily said as I stepped all the way in and closed the door behind me. "But ALE is out there... demanding to talk to you. They want to search the place."

"Fuck," Simon muttered and glanced at his watch. Lance shifted and adjusted Carla's weight in his arms.

Simon's eyes narrowed on me, and I let my gaze dart over to Lance and Carla before looking back at him.

"What can I do to help?" I asked boldly... help-fully... trying to calm my pulse. There was no doubt that I had just walked into the middle of an abduction, and my head was spinning over what to do.

He was sizing me up... I could tell. His eyes held me with keen inspection, and I held his stare with confidence and an eager look to please my master.

Simon strode across his office and got right in my face. "You fuck this up and you're a dead man."

"I won't. Just tell me what to do," I said confidently.

"Take Carla... put her in your car and drive. Don't go too far but get to the outskirts of town. Be careful and don't get stopped. I'll call you when I'm ready for you to come back with her."

I nodded quickly and stepped over to Lance, taking Carla from him and hauling her up over my shoulder. By the way her body rolled, I could tell she was passed out cold.

"Lance... I need you to get rid of the shit in my safe. No clue if they have a warrant but get it out of here. I'll go stall ALE for a few minutes but be quick. And then call our buyer. Tell him there's a delay, and we'll deliver the package mostly likely in a few hours."

I had no clue what kind of "shit" Simon was referring to in his safe, but I bet it was documentation about the slave sales he'd made.

"Got it," Lance said, heading toward Simons' safe behind his desk. Lance was really within the circle of trust because he spun the combination dial efficiently.

"Need me to do anything else?" I asked as I grasped onto the fire exit door that led out of the back of the building from Simon's office.

"No," Simon growled, sparing me a brief glance. "Just keep your phone on and I'll call soon."

I didn't respond just pushed my way out of the door and headed across the darkened parking lot toward my car. After unlocking the door and carefully laying Carla across the backseat, I pulled my phone out of my pocket and called my handler, Special Agent Mike Gomez.

He answered on the second ring with obvious worry in his voice because I wasn't to call unless it was a dire emergency.

This constituted dire emergency.

"Raze?" he answered, careful to call me by my alias.

"I need you to meet me out on Six Forks Road, north of Durant… there's a small country gas station about quarter of a mile down on the left."

"I'm familiar with it," he said.

"I'll be there in twenty minutes. Have EMS there and tell them they'll need Narcan," I said quickly as I got in the driver's seat and started the engine.

"What's this about?" Mike asked quickly.

"I just walked into the middle of an abduction. Simon and Lance drugged the girl. I've got her in my backseat."

"Fuck… are they on the run?"

"No. He asked me to get her out of there when ALE showed up. Wants me to bring her back when it's clear."

"Then that's what the fuck you do," Mike growled. "If you don't return her, you blow this entire operation out of the water."

"We are not turning her back over to them. I overhead Simon… he was taking her to a buyer tonight."

"Wyatt… we have to let him take her to the buyer. We can follow and make the bust there."

"No fucking way," I snarled. "You're not putting her at risk. You said we had an agent ready to come in on the inside. We need to go that route."

"And just how do you think you're going to explain this girl's disappearance to Simon?" Mike asked skeptically.

I took a deep breath and blew it out. Putting the car in reverse, I started to back out. "I'm not sure yet, but I'll have something figured out by the time I meet you. Just get there on time."

Disconnecting the call before he could argue with me, I pulled my car slowly out of the parking lot of The Platinum Club onto Kramer Street, heading toward the outer beltline. My mind was racing but by the time I met Mike and several other agents at the gas station, I knew what I had to do.

Mike had made a judgment call and did not bring

in an EMS unit. He felt it would call too much attention and didn't want it out on the airwaves. Instead, he insisted they'd take the girl to a hospital for treatment.

We made the transfer quickly as I assured Mike I had a plan. He accepted me at my word although his face held worry, and as soon as they were out of sight, I pulled my phone out and called Simon.

"What?" he whispered harshly into the phone, so I knew ALE was still there.

Putting on my best frustratedly panicked voice, I said, "Fuck, Simon. We got a major problem."

"I'm listening," he said quietly.

"She started convulsing, man… vomit and foam coming out of her mouth… shaking and shit. I tried, man… I tried to save her. Fucking did CPR… got her fucking vomit in my mouth. SHIT," I yelled for good measure and then groaned into the phone. "She's fucking dead, Simon. What in the hell did you give her?"

I heard some shuffling noises, and knew Simon was moving somewhere for privacy. "You're sure she's dead?" he asked urgently.

"Yes," I yelled into the phone. "Fuck, what in the hell do we do now?"

"Just ease the fuck up, Raze. Listen… you dispose of the problem, you hear me?"

I took a deep breath and let out a shaky breath, but I was smiling on the inside. Simon just bought

my panicked lie hook, line, and sinker. "Yeah, man...
I got it."

"Don't fuck this up," he warned.

"I won't," I said with confidence. "I got this.
Don't worry."

"Come straight back here when you're done," he
said and then disconnected the call.

I leaned back against my car and looked up at the
stars in the night sky, immensely relieved I just saved
Carla's life and kept the operation intact.

So yeah... I was now fully in the circle. I went
back to the club and relayed again in detail to Simon
and Lance what happened. They didn't seem to have
a doubt over my veracity, and in fact, Lance muttered
that he was afraid they'd given her too much of
whatever drug they had pumped into her, hypothesiz-
ing she was probably high on something else and
overdosed.

I assured them both that I weighted her body
down and dumped her in Falls Lake, and that she
would never be found. I said it with almost a pride in
my voice over having done such a bang-up job for
Simon, sounding like an eager puppy looking for
praise. They accepted that as well, and then proceeded
to bring me in on the details of their sex-slave trade.
There was some concern that Carla's buyer would
turn tail and run, but after a call to him to explain the
situation, he said he'd wait for another girl.

So, as Lance just instructed me, I am now in

charge of getting some new talent.

Operation Bust Simon's Ass is now in full force. I've got a meeting tomorrow with Mike and the female FBI agent they've brought in to go undercover, so I can fill her in on the details of the case so far. Since I'm in charge of all hires now, it won't be a problem to get her in the door. I just hope the FBI chose someone that could handle the delicate, yet stressful nature of this situation. I wasn't worried about the background alias they would provide for the plant. The FBI is good at that shit.

I just hope the woman is tough enough for what is about to be thrown her way. She's going to be playing an important role in this operation, and she's going to be in incredible danger. While I will do everything I can to protect her, if we're lucky enough for Simon to target her as an appropriate item of merchandise, she's going to need to be prepared to see it all the way through to the end.

CHAPTER 4

Andrea

RUBBING THE BRIDGE of my nose, I close the file I had been perusing and toss it on the couch beside me. It's probably the fourth time I've read the investigation into Simon Keyes in its entirety, and I feel like I have a good bead on this man. I think I know exactly how to handle him, although I'll have to wait to meet my undercover partner to be sure. His insight will be invaluable.

I glance at my watch.

1:23AM.

It's a cheap Timex I bought at a thrift store a few days ago, where I used some of the cash I was provided by the FBI to extend my wardrobe a bit. Upon my arrival in Raleigh, I was immediately deposited into my new home, a hovel of an apartment in the worst area of downtown imaginable. Every night, I could hear other tenants screaming at each other, booming music, and once, even a gunshot.

All the clothes I brought with me were going to be

taken tonight, assuredly stored back in the Raleigh field office, along with my suitcase. Two days ago, I was told to buy a new wardrobe that was more in line with what a down-and-out stripper might wear. That meant tiny Lycra miniskirts, tank tops that were two sizes too small, and slutty red bras to wear underneath said small tank tops. I bought a good chunk of my attire at a thrift store and the rest from Wal-Mart. My new ID was handed to me, which I deposited into a beat-up old wallet I got for two dollars, which was housed in an ugly, brown leather purse with leather fringe along the edge that I got for six. I bought garish makeup, also at Wal-Mart, and hot curlers for my long, blonde hair. However, until such time as I had to step foot in The Platinum Club, I was still Special Agent Andrea Somerville and was dressed accordingly.

But when the time came, make no doubt, I was ready to display trashy Andrea to the world.

I mean… trashy Nikki O… my new alias. The "O" stood for Oliver, but I was prepared for it to stand for "Orgasm," which was my even trashier stripper name.

Nikki O.

Nikki Orgasm.

Ugh… I didn't have to deal with something so terribly perverse when I stripped through college. There I was just good ol' Andrea, dancing her way to a higher education. I showed up to work in my faded jeans and UVA t-shirts, and went home dressed in the same with my pockets stuffed full of green, green cash.

Sliding my gaze to my watch again, I see it's now 1:27 AM, and I let out a tired yawn.

"He should be here soon," SA Mike Gomez says from his seat at my kitchen table. He's typing away on a laptop, his blue sport coat draped over the back of a ratty recliner that sits perpendicular to my couch and his tie loosened.

Mike arranged for this meeting with my undercover partner, who I've only been told is a member of a local police department on the east coast of North Carolina and has been undercover at The Platinum Club for just shy of four months now. I don't know much about him other than his real name is Wyatt Banks, but his undercover name is Charles Hawkins, but as with any good criminal alias, his nickname is Raze.

So much cooler than Nikki O, I have to admit.

Standing up from my couch, I raise my hands over my head and arch the stiffness out of my back. My vertebrae pop one by one, straight up my spine, and I groan in relief. I'd been on that couch for a good three hours.

Padding into the kitchen, I open the rusted, avocado-green fridge and snatch out a Diet Coke. "Want one?" I ask Mike, holding up the slightly chilled can because the refrigerator only works sporadically and I don't trust it to keep any actual food in there for safety reasons.

"Sure," he says as he looks up from his computer.

I pull another one out and take a chair next to him at the table, popping the top of mine and pushing his can across the table toward him. "Anything else I need to know about Wyatt before he gets here?"

"Raze," Mike says sternly. "Purge the name Wyatt from your vocabulary."

"Right... Raze," I mutter, my cheeks turning warm over such a stupid mistake. I had been told from the minute I walked into this craphole apartment that I needed to assume my role completely, which means I should have ditched the FBI suits and started wearing my Lycra.

I had spent hours and hours over the last four days, going over my backstory. I was Nikki Oliver, age twenty-six, born and raised in a podunk town in western North Carolina. My mom was a drug addict who had OD'd when I was seventeen, and I'd been on my own since then. I didn't graduate high school but had made somewhat of an attempt at an honest living, at least, that is what my fake work records show. Little stints at fast food joints and gas stations. But my criminal record shows an arrest for petty larceny when I was nineteen, and then solicitation when I was twenty. Since then, I've worked at various strip clubs around North Carolina, and even one in Georgia when I supposedly followed my no good, drunk, abusive boyfriend down there when I was twenty-three. Now I was back in my home state, where I had been fired from my last stripping job for selling drugs to the other dancers and shed of my no-good, drunk, abusive boyfriend.

This spotted history, I was assured, would get me hired on the spot at The Platinum Club.

That is... Mike told me... if I could do a half-assed job at dancing.

Luckily, no one in the FBI required me to prove those skills and just accepted my word and my history that I was good enough to hack it.

"Not much to tell about him," Mike answers my original question about Raze. "He's a cop with the Nags Head Police Department over in the Outer Banks. We needed someone that wasn't local, and he was highly recommended. Had done undercover work before. He's been working for Simon almost four months and was brought into the slave-trade operation just about a week ago. He's been tasked with finding some new girls for Simon to sell. He wants to move one pretty fast... within a few weeks, is what he told Wyatt."

"Raze," I correct automatically, and Mike shoots me a grin.

"Good girl," he praises.

I swallow hard, because I happen to be one of those new girls. "And how is Raze going to ensure that I'm the one that Simon will want to sell?"

Mike shrugs. "We're just going to have to assume Raze has enough pull. But he knows exactly what Simon is looking for. He's the one that helped to create your new identity, and I'm assuming a key component is that you don't have any family members who would notice you missing. That seems to be the pattern so far. Plus, the fact you had an abusive boyfriend means you'll probably swear off men—aka attachments—for a while."

"Makes sense," I say and take an idle sip of my soda.

At a soft knocking at the door, Mike and I exchange looks. He nods, and I go to answer it.

I open the door, the safety chain still in place, and take a peek. With only a few inch gap within which to spy my visitor, he shouldn't make that big of an impression on me.

Yet, that tiny glance at Wyatt Banks... I mean, Raze Hawkins... causes my stomach to flip and my pulse to pound. God, he's stunning and so not what I imagined.

I had thought that anyone being put undercover in a slimy strip club fronting as a slave ring would look... slimy. Short, thin, and balding... with a massively hairy chest. You know, slimy.

He's tall... I mean, really tall, and golden from head to toe. It was the briefest of glances but I caught warm, brown hair cut short and spiky on top, lean muscles, and a hard jaw line. He was a brief vision of spectacularity. That's all I need to see before I shut the door, pulling the chain free, and mentally willing myself to chill out.

When I open it, he is even more gorgeous than what little I had seen. Clear, hazel eyes swirling with green, gold, and a warm earthy tone appraise me. His eyes travel down my body… slowly… in a most calculating way, and his lips… which I notice are very full… flatten out.

I glance down at myself, taking in the pressed black slacks, French blue shirt with ivory buttons, and low-heeled black loafers. My hand subconsciously comes up to pat at the tight bun I had wound my long hair in that morning, ensuring no stray hairs were falling out.

"You're my stripper?" he asks slowly, a slight censure in his tone.

It gets my hackles up, being judged for looking so prudish, which is insane, I know. I hold my hand out to him. "Nikki O at your service. That "O" stands for Orgasm, or Oliver if you go by my newly acquired license. Sorry I couldn't greet you in my stripper gear and all."

There it is… a lip twitch… and his eyes crinkle slightly at the corner.

"Wyatt," Mike says from behind me. "Come on in… we got work to do."

Wyatt's… I mean, Raze's eyes flick over my shoulder, and he gives a head nod to Mike. Gone is the threat of a smile and he ignores my hand, stepping past me into my apartment.

"Come on in," I mutter under my breath and close the door, sliding the chain back in place.

By the time I turn around, Raze is sitting at the table with Mike... in the seat that I had just vacated. Sighing, I walk over to the couch, grab the FBI file on Simon Keyes, and head into the kitchen so we can get down to work.

"Want a soda?" I ask Raze.

"Sure. Pepsi if you have it," he says, his eyes watching me intently as I walk toward the fridge.

"Sorry... it's Diet Coke or nothing," I respond, but I'm brought up short just before I reach for the handle.

"Jesus... you walk like you have a stick up your ass. Please don't tell me that's your sexy strut?" Raze growls.

"Wyatt," Mike says in a low warning before I can open my mouth to defend myself.

"No, Mike," Raze says as he holds his hand up to cut him off. "Look at her. She reeks of FBI... probably prior military by the way her spine is ramrod straight. She's going to blow this whole operation out of the water. Simon will spot her for what she is a mile away."

"Ease up," Mike says with a sigh. "She's got the skills... trust me."

Raze snorts in skepticism and for a brief, crazy moment, I have the wild urge to start a sexy dance right then and there to prove to him that I can handle this. But the moment fizzles because standing here in my plain black suit with my hair done up tight and not an ounce of makeup on, and with Raze's hard eyes on me, I don't feel an ounce of sexy within me.

Instead, I decide Raze doesn't deserve one of my lukewarm Diet Coke's and take the chair opposite of him at the kitchen table.

Clasping my hands together, I force my shoulders to relax a little and give him a focused stare. "Look… you're just going to have to trust the FBI knows what it's doing and that I'm qualified to handle this job. I'm ready for this, and hear me when I say that they will never in a million years guess what I truly do for a living. Now, let's quit wasting time with your doubts and how about you tell me what I need to do."

Mike gives a little cough behind his hand, and Raze narrows his eyes at me. He holds my gaze, and while I can still appreciate his male perfection as he sits across the table from me, I have decided that I don't like this man very much.

Raze pops his jaw and then slouches back in his chair. Drumming his fingers on the table, he looks at me intently. "You prepared to go all the way with this?"

"You mean—am I prepared to let myself get kidnapped and possibly sold into slavery under your nose if things don't go according to your brilliant plan?" I ask calmly. "Because yes… I am."

His gaze is shrewd. "You're prepared to get up on stage and flash your tits to a bunch of strangers? Have their hands on you... shoving grease-covered dollar bills in your G-string, hoping to cop a feel of your pussy?"

I flinch hard over his crude words.

Sitting up quickly, he leans over the table in a menacing gesture and growls at me. "You can't fucking flinch over words like 'tits' and 'pussy'. That's the business you're in now, Special Agent."

"Okay... that's enough," Mike says in exasperation. "Agent Somerville—"

"That's Nikki Orgasm," I snap at Mike as I cross my arms over my chest, and I see Raze's lip twitch again.

Mike shoots me a glare and continues, "Agent Somerville will be fine. Once she's in role, she'll be able to carry herself accordingly. Let's quit dicking around. I need you to instruct her, Raze, on what to expect and how she has to act, and you're just going to have to fucking trust she can do it. Okay?"

Raze keeps his eyes pinned on me, but he finally acknowledges Mike. "Fine. But one fuck up and months of hard work are down the drain... and a very dangerous man is going to walk free."

I don't bother acknowledging his threat, just continue to stare at him. With a frustrated grunt, Raze pushes his hands through his hair, scratches the back of his head, and then slouches back down in his chair again.

"Okay," he says, his voice now sounding a bit more professional. "You're going to come in tomorrow afternoon for an audition before me, Simon Keyes, and his second in command, Lance Portman. I make the hires but the ultimate decision to nix one of my choices is in Simon's hands, so you need to impress him. I'll lay your background out to him ahead of time, and tell him that I've targeted you as one of the marks."

"What's going to make me so appealing to him?" I ask.

"Because you're expendable and no one will care. You have no family, no close friends, and no ties. You've been arrested before on drug charges, so he's going to assume you use, which makes you more vulnerable."

"What's my demeanor supposed to be? Harsh? Meek? Confident?"

"Be confident when you're on stage," Raze says thoughtfully, "but not when you're off it. You can come across as a bit of a scared rabbit, but mostly, you need to be desperate for this job. Willing to do anything to land it and keep it. He needs to have the feeling of complete power over you right away, that you're not going to be scared away, and that you're in this job for the long haul. He wants to have confidence that you're going to keep coming back for his brand of shit until he's ready to sell you."

"So I need to give him a bit of my backstory... convince him of my desperation?"

Raze gives me a short smile, and it's starting to become clear to me... maybe he's testing my mettle.

"Sweetheart, the only thing you need to do is give him a lap dance that produces a hard-on. That's all he'll be looking for. He will then look to me to verify that you fit the profile of what he wants."

I don't flinch this time over his crudity, possibly because it was said with a twinge of humor. But I have had enough of his doubts over my abilities, deciding to show him that I can hang with him and all his undercover debauchery. Leaning across the table, I murmur in my sexiest, southern voice. "Baby... any man within a twenty-foot vicinity of me tomorrow is going to have a raging hard-on when I'm done dancing. I suggest you learn how to discreetly adjust yourself so *you* don't get embarrassed."

Mike coughs again behind his hand and shifts in his seat. God, I hope that didn't give him a hard-on, but I don't spare him a glance. I hold Raze's stare, which I'm happy to say is not as smug as it was ten seconds ago, and then he surprises me with a full and genuine laugh.

Giving me a nod of approval and still smiling with good humor, Raze says, "I've been duly warned. But we have a lot more to discuss. I want to fill you in on every person at the club, and even though you can't trust any of them, there are a few girls that will help to look out for you, and I want you to make friends with them. I want to go over your cover again and again until I'm satisfied that you know it inside and out and that you don't flinch when you hear the word 'pussy' because you'll hear it several times a night while you're working, and then I want to discuss how we can communicate safely if it becomes necessary."

I take a shallow breath and blow it out softly. "Okay, then... let's get to work."

"One other thing," Raze says softly. "I'm going to have to assume you know what to wear tomorrow?"

"She's got it covered," Mike asserts. "Whole new wardrobe."

"It's more than that," Raze says, shaking his head. "You need makeup... get some long, fake fingernails... do something sexy with your hair."

"Okay," I say confidently. "That's not a problem."

"Wax," Raze says, still holding my gaze firmly.

"Wax?" I ask, dumbfounded, and I notice Mike shifts in his seat again.

"You need to get waxed... everywhere. Simon requires it."

Crap. I hate getting waxed. Hurts like a bitch, but I also know in this line of business, it's the easiest way to maintain a well-groomed crotch line.

"Fine," I grit out. "Anything else I need to do about my appearance?"

"Just try to remove that steel pole out of your spine and I think we're good."

I don't rise to his goading and instead give him a sweet smile. "Consider it removed. Now, let's get to work so we can bring this son of a bitch down."

CHAPTER 5
Wyatt

C HRIST, I'M NERVOUS.

Not once in the past four months have I had an attack of nerves, but fuck if I don't have them now. I take a sip from the can of Pepsi sitting in front of me, and then surreptitiously wipe my sweaty palms on my jeans. One of the dancers I had interviewed yesterday is on the stage. A beautiful girl named Amy with mocha-colored skin and small breasts that she more than makes up for by the way she can twerk her hips.

Club music is thumping, but the lights are all on brightly, not affording them subtle mood setting to go along with their routine. She's spinning on the pole as I watch her with shuttered eyes, my nerves doing a twerk of their own because Andrea Somerville is up next.

Fuck, she better land this audition for Simon or we're screwed. I won't have time to get another undercover plant in place before Simon is ready to make the next sell.

With a quick glance to my left, I see Simon and Lance with their heads angled in toward one another, quietly discussing the girl up on the stage. Their eyes stay pinned on her while they talk in low voices about her performance. I hear words like "looks too proud" and "she'll be a fighter," and based on those snippets, I'm sure she won't be offered the job. While Simon can use the extra talent up on stage, these auditions are strictly for sex slaves, whether those poor, unsuspecting girls know it or not, and "proud" and "fighter" don't make for easy marks.

I am pleased to hear this, though, because while Amy's social background is perfect for what Simon is looking for, I knew that the haughty tilt of her head and the pride in her eyes would make him uneasy. He wants marks that, while beautiful and sexy, won't make trouble for their soon-to-be captors. I figured just such a girl thrown into these auditions would increase the likelihood of Simon choosing Andrea.

As long as she could dance.

Fuck... more sweat on my palms and I wipe them again.

I'm not only nervous over the possibility that Simon won't hire Andrea. I'm also nervous over the possibility that Simon *will* hire Andrea, because the minute that happens, she's going to be in danger.

Serious fucking danger.

My plan is tentative and still needs some thinking,

and all of this hinges on my ability to be present at Andrea's sale. But as long as that works out, then the plan is just to take them down right then and there with a carefully concealed weapon and a surprise reveal of my law enforcement status.

But there is a huge unknown, and that is I don't know what to make of Andrea. I just couldn't see her being a stripper, and about the only thing I felt she had going for her was a sweet, southern accent that was not faked. That fit in nicely with her backstory. But past that, she screamed law enforcement from the clear higher education in her voice to the military-like stiffness of her posture to the confidence brimming in her eyes.

She was going to have to do a world of great fucking acting to pull off this charade.

And Christ… I hope to God she can pull sexy off. She came off as a bit of a plain Jane to me when I met her in the wee hours of this morning, wearing her starched FBI-ware and a severe bun at the back of her head. No makeup but she had clear skin, gorgeous blue eyes, and full, fuckable lips. I could only hope Simon was calculating the way they'd look around his buyer's cock when he was making his decision, a thought that causes my stomach to curdle.

The music starts waning and I realize Amy is at the end of her routine. She ends it by hooking her fingers in the strings of the thong that rest at her hip, shimmying them down her long legs. She steps out of them, catching the edge on one manicured toe encased in silver, high-heeled sandals, and flicks it out so the material goes sailing at Lance. He deftly catches it and just like the schmuck that I know him to be, brings it to his nose and inhales deeply with a sensuous look on his face. That earns him a cheeky grin from Amy, bare-assed naked and staring boldly down at us.

Cocking one hand on her hip and letting the other hang loosely at her side, she says, "So what did you think? Do I have the job?"

Simon and Lance bend their heads toward one another, voices so low that I can't hear a damn thing now. They don't bother to conference me in because my opinion doesn't matter at this point. I did my job… brought the prospects to the table, and now it's Simon's decision.

Pulling back, Simon looks up at Amy and gives her a smooth smile. "You're hired, baby. Head back to the dressing room and get your clothes on. You can go over the details with Raze a bit later. We have two more auditions."

Fuck.

He hired her, and that just decreased Andrea's chances.

"Who's up next?" Simon asks me.

I glance down at the application I had filled out the day before and pretend I'm not overly familiar with the fake person it belongs to. "Nikki Oliver, but she goes by Nikki O… She said it means Nikki Orgasm," I say with a snort, and Simon and Lance laugh along with me.

"That's right," Simon muses. "I thought that one had particular promise when you told me about her."

I shrug my shoulders carelessly, as I don't want him to get a hint of how much I want him to hire her. "No better than any of the others. I think they're all easy marks."

"That last one won't be easy on the buyer we have in mind," Lance says darkly. "But he's got a bit of a whipping fetish, so he'll enjoy knocking that smug smile off her face."

My stomach cramps hard over those words, and I take another swallow of my Pepsi to coat my dry tongue.

Fuck, fuck, fuck. I hope I didn't just condemn that girl to a nightmare of a life. My only hope at this point is that her potential buyer won't be along soon to collect his toy.

"Nikki Oliver," I yell out toward the stage. I know she's standing just behind the curtain… ready to go. "You're up."

A slow, sexy beat of music starts… thumping almost ominously, rising in crescendo, until it's taken over the loud pounding of my own heart. And there she is… striding out onto the stage.

And holy fuck… I almost don't recognize her.

My jaw drops, but I pick it back up quickly,

slamming my teeth together. Her golden hair is loose… long… flowing down her back in sexy waves. Her makeup is flawless with long lashes that make her blue eyes pop and fuck-me red lipstick is painted onto those full lips.

She chose to come out with guns blazing, because she didn't bother with any type of clichéd fantasy costume—naughty nurse, spankable schoolgirl, or dominatrix professor. No, instead, she chose to come out in a sexy-as-sin, black bustier with a simple and very, very tiny black G-string.

The bustier was perfectly chosen… the cups covering yet plumping up what I now understand to be luscious breasts that she must have had flattened down behind a sports bra when I last saw her. The bottom half of the bustier is in black lace, coming to just above her belly button, and trimmed in dove-gray lace around the edges. It's not an expensive piece of lingerie, the cups done in some type of faux leather, and I realize with admiration that she wore something sexy yet of obvious cheap quality so as to enhance her "down-and-out" character portrayal. My gut tightens as my eyes sweep over the G-string, the tiny triangle of black cotton stretched precariously between her legs, with thin straps arching over the most perfect-looking hipbones I've ever seen.

I've always had a thing for a woman's hips.

She walks—no prowls—down the center of the stage, her eyes sweeping briefly over Lance, then

Simon, and finally me. Her lips quirk up sexily and her eyes flutter closed briefly as she reaches a lazy hand out to the metal pole, and then reels her entire body inward toward it. Looping one long leg around the pole, she releases her hand's grip and arches her back, tilting her head way back so that her the ends of her hair brush the lacquered floor.

Smoothly... sexily, she pulls her body up, un-wraps her leg from around the pole, and starts a slow, gyrating dance. Her movements are silky... fluid, almost with a touch of hard-edged grace about her. Her body moves in perfect synchronicity to the slow beat of music, undulating like the current of a lazy river.

She moves with her shoulders squared proudly, yet with none of the stiffness I saw yesterday. She tempers that confidence with an almost coy attitude on the stage. It's an enchanting mixture, and my eyes follow her avidly.

I can hear Simon say, "Fuck, she's hot," and Lance say, "I bet she'd fucking blow like a rock star with those lips," and I while I don't like hearing that about my partner, I can't say as I disagree with them right now.

I'm mesmerized when Andrea... I mean, Nikki... reaches behind her back and with a well-practiced and highly coordinated move, releases the clasps of the bustier. In typical, teasing fashion, the back springs open and she deftly holds the material to her breast, hinting at what we might see, yet denying us what I'm betting will be fucking perfection.

Her body spins—a flash of a perfect ass—and the bustier drops from her hands. Her arms rise above her head, scooping up her hair while her hips dip and tilt to the cadence of the movement, only giving us the vision of her beautiful backside. When her arms are stretched sky high, she releases her hair and it floats down over her back.

The music picks up in speed… gets a little more raw, and when Nikki spins back around to face us, her breasts are even more spectacular than I could have imagined.

Full, lush, perfect pink nipples that are pebbled hard and I feel a tightening in my groin for the first time since she walked out on stage. Luckily, I'm sitting behind a table, and she'd never know that she's starting to give me a hard-on. A quick glance to my left, and I see Simon isn't hiding any such thing. He sits to one side of the little, round table he shares with Lance, his long legs stretched out in front of him, and his dick tenting the wool-and-silk blend dress pants he's wearing.

Anger burns through me that he'd dare to get aroused over my partner, and a protective instinct rears up inside of me. My eyes cut back to Nikki, flaring wide as I watch as her one delicate hand— adorned with garishly long, red nails per my instructions—flutters over her belly. Her other hand rises to her mouth and she sucks her index finger in deep. Fluttering her eyelashes down at Simon, she appears to be eating him up with her eyes.

Another surge of anger flows through me, and this time, it has nothing to do with over-protectiveness and everything to do now with the lengths to which Andrea is going to secure this job. She is eye-fucking Simon, and I can't tell if this is real or part of her act.

It's an act... it has to be an act, and her zeal is about doing her mission for the greater good.

Right?

Nikki O—because that is how I *must* think of her—moves her hand down, all the while spinning her body, gyrating her hips, and sucking on her finger. The tips of her fingers sink into the low-cut triangle of material between her legs. When they disappear completely from view, she throws her head back, closes her eyes, and mimes a moan of ecstasy while her hips pump against her hand.

She's dancing out a slow act of masturbation, one I'm quite sure is an act. Her fingers are not actually lodged anywhere of particular sexual importance, but still... the effect fills the room with a current of thick lust.

My cock goes stiff, swelling instantly, and I grit my teeth, uncaring if I crack a molar.

Nikki's head lifts back up, her stare going back to Simon, and she removes her hand from down below, only to scrape her nails along her body over to her hip. Her fingers latch into the string at her side, and she gives a sharp tug, never once missing a sensual beat of the dance.

The G-string is of the rip-away variety, probably held only by tiny snaps or Velcro, and I suck in oxygen as she turns toward me, giving me a smirk and tossing the tiny panties my way. They hit me square in the chest, and I catch a subtle fragrance of gardenia before they fall to my lap.

Right across my aching dick pushing against my jeans.

Can't help it... my eyes go to her body, briefly taking in her bouncing breasts, straight down to that area I told her to wax.

And wax she did.

She's beautifully... stunningly... amazingly... bare, and I have a wild, insane urge to pull her off the stage. Not to cover her body with clothing but with my own.

Shaking my head hard, I bite down on the inside of my cheek and attempt to will my hard-on away. But it's a no-go, because now Nikki looks back down at Simon and with the thump of music egging her on, she walks down the three steps that lead off the stage and down into the lounge area. She walks right up to Simon, who is sporting the most lecherous grin I've ever seen, and proceeds to give him the dirtiest lap dance I've ever seen.

Nikki drapes both of her arms over his shoulders,

resting her elbows on his light blue, silk shirt, and swings one leg over his lap to straddle him. Simon's hands come up and grab her by the hips, an absolute no-no with club patrons as we have a strict, no-touch policy—outside of the prostitution, that is. That clearly doesn't apply to the owner, though.

Her hips pump inward and out again, hovering just over his straining hard-on, never making contact but coming whisper close. She stares down at him, pursing her lips and eye-fucking him… making every fantasy of his come true. I watch, appalled, as Simon's fingers dig into her flesh and his arms stiffen in an attempt to push her down on his cock… to make her grind against him.

I watch, equally fascinated, as the muscles in her legs bunch and quiver, pushing against his strength and absolutely refusing to let her crotch touch his. Before he can demand her obedience though, she shoots him a coy look, shakes her head in sexy reprimand, and swings her leg up and over his lap until she's standing in front of him.

The music starts to wind down and she finishes her dance with a few more spins and twist of her hips, finally walking back up onto the stage as the last note of music flutters away.

Nikki immediately looks to me, holding her hand out, and I don't hesitate a moment. I pick up her G-string, tossing it back up at her, and she efficiently puts it back on.

She bends over to pick up her bustier but before she can straighten her body, Simon stands from his chair and says, "You're hired. We can discuss the details of your employment in my office."

Oh, fuck no, that is not going to happen, because he's going to try to fuck her, no doubt about it. And I don't know much about Andrea, but what I just saw on that stage, she intends to get this job… and I'm not so sure she won't lay down her body to ensure she gets her foot in the door.

Standing quickly from the table, I remind Simon, "Don't forget you have that meeting with Darren in five minutes."

Thank fuck, he has that meeting with Darren.

"Lance can handle that," Simon says, his eyes raking over Andrea's body while she puts on her bustier with practice movements. My pulse skyrockets and my mind starts going into overdrive figuring out how I can swoop in and save her.

"Actually, I can't," Lance says. "I have to go meet with our supplier over at the bakery."

Relief courses through me. "Supplier at bakery" translates into the pipeline of chemicals that is trucked in to Simon's meth operation, something that he has never asked me to handle before.

"Fuck," Simon says and glances at his watch. He shoots a last, longing look at Andrea and turns away. "Fine. Raze… get the new girls set up."

"What about the last girl's audition?" I ask as I

reach down to shift my still-hard cock before standing from my chair.

"Hire her if you want," he says as he looks at me with a smirk. Leaning in closer, he whispers, "But these last two girls are perfect for our 'export' business."

Satisfaction and relief courses through me that Andrea landed the job, not as a dancer, but as a potential sex slave, and we have crossed a major hurdle. On top of that, I've averted the opportunity for Simon to get his hands on Andrea. He may come after her again, and I'll worry about that later, but right now… our foot is in the door and we are one more step closer to taking Simon Keyes down.

Turning to look back over my shoulder, I see Andrea standing there with a hopeful look in her eyes as she puts the bustier back on. "Okay, Nikki. Go get dressed, then I'll get you and Amy to sign the final employment paperwork, and we'll get you both on the schedule."

"Thank you," she says to me and then turns to scurry to the back of the stage and through the black curtain that houses the dressing area. I watch until she disappears, my gut rolling over the thought of what she was going to have to do with her body, night after night. I respect the shit out of what she just did to get her foot in the door, but an unpleasant feeling of anger and fear, along with a twist of something vaguely close to jealousy, permeates me through and through.

CHAPTER 6

Andrea

I UNLOCK THE deadbolt and then the door lock of my apartment, needing to give an extra hard twist on the rusty knob before pushing my door open. It's almost 2:30 AM and I'm exhausted. Closing the door behind me, I re-lock it and slide the safety chain in place. I drop my purse on the floor and kick off my hooker heels. They can stay there until morning for all I care, I'm so tired.

Three days of dancing, and when not dancing, serving cocktails to drunk patrons. While I have to strip entirely naked when on stage, I'm left with a small measure of dignity by being allowed to keep my bottoms on while playing waitress. Still doesn't stop horny men from pawing at me after I set their liquor down in front of them, but at least I don't have to worry about their eyes dropping to crotch level all the time. It's barely manageable with having to suffer their lewd gazes at my breasts.

I fell back into the dancing easy enough. Just like

riding a bike, and just like when I was in college, I was able to let my mind drift away with every article of clothing I shed. When I'm up on that stage, I may have hundreds of men leering at me and imagining the dirtiest things in their mind, but I'm never mentally present when I dance. I always have had a good knack for letting my mind float away while under the spotlight, only coming back to cognizance of my surroundings when the music died away and I could get off stage.

Nothing of interest has happened since I started at The Platinum Club, at least not that I know of. Raze has kept his distance from me, giving me no more interaction than he does the other dancers. Each night, he makes an accounting of my tips, along with the other girls, and parcels out our shares. We are only paid in what we make in tips for dancing, less a thirty-percent commission for Simon. After every dance, of which I do three each night, I pull out all the cash stuffed in my garters and put it in an envelope that I hand to Raze. He doesn't say a word, just sometimes gives me a nod of his head. Each night before I leave, he hands me a fat envelope with my take and murmurs, "Good job."

He says that to every girl though.

Outside of those brief interactions, I haven't had a single conversation with Raze. He watches me dance... every single time, but then he watches all the girls dance unless he gets called away to a problem in one of the VIP rooms. He's there to keep his eye on things, and while he has plenty of bouncers to do the heavy work if the patrons get rowdy, he's always there for every one of my performances.

As I said, I let my mind drift away when I'm on stage, but once… just last night as a matter of fact, I happened to lock eyes with Raze. My blank eyes had passed around the club, vaguely tracking the men waving the money and dutifully bending when appropriate at the edge of the stage so they could slip ones, fives, tens, and sometimes twenties in my garter. My eyes passed right over Raze and for a split moment, kept right on moving. But then a jolt went through me, and I looked back at him.

He was standing in a corner, leaning one shoulder against the wall, with his arms folded over his chest. He was watching me dance with glittering eyes and a hard line to his jaw. Our gazes melded and held firm, and for several seconds, I was dancing just for him. I saw him suck in a deep lungful of oxygen and hold it while he watched me.

My skin started tingling, and my nerves hummed. He was across the club, yet I could feel the intensity of his presence as if he were inches away from me.

It was easy to get lost in that feeling. Get lost in Raze's stare. Or was it Wyatt's stare I was succumbing to, because while he was putting on an act, I knew his true identity. I knew he wasn't a slimy, flesh-peddling scumbag.

I know he is dedicated and loyal, and if I'm going to go ahead and lay all of his golden attributes at his feet, I might as well admit that he is freakin' gorgeous and sexy as hell, and he makes me long for something that I know I have no damn business longing for.

I've thought that from the moment I laid eyes on him.

It was reiterated to me when I had my audition dance. While I played the part for Simon's benefit, and I focused my eyes on him, I couldn't help but pour every ounce of sexiness I possessed into my performance. I did that not for Simon, but for Wyatt.

Yes, Wyatt.

Not Raze.

Wyatt.

For some compelling reason, I wanted him to be attracted to me. I wanted him to get that raging hard-on I threatened him with. I wanted his eyes to be fevered as they gazed upon me, and I wanted him to succumb to lustful thoughts.

I did all of that, knowing it was wrong, knowing that it didn't have a damn thing to do with my job, and knowing that it was dangerous to let those feelings flow.

But I did it anyway.

And all of those feelings overwhelmed me last night as I held his gaze while I danced, and he watched me from a darkened corner with something other than a law enforcement partner's interest. I felt it straight down to my toes.

After the dance, I tried to analyze my feelings, and then I thought of David. He was the love of my life… or so I thought, and yet in the almost eighteen months we had been together, I don't ever recall having such an electric connection to him such as I felt when Wyatt was watching me dance. That was fascinating to me, and the mere fact that I don't have a shred of guilt over that connection makes me wonder if I'm beginning to finally accept that David and I are really through.

Padding down my short, narrow hallway that houses just my room on one side and a small, dingy bathroom on the other, I start pulling off my clothes… micro-stretch denim skirt, off-the-shoulder rayon shirt, slutty red bra. By the time I reach into the shower to turn on the water, I'm ready to shimmy out of the matching, bright red panties and wash the heavy layer of scummy job off my body.

The water is pleasant and soothing, but I make quick work of it, as the hot water doesn't last more than five minutes. Another ten minutes and my body and face are moisturized and my hair is dried to a sufficient level of dampness that I don't mind going to sleep on. I cross the hall into my bedroom and slip on a pair of cotton pajama shorts and a matching white camisole, then turn toward my bed for some much-needed sleep.

Just as I reach out to pull back my blanket, I hear

a knock at the door. Instantly, I go on high alert, because there shouldn't be anyone at my door. Best-case scenario—it's a neighbor needing a poorly timed cup of sugar; next best—a potential rapist; and worst-case—it's Simon Keyes, who has found out that I am not Nikki O.

I walk softly toward the front door, pausing at my couch, where I reach under the cushion and pull out my Glock 22 .40 Caliber handgun. A quick pull on the slide to chamber a round, and I have it cocked.

There's no safety on this gun so I hold it loosely at my side, my forefinger grasping around the stock rather than the trigger. I walk to the door and curse to myself that there's no peephole.

"Who is it?" I call out.

"Raze," I hear back, his voice low.

I reach up and slide the safety chain off, unlock the door, and open it. And God… how can a man be that gorgeous, particularly at 2:45 AM, after spending all day and night in a slimy strip club. His hair is perfectly spiked, his black t-shirt pulled tight over a broad chest, and a darkening of scruff over his jaw and chin.

"Gonna invite me in?" he asks, and I blink at him stupidly.

"Andrea?" he prompts, and I blink once more before I give a slight cough and step back from the door.

"Yeah… of course. Come in."

He walks past me and I shut the door, relocking it but foregoing the chain. He turns, and his eyes glance down at the gun in my hand. "Good girl," is all he says.

I give him a nod of my head and then eject the magazine. A quick pull of the slide and the lone round pops free and clatters to the floor. I deftly pick it up, push it back into the top of the magazine, and slide it back home. Now I have a fully loaded gun but without a round in the chamber, that I can safely store back under my seat cushion and not worry about it inadvertently discharging and shooting me in the ass while I watch TV.

"What are you doing here?" I ask as I turn away from him and walk back to the couch to hide the Glock.

"Just needed to touch base... fill you in on some things. See how things are going on your end."

"Should you be here?" I ask him skeptically. "I mean... what if Simon had you followed or something? That would look suspicious."

Wyatt shrugs his shoulders and walks over to sit in the old recliner, his fingers idly smoothing the patch job over a hole in the armrest that is repaired with duct tape. "Nah... I'd just tell him I was sniffing around you, hoping to get laid."

I sit down on my couch, feeling the lump of the gun under me, and cock an eyebrow at him. "He doesn't care if you bang the hired help?"

"Nope," he says candidly. "He sort of expects all the guys to sample. Sort of a perk of the job, so to speak."

"And have you sampled?" I ask before I can even help myself.

His eyes appraise me, even raking over my body to take stock of my pajamas. I pull my bare legs up under me, suddenly self-conscious, which is ridiculous. He's seen every inch of my naked body, a thought that causes my face to flame red as I sit here in close proximity to him.

"Undercover work is hard," he says with a smirk. "We have to do things to maintain that cover. Play a role, so to speak. Sacrifice our principles."

"And I suppose you're all about the role play?" I ask candidly.

Wyatt gives a low chuckle and scratches at his chin, his eyes lowering to the floor. When they rise back up, he looks me dead in the eye. "I didn't sample. Didn't sacrifice my principles. Wasn't necessary, as it's not something Simon watches, per se. But if it was required of me to get this job done, I'd sample the entire stock."

I give him a dim smile, although I'm immensely relieved for some reason that he didn't sleep with any of the other girls. "I get it. This operation is too important. I mean… we've all heard of the undercover cop that has to use drugs to get in good with the drug dealers. It's a necessary evil."

"Did that evil," Wyatt mutters, and my eyebrows shoot sky high.

"You did undercover narcotics?"

He nods with a hard glint in his eye. "For an operation that lasted almost a year. Was in pretty deep but it was a successful bust."

"Did you have to…?" I start to ask, but then let the words taper off. It's none of my business.

"Yeah, I did," he says quietly. "There's not anything I wouldn't do to see it through."

"I'm the same way," I tell him. "There's not anything I won't do now that I'm in to see this through."

I see something flick through Wyatt's eyes… maybe respect… maybe fear… and he grimaces.

"Look… that's what I want to talk to you about. You're doing a phenomenal job so far… playing your role perfectly. If we're lucky, things will continue on as is until your sale can be arranged, and you won't have to suffer anything more than baring your body to those douchebags."

"What do you mean… if we're lucky?"

Wyatt takes a breath, leans his head back to look at the ceiling, and then lets it out. When his eyes meet mine again, he says, "Simon has your buyer locked down. They're planning on making the exchange next week."

"Okay," I say carefully. This is good news, but something about his voice causes my skin to break out in chilled goose bumps.

"Simon told me today that he wants to do a little sampling of his own before the sale," he says, his voice sharp as a knife's blade. "The lap dance you gave him during your audition was just a little too good."

"Oh," I say, lowering my eyes to my hands, which are clasped in my lap.

Simon Keyes wants to fuck me. Dismay and disgust course through me. I had imagined something like this could happen, even imagining worst-case scenario that I get sold, our bust gets foiled, and I endure being raped by my captor. But no amount of imagining really prepared me to accept the cold, hard reality of my situation.

Yet, we are too close to let this all go down the drain. It won't mean anything if I have to do it. I can let my mind drift away as it does while I'm dancing, and I can compartmentalize that horror away from my psyche. I can do this.

Squaring my shoulders, I raise my gaze back to Wyatt's. "I'll do whatever is necessary so this doesn't go down the drain. You don't have to worry about me holding up my end."

Wyatt surges up out of his chair and glares down at me. "For fuck's sake, Andrea. You are not fucking Simon Keyes."

"But we can't get him angry… or suspicious. I have to—"

"You are not fucking him," Wyatt snarls at me. "We'll figure something out, but I just wanted you to

SAWYER BENNETT

be aware of his thoughts. I don't know if he'll approach you. For all I know, he could have just been spouting off. But I want you to be alert and careful."

"But—" I try to say, and he cuts me off again.

"Starting now, I'll cash out your tips first each night so you can hurry up and get the hell out. He normally stays locked up in his office until all of that accounting is over with."

"But don't you think—?"

"And you do not open that door for anyone that knocks on it," he rolls right over me, thumbing back at the door over his shoulder. "If I have to see you again, I'll always tell you it's me when I knock. Otherwise, you keep silent and pretend you are not home for anyone that knocks. Understand?"

"Wyatt, you have to consider—" I try again, but he lunges at me, taking me by my shoulders and leaning his face in close to mine.

"Just shut the fuck up and say you understand," he commands in a deadly voice that causes a shiver of dread... or is that desire... to race up my spine. "It's not negotiable."

"Okay," I whisper.

Wyatt releases his hold on me and starts to turn away, but I make sure to hastily add on, "But if I'm in a situation where I have to make that decision, you have to know I'll do what's best for the operation."

Spinning back on me, Wyatt starts to say something, but then slams his mouth shut. He glares at me a moment, and I lift my chin higher to him in defiance. His eyes bore into me, trying to cow me into submission.

I lift my chin higher, and then something shutters over his eyes.

With a shrug of his shoulders, he says, "Whatever. It's your body... do with it what you will."

"I'll do what's best for this mission," I reaffirm.

"I'm sure you will," he says softly before heading toward the door.

"Is that it?" I ask as I jump off the couch to follow him. "Is there anything else we need to discuss about the sale?"

His fingers work at my locks, but he says over his shoulder, "I don't have any details on the time and place yet. Once I get that, I'll get with you and we'll have to come up with a fast plan of action. But there is one thing I need you to start doing."

"What's that?" I say, and my breath catches as he turns to face me. Again, I'm struck with just how beautiful he really is.

"Start wearing more casual clothes when you come in to work. Not the hooker wear. Jeans, baggy t-shirt, running shoes."

"Okay, but why?"

"Because if Simon follows the same pattern, the abduction will happen after you get off duty... at the Club. I'll need you to be wearing clothes where we can conceal a weapon on you. There's nowhere to hide that Glock in those skirts you wear that barely cover your ass."

"Got it," I say, marveling over his foresight at this point in the game. He's not telling me this to be prepared for an unexpected abduction. No, he'll have notice of when that's going to occur, and I'll have time to be dressed accordingly. He's telling me to start wearing casual clothing now so that it becomes my norm... my habit... and it won't seem out of place later on down the line.

Wyatt turns away and opens the door. He turns to me after he steps into the hallway. Our eyes lock, and his gaze flits for the barest of moments down to my lips and then back up again. "Lock up. And stay safe, okay?"

"Okay," I say. "You stay safe too."

I start to shut the door, but Wyatt's hand shoots out and stops the progression. I look at him in surprise.

"I'm not going to let anything bad happen to you, okay?"

"Okay," I whisper, and then he's gone.

CHAPTER 7

Wyatt

ALMOST A WEEK to the day after I went to Andrea's apartment, I push on the handle to the back door from Simon's office and step out into the parking lot behind the club. When the door closes behind me, the music is immediately drowned out and I don't waste any time, because right now... it's a precious commodity.

Pulling my phone out, I dial Mike Gomez and he answers on the first ring. "Talk," is all he says.

"It's going down tomorrow night," I tell him while I keep my eye on the back door to make sure no one else comes out. "Simon just left about five minutes ago to iron out the details with the buyer."

"Where will it go down?" he asks, his voice now on high alert.

"No clue yet, but I will try to call or text the minute I find out," I tell him.

Chances of me being able to do that though are nil, and I tell him that as well. While Simon is going to utilize me to help make the transfer, he told me he'd fill me in on the details tomorrow night. This tells me, that while I'm in the circle of trust, I'm really only standing with one foot in and the other foot still hanging out.

He had just met with Lance and me not fifteen minutes ago in his office and told me that Andrea's buyer had committed. Unbeknownst to me, he was apparently in the club tonight and watched her dance, liked what he saw... very much, according to Simon... and made a tentative offer.

Lance and I were told to make arrangements to get her into Simon's office tomorrow night after she gets off duty, and then the only other thing I was made privy to was that I would go along with them to make the transfer. Simon was nervous about drugging her, especially after what happened with Carla, and I suggested maybe something a little less dangerous. A small dose of Ecstasy to make her compliant and to take away her inhibitions.

He thought it was a brilliant idea, and he clapped me on the back like a proud father.

My adrenaline spiked with the knowledge that this bust was very close to going down. It also spiked with fear for Andrea's safety, and my mind started whirring, trying to come up with some type of game plane. But unfortunately, we were going in blind and I figured we'd be winging much of this.

One other emotion coursed through me, and it

took me by surprise.

I was immensely relieved when Simon said that he was leaving to meet with the buyer in a quieter place where they could continue negotiations on the price and maybe have a celebratory drink. That meant that I didn't have to worry about Simon trying to fuck Andrea.

While he had made mention of it last week, and part of it was done in a cocky, egotistical manner as he, Lance, and I sat around after the club closed—shooting the shit—I decided I was going to take him seriously over his interest in Andrea. While she made it clear she would do whatever was necessary not to screw up this operation, I was going to move heaven and earth so she wouldn't have to sacrifice her body... probably her soul... in that manner.

True to my word, I cashed Andrea out first every night since our talk, getting her out of the club as quickly as possible before Simon could come out of his office to make a move on her. And now that Simon was gone from the club this evening and wouldn't return tonight, it meant that she was safe from his clutches again. Temporarily, of course, because tomorrow night the stakes were going to be astronomically high and she'd be in more danger than ever before.

Still, I welcomed the relief that Simon wouldn't know her body.

A body that I have been constantly obsessing

about… fantasizing about.

It's absolute fucking torture watching her on the stage, night after night… her skin glowing, her body undulating, completely fucking naked and moving so provocatively. It causes me to have to go home each night and jack off my frustration.

I have never in my entire career been attracted to another fellow law enforcement officer. Not that there haven't been some beautiful women that I've worked with, but I've never chosen to look at them as anything more than an extension of myself.

But Andrea's different. While she's playing her role to perfection, it doesn't mean that elements of her true personality don't shine through at times. It may be in the way that she gives a soft smile to one of the few patrons that actually treat the women with respect, or the way that she jokes around with some of the bouncers. Sometimes, it's even in the way that I watch her on stage, and she's entrancing every man with her eroticism, yet I can tell by the look on her face that she's far away in a safe place. I admire the way that she can compartmentalize, and that shows me a lot about her moral fiber and her dedication to the job.

Yeah… my attraction for her goes way deeper than just her sex appeal, which is through the fucking roof. I search my memory and can't think of a single woman I've ever been with that I wanted more than I want her. I can't fucking help it… she's a temptation that while I can't have, I still desire very much. While I'm anxious to get this job over and get back to my life in the Outer Banks, I'm most anxious to actually part ways with Andrea so I don't have to suffer from wanting that proverbial cookie in the cookie jar that I know I really can't have.

"What's the game plan if you can't get information to me in time?" Mike asks, and this is something I've given some thought to over the last few days.

"I'm going to meet with Andrea tonight and discuss it. I'll have both of us armed. Simon's entrusted me to ensure she's drugged properly. Then we're just going to hope the element of surprise and quickly drawn guns works."

"Clearly, that won't be a problem if you can alert me to where the sale will take place. I can have a tactical team in place, but you two may have to do this on your own. At the very least, I can follow your GPS signal as long as there's no jammer in use, and we can move in after you become stationary. Set up nearby but probably not close enough to help if things go sour quickly."

Yeah, by sour he means if a shootout ensues. He could be half a block over and that wouldn't be close enough to beat speeding bullets. This, I knew and accepted.

This could end badly for Andrea and me but that's part of what you accept as a cop.

"Let's just hope I can get you some details. If not, from what I gather, it's just going to me, Simon, and Lance at the exchange with the buyer. The unknown is whether the buyer will have anyone with him."

"Do the best you can, Wyatt," Mike says. "We're almost there, buddy. It's almost over."

"Almost over," I concur. "I better get back in the club. Hope to talk to you soon, man."

I disconnect and start toward the back door when my beeper goes off. Glancing down, I see the message.

Customer complaint. VIP 5.

"Fuck," I mutter to myself as I unlock the back door and step inside. "Just another day at the office."

I make my way through the club, past the stage where two of the dancers are grinding against each other. My eyes sweep the area, looking for Andrea. She danced about twenty minutes ago and wouldn't be back on for a while. She was probably in the back changing into something so she could serve drinks until her next number.

I jog quickly up the stairs, turn left, and head down to VIP Room Number 5.

After giving a soft knock to announce my presence, I open the door and step inside. My blood immediately boils when I take in Andrea, naked but clutching a discarded corset over her crotch with her other arm covering her breasts. She looks fearful as she glances at me and then back at another man in the room.

My stomach tightens when I see Peter Cantz, one of Simon's best friends and closest criminal allies. Lance told me once that he is heavy into the gun trade and he scratches Simon's back with cut-rate deals on arms and munition, while Simon repays the favor by offering him in on his meth operation.

He's a frequent visitor at The Platinum Club, and is one of the heaviest spenders.

My gut tightened when I first saw him because every time he visits, he ends up fucking one of the girls. He pays well because he always wants the dirtiest kind of kink, and he always walks away a happy man.

"Peter," I say in a friendly tone as I walk over to him with my hand outstretched. "Is there a problem?"

He shakes my hand and gives me a tight smile. "Bitch over there isn't willing to play. I put three hundred in her hand, and then she went all shy virgin on me."

Fuck, fuck, fuck.

I think back to that relief I felt when I realized Simon wouldn't have an opportunity to get at Andrea, and it's completely gone. I thought Simon was the only threat and never in a million years thought Andrea would be in any other type of danger while working here. Sure… a lot of Simon's girls fuck the patrons for money in these VIP rooms, but that business is all very closely regulated by me. Because I am the one that approves which customers are allowed in on this action and the one that approves which girls whore themselves out, I just never worried that this would touch Andrea. The plan was for her to be one of the four or five girls that work here that don't sell their bodies, and it was something that I just didn't worry about.

Apparently… that was a critical error in not taking it more seriously.

Putting on my most apologetic and sheepish look, I say, "Sorry, man… Nikki here is new. She's not aware of that part of the business."

Peter's face flushes red with anger. "She's fucking aware of it now. I gave her my money and told her I want to fuck her bent over the couch. How much clearer does it have to be for her?"

"I'm sorry, Peter," I say in apology but in a much-firmer tone. "She's not part of that business. Simon entrusted me with making sure that all the girls are properly vetted for this line of work, and Nikki hasn't been approved. Let me get another girl up here—"

"No fucking way," Peter roars. "I want that bitch, and you know Simon doesn't deny me anything."

"Raze," I hear Andrea say from behind me and by the tone of her voice, I know what she's getting ready to do.

I give Peter my back and turn to look at her. I pin her with a glare that says, *Shut the fuck up*, and her mouth slams closed.

"Let's go," I say to her firmly, and she starts walking toward me. When she gets near enough, I reach out to grasp her arm and push her toward the door. Looking back at Peter, I say, "I'll send another girl up."

Peter opens his mouth to argue, so I continue, "In fact, I'll send two girls up, and it will be on the house. You can have them all night."

He's no dummy, and from what I understand, quite the savvy businessman, so I'm not surprised when his mouth closes and he gives me a nod of acquiescence.

"I'll send up a bottle of Chivas for you as well. That's your favorite, right?"

Again, he nods, and I exhale a quiet breath of relief as I pull out my phone and dial. Leon picks up. "Send Misty and Layla up to VIP 5 as well a bottle of Chivas. Charge it to the house."

I don't even wait for Leon's answer, disconnecting and pushing Andrea out of the door. When I close it behind me, I turn my back on her.

"Get dressed," I tell her.

I hear her rustling into her clothing and after a few minutes, she steps around me and looks at me with censure. "You didn't have to do that. You could have jeopardized—"

"Not another word," I growl at her as I take her by the arm again.

I escort her firmly toward the staircase that leads down into the club but before we can start our descent, I see Lance walking up toward us.

"What's going on?" he asks in a tight voice as his eyes flick back and forth between Andrea and me. "Manny said that Peter was in VIP 5 and had a complaint."

"I took care of it," I say as I watch Lance continue to walk up toward us.

"I won't ask again," Lance says in a dangerous snarl right to my face. "What the fuck was the problem?"

Andrea tenses up beside me, and I stroke my thumb on the inside of her upper arm in reassurance. "Peter paid her money and wanted to fuck her. She said no, and he got pissed. I told him she wasn't a part of the—"

I'm cut off as Lance lunges past me and grabs ahold of Andrea's other arm. "Fucking snooty-ass bitch thinks she's too good. Is that it?"

Lance rips Andrea away from my grasp and starts pulling her down the stairs. "Send someone else up to Peter," he calls out over his shoulder.

I bound down the stairs quickly behind them. "I already did," I say hastily, hoping to quell his sudden burst of fury.

"Then it's time this cunt learned her place," Lance snarls as he reaches the bottom of the stairs.

Fear and anger surge through me as I watch Lance haul her through the club. Other dancers watch in interest… some with amused smirks, others with a look of pity in their eyes.

My eyes catch Leon's across the room, and he raises his eyebrows at me in a silent question, *Do you need help?*

I give a shake of my head and lengthen my stride to keep up with Lance. He pulls her down the back hallway to the left of the stage, straight toward Simon's office, and then he's pushing her through so roughly that she stumbles and almost falls. Luckily, she catches herself on the corner of Simon's desk and rights herself.

I grab ahold of Lance's arm and pull him around so he faces me. "What the fuck are you doing?" I whisper urgently. "Peter's taken care of. He's not mad anymore."

The fucker gives me a wink in return. "I know. He's satisfied with any pussy."

"Then what are you doing to Nikki? You know she's not part of the prostitution... She didn't do anything wrong."

Lance steps in closer to me, a maniacal smile on his face. "I know. But I'm not about to waste a chance to beat this bitch down into submission a bit. Make her a little easier for us to handle tomorrow. I want to see what kind of fighter she is."

"You are not going to—?" I start to say, intent on blowing this whole operation out of the water if I have to save Andrea from being raped by Lance.

"Relax, dude," he says with a chuckle. "I like my

women willing. But I am going to test her."

With that, Lance turns away from me and walks into Simon's office. I follow him in and watch as Andrea raises her head and pushes her hair out of her face. I don't know if it's an act or not, but she looks scared. This causes my own fear and anger to surge again.

Lance stalks up to her and wraps his large hand around her throat, pulling her up straighter. Leaning his face in, he hisses at her, "You think you call the shots around here, Nikki?"

"No," she whispers fearfully, now standing on her tiptoes to try to keep balance with the way Lance is holding her up by her throat.

I stand poised... ready to attack if Lance makes a move to hurt her. The fear in her voice has me on edge, and every protective instinct I have as a man rears up inside of me. Andrea's eyes are flared wide, her bottom lip quivering. I take a step toward Lance to put an end to this, but then I look down at Andrea's hands. Both of her arms hang loose beside her body, but her fists are balled up tight. I watch as she opens her hands, and then curls her fingers inward again in tight reflex.

Open... close. Open... close.

She's not scared.

She's pissed, yet she's still maintaining an act.

Immediately, my pulse calms somewhat, because her body language is telling me that she has a grip on the situation and she is not fearful as to where she's at right now.

Reluctantly, I decide to trust my partner and let it play out.

Wanting to appear nonchalant and vaguely interested in what Lance is going to do to "test her," I walk over to one of the chairs and sit down. I stretch my legs out in front of me, casually resting my elbows on the armrests.

"You are the fucking employee, Nikki," Lance snarls in her face. "You do not say *no* to the customers."

"Okay," she says quickly… fearfully… giving him no fight.

"You want this fucking job?" Lance asks, his nose just an inch from her own. He gives her a tiny shake to further bully her.

"Y-y-y-es," she stammers, and her fists clench and uncurl.

Clench and uncurl.

"Then you better do anything Simon, Raze, or I tell you to do, you hear me?" he says with menace.

"Yes," she blurts out. "Yes, of course. I'm sorry. I'll go back to that man now, if you want."

Lance doesn't say anything, just stares at her intently. I see his eyes roaming back and forth between her own, gauging the truth of her words.

He releases his grip on her throat and her heels go back down until she's standing on her own again.

"No, that opportunity is already ruined," Lance says quietly, and I let out a sigh of relief. It appears Lance just wanted to scare the shit out of her.

Reaching out, he skims his knuckles down her arm. His voice is thoughtful when he says, "But I'm not sure if you really mean what you say."

"I do," Andrea assures him.

Good girl. She sounds completely obedient.

"Let's test that out," Lance says, and I immediately go back on alert again. I sit up straighter in my chair, prepared to strike if necessary.

Lance grips Andrea by the arm and then gives her a push my way. She stumbles... rights herself again, and then straightens up, looking back over her shoulder at Lance.

"Give my boy Raze here a blow job," he says with an evil grin on his face. "A stellar fucking blow job. In fact, get on your fucking hands and knees, crawl your ass over to him, and beg him to let you blow him. You do that, and then I'll believe you when you say you'll do anything to keep this job."

Jesus fucking Christ.

No way.

No fucking way is this going to happen.

CHAPTER 8

Andrea

"**D**O IT," LANCE barks at me, and I jerk in response.

Conflicting emotions run through me. Fear that this isn't just Lance fucking with me... that he has something more nefarious planned.

Relief.

Relief that he's not the one interested in getting a blow job, and relief I didn't have to prove my loyalty by going back upstairs to fuck that guy.

Guilt.

Guilt that Wyatt has no say so in any of this, because what little I've come to know about this man... I know that he, more than anything, doesn't want me to be violated in anyway. Even if I have to give him a blow job, and he's the one receiving pleasure, he will still feel like he's violating me.

Shame.

Shame because the thought of giving Wyatt a blow job causes skitters of pleasure to course through me. Odd… I never much enjoyed it with David but for some reason, my mouth waters thinking about doing that to Wyatt.

That is wrong on so many fucked-up levels that I have to immediately dismiss it from my mind, and instead, I choose to focus on the last emotion coursing through me.

Fury.

Fury that this prick Lance thinks he can bully me around. Fury that Simon kidnaps and sells women as sex slaves. Fury that someone as good and decent as Wyatt even has to immerse himself in this untenable situation.

I slowly drop to my hands and knees and start crawling toward Wyatt. His face is hard, a muscle popping at his jawline. He gazes down at me intently, and I see the subtle grinding motion of his teeth, silently gnashing at each other.

If I were really Nikki O, a down-and-out stripper who needed this job and would do anything to keep it, I would think Wyatt was looking down at me with barely uncontrolled lust. But as FBI agent Andrea Somerville, who knows exactly what stakes are at risk here, and who remembers when Wyatt told me the other night that he wouldn't let anything bad happen to me, I see a man that is furious and regretful all at the same time that I'm crawling toward him.

Lance gives a dark chuckle behind me. "She looks phenomenal from this angle, Raze."

WITH A TWIST

Closer and closer I get to Wyatt and my heart is thundering deep within my chest. My heart aches for him as I take note of the very clear erection pressed against his black jeans, showing his traitorous body.

"You're forgetting something," Lance says thickly.

I pause in my crawling and turn my head to look back over my shoulder. Lance's eyes are pinned onto my bare ass since I'm wearing a thong, but then his eyes slide to mine. "You need to beg him."

I give Lance my most capitulating look coupled with a smile of assent and turn back to Wyatt.

Looking him straight in the eyes, I start crawling toward him again.

"Please... Raze... let me give you a blow job."

His jaw muscle pops again and his fingers curl tightly into the armrest.

I crawl closer.

"Please... let me suck you down."

Teeth grinding, his legs spread apart to give me room to crawl right up to him.

Reaching out, I place one hand on his knee and use it to pull myself up in between his legs. I hope he can see the apology in my eyes when I say, "Please... Raze... let me make you come with my mouth."

"That's it, baby," Lance murmurs behind me, and a shudder of disgust over the lust in his voice floods through me.

My eyes flutter closed, and I swallow hard. When I open them back up, I don't dare to look at Wyatt.

101

Instead, I look down at the straining fly of his jeans. My hands are shaking when I reach out and pop the button, and his hips shift slightly as I lower the zipper.

"Lift your ass," I say quietly, and he does as I ask. I hear his teeth grind together harder, and I internally wince because I know that hurts.

My fingertips slip into the waistband of his underwear, and I gently tug them and his jeans down. His erection is revealed and when the constraining material is removed, it stands up tall, thick, and hard as a rock.

It's fucking beautiful and even though this is an act... a part of the job... the tingling sensation between my legs tells me this is not going to be a hardship.

"A little privacy," Wyatt says thickly, and my eyes jerk up to his. He's not looking at me though. His gaze is focused over my shoulder at Lance, and the hard glint I see reflecting leaves no room open for Lance to argue.

"Enjoy," Lance says, and then I hear his shoes quietly whispering over the carpet. I don't turn to see him leave but instead watch Wyatt's gaze as he follows Lance's movement. I hear the office door open, then close again, and we are alone.

Wyatt's eyes slide to mine, and I expect to see relief that Lance is gone. Instead, his face is awash with regret.

His hands come up to clasp on either side of my head, and he pulls me up as he leans down toward me. I'm stunned when his mouth comes down on mine, and he gives me a swift kiss. His lips are velvety against mine, and lust courses through me. I open my mouth, but all too quickly, he pulls back and sticks his lips near my ear.

"I'm sorry," he says in the barest whisper that I almost can't hear him.

"Me too," I whisper back. "Thank God he's gone and we don't have to—"

"No," he says urgently, still in a voice so low that it sounds like it's being carried away on the wind. "I'm sorry because there's a camera over your shoulder. He's watching us."

"What?" I breathe out in surprise while Wyatt moves his lips across my skin. I realize he's hiding his mouth so Lance can't see what he's saying to me.

"He's testing me as well."

And understanding slaps me silly.

He's watching to make sure that Raze is fully on board with showing dominance over the women here. He's making sure that Raze has no problem in taking advantage of me... of abusing me.

My mind is spinning and then spins harder when Wyatt brings his mouth back to mine. Another hard kiss and then he's murmuring softly against my lips. "Listen closely... the camera is to your back so if you bend over my lap, we can fake this. He can't hear us… just see us. Your hair and the camera angle will hide what you're really doing. It's time for both of us to put on a performance. Just follow my lead and fucking fake it."

I take in everything he says to me in a mixture of part relief, part disappointment, but ultimately acceptance as this is the best thing possible so that boundaries aren't crossed. I nod and before I know it, Wyatt's hands move to my hair where he grips my head roughly.

He pushes down on my head, and I know that his face is visible to the camera again because he clearly says, "Time to put that mouth on my cock, baby."

This is said with another low murmur, as it's doubtful that Lance is at the door listening. Instead, he's in the security room watching the silent feed on this office's camera, but if he's adept at reading lips, Wyatt is giving him what he wants.

I bend my head down toward Wyatt's lap and my long hair floats all around me, shielding my face and Wyatt's cock that's sitting inches from my lips. It's dusky with a thick vein running along the bottom, and I feel terrible that Wyatt is suffering right now.

Bringing my right hand over, I slip it under the curtain of my hair and lay it on his pelvis, so that it looks like I've taken him in my grasp. I bend over further, and it's my hope that as Lance watches, he thinks I've taken Wyatt deep into my mouth.

I start a fluid bobbing motion with my head,

keeping my eyes wide open so I don't actually make contact with Wyatt's skin. I watch that beautiful cock come close to my lips, then get further away as I raise my head. He shifts slightly under me, and I can imagine his head is thrown back. His hands tighten in my hair, and he actually exerts slight pressure to help keep me from touching him.

My heart thumps with exhilaration that we are pulling this ruse off, and with a weird, achy need for something more to happen. I also feel tremendous guilt that, while this is hard on me, Wyatt is the one with the straining erection that isn't going to get a damn bit of relief.

I bob up and down, and in my zeal to put on a star performance, I push down a little too hard and my chin grazes against the tip of his shaft. Wyatt hisses… almost as if he's in pain, and my body freezes. I raise my eyes even as his fingers dig sharply into the back of my neck and side of my head.

His look catches me off guard, and the oxygen is pulled from my lungs. His eyes are filled with lust and frustration, yet he says to me softly, "You're doing great, baby. Keep going."

Anger, guilt, shame, and fury roll back through me again, and I am pissed that Wyatt is being made to suffer this travesty.

"This isn't working," I whisper.

"Sure it is," he says through gritted teeth, pushing back down on my head so I can resume my ruse. "Just a little more and I'll fake the world's biggest orgasm."

"I'm sorry," I murmur, and our eyes lock. I hope he can see how truly, truly sorry I am for what I'm getting ready to do.

I lower my head and move my hand to grip him at the base of his cock. The minute my fingers touch his warm flesh, his entire body tightens. I open my mouth and guide the tip of him inside of me, taking him deep inside… straight to where my tongue ends and my throat begins.

"Fuck," Wyatt groans, and his hips buck up hard against me.

His shaft is warm and pulsing within my mouth. I start moving… desperately, with purpose. I want him to come… I want him to have a moment of peace and pleasure, and I want more than anything for us not to fuck up this operation when we are too close to the finish line.

Mostly, however, I want Wyatt to feel good. I want to make him feel good.

I move over him, licking and sucking. Pumping him hard with my hand, I moan low in my throat so he feels the vibrations against his skin. I want this to go quickly, because I want us both to get past this, and because the longer I keep him in my mouth, the more I yearn for something more.

I feel twitchy and unsettled, a deep, empty feeling within me. I want the world to melt away so there's no Lance watching us, no strip club music thumping outside the doors, no jilted fiancée feelings within me. I wish this were just Wyatt and me… two people that are attracted to each other. Two people that could bask in physical pleasures.

"Fuck, fuck, fuck," Wyatt starts chanting. A quick raise of my eyes reveals his head to be thrown backward and the muscles in his neck corded tight. His fingers dig into my scalp, and then relax in spasms. His hips gyrate underneath of me with need, and I move up and down on his warm, slick shaft.

"Fuck, fuck, fuck… coming… fuck… I'm coming," Wyatt groans and pushes down hard on my head. I suck him in extra deep, feel the first shot of him against the back of my throat, and I take every bit of him down. His breathing is erratic…sharp blasts of air that I can feel fluttering against my hair. I softly lick against his skin before pulling away from him… terrified to look up in his eyes.

He doesn't give me a chance to face my cowardice though because his hands come under my armpits and he's hauling me up his body. His mouth meets mine brutally, and his tongue dives in deep. Wyatt kisses me savagely… so invasive I feel him everywhere, and my fingers clutch hard onto his t-shirt.

I'm dazed… aching… confused over how much pleasure I took in that. Wyatt pulls back slightly, bringing his lips to my ear. "You didn't have to fucking do that," he growls, and I'm surprised at how much rage I hear in his voice.

Pushing down on his chest, I rise up from the floor, gain my balance, and stare down at him. His eyes are blazing, but I know his face is blocked from the camera.

"I'm sorry," I blurt out softly, unsure of what to do.

His eyes harden further, and he grits out. "Too far. Too fucking far, Andrea."

I know he's seriously pissed and it sucks… because that's the first time he's used my real name, so I know he's serious. I know he's angry. I know Wyatt is angry… not Raze.

He surges up from the chair, tucking himself back in and zipping up his jeans. Grabbing me by the arm, he steers me toward the office door. With both of our backs to the camera, he says, "Sale is tomorrow. I'll be by your apartment later to discuss it. Now get back to work."

He gives me a little push out of the door and then it's closing in my face. I stare at the scarred wood and faded brass plate that says "Office," my eyes misting with emotional tears. I blink hard, push them back, and square my shoulders.

Fuck, that didn't go well at all.

Turning around, I run smack into Lance coming out of the security office. Just as Wyatt predicted, he was in there watching.

"Good girl," he murmurs as he reaches out and rubs a thumb over my bottom lip. "I think you'll do just fine."

I give him a tremulous smile. "Thank you, and again... I'm sorry about earlier."

"No worries, baby. Now get back out there. I believe you're on stage in about fifteen minutes."

My stomach pitches at the thought of doing yet another dance, but then a surge of relief washes through me. Wyatt said the sale is set for tomorrow night. We're on the verge of making this happen. One thing is for sure, tomorrow night... it will all be over.

CHAPTER 9

A FTER PUSHING THE door closed on Andrea, I walk back over to the chair I had just vacated and plop back down in it. Rubbing my hands vigorously over my face, I take a deep breath and let it out in slow frustration.

Damn… that fucking felt amazing.

Best. Head. Ever.

And yet it was so very wrong to go there.

I should have stopped her. I should have had the strength to pull her off me. Should have done something to prevent her from wrapping those beautiful lips around my dick.

Yet, I didn't do a damn thing except thrust my hips up to hit her mouth harder, and I'm pretty sure I did a hell of a lot of groaning.

What in the hell was Andrea thinking? We were doing an adequate job of faking it. I knew the camera angle, fuzzy resolution, and positioning of Andrea's body wouldn't give Lance a clear-cut picture. I knew he'd be watching a grainy image of her bobbing her head up and down over my lap, and I was pretty sure that he couldn't clearly see facial expressions or read my lips. Still... I was cautious about it, choosing instead to kiss the fuck out of Andrea first before moving my lips closer to her ear to communicate.

Don't regret that kiss a damn bit. It was wrong as well, but it's easier to justify a kiss and I couldn't fucking help myself. I've been fantasizing about kissing every inch of her body since that first time she danced, and I wasn't about to let an opportunity to have her lips pass by.

I'm still pissed at her though.

I'm pissed because she took away my control.

Yeah... the minute her hand wrapped around the base of my cock, I was done. I knew there was no way I was going to stop her. I wanted it too much... I was too weak... fucking consequences be damned.

And it was fan-fucking-tastic. She was a fantasy come true and if I'm completely honest about it, the only thing I'm regretful about is the fact that she felt it her duty to go all the way. That she felt pressured to make sure that our duplicity would not be discovered. That she ultimately sacrificed her body so Lance would not be suspicious of us. Yeah... I'm fucking regretful that all of my grandiose plans to make sure she would never have to go too far in her role were a complete, fucking bust, and all because I was too weak to insist she stop.

Simon's office door opens, and Lance walks in with a shit-eating grin on his face. He takes the seat next to me. "So, how did our girl do?"

He knows fucking well how she did. He was watching—I'm sure of it.

I'm also sure that he was able to see enough to know that it didn't take me long to get off, and that I came hard, so there's no hiding the fact it was fucking great.

"Man… she's got some mad skills with that mouth of hers." And then, because I want to turn the conversation to something far more interesting to me, I say, "Her buyer is going to be very pleased with her."

"As long as she doesn't bite his dick off as a means of rebelling." Lance snickers.

I could so imagine Andrea doing that, but then I put that out of my head. To imagine her biting off her captor's dick means I would have to imagine that she actually gets sold to him, and I'm not going to let that fucking happen.

"Speaking of rebelling," I say to turn the conversation toward the actual abduction in an attempt to see if Lance will give me any further details that could be helpful to my planning. "I'm going to slip Nikki the drug after she finishes her last dance tomorrow night. It takes about forty-five minutes to take good effect, so I figured I'd just bring her back here to Simon's office and hang with her. Do we have a long drive ahead of us to make the exchange?"

"Not a long drive," Lance says dismissively of my question. "Hey... maybe you'll get another blow job from her before the transfer. I've never tried it, but I know X takes away your inhibitions."

Lance laughs and gives me a brotherly punch to my arm.

"Yup... definitely lowers inhibitions. Wouldn't say no to another blow job, either," I tell him with a fake, toothy grin of slimy brotherhood even though I'm disappointed as fuck he won't tell me any details about where the transfer will take place.

"It was a good call to suggest the X," he says as an afterthought. "She won't be knocked out, but I'm still a little worried she may put up a fight."

"Nah... Ecstasy generally produces euphoria. She'll be too happy to fight. I scored some with a little bit of ketamine mixed in, so she'll be a little loopy. I'm going to tell her we're taking her to an after-hours party for her to dance. She'll be totally compliant."

"That's a good plan," Lance says soberly. "That shit with Carla was a fucking fiasco. You did a good job handling that too."

I learned pretty quickly that Lance and Simon both value humility, so I shrug my shoulders carelessly. "Wasn't a big deal."

"Will you have any problem giving Nikki the drug?"

"Nope. She drinks a Diet Coke after every dance.

Creature of habit. I'll just slip it right in."

"And you don't think she'll fight at all?"

"Definitely not. I've used this drug on a lot on women," I tell him with a lecherous grin. "She'll be like putty in my hands."

Lance stares at me a moment, and then says, "That's good. Because I'm not going to be at the transfer, and I need to make sure you can handle this alone with Simon."

A jolt of euphoric adrenaline over this news spikes through me, but I carefully school my features. I appear bored when I say, "It'll be fine. Trust me... she'll do anything I tell her to after I give her the dose."

"You do a good job with this... Simon's going to bring you into the operation. You'll get a cut."

"Fucking awesome," I say with fake glee. "I'm so ready, dude. You both can count on me."

Lance nods his head in agreement as I move my way further inside the circle of trust. Stupid fuck.

"I know we can count on you. I felt good about you the minute we brought you in."

Lying fucker. Forcing Andrea's blow job on me was a means of testing my loyalty. Thanks to Andrea... I passed with flying colors, so he might trust me now, but he didn't just half an hour ago.

"So, where are you going to be?" I ask casually.

"Simon wants to expand this business outward. He has a connection that has stock down in Mexico.

Kidnapped tourists or some shit like that, and they want a pipeline to move them here in the States. We'll have to share a cut with the Mexicans, but we can move more stock so we'll make it up in volume. We actually need to cut back on the amount of girls that we're taking from the club. Don't want to get on the police radars."

I nod my head thoughtfully toward him, but my mind is on overdrive trying to process this development. It doesn't have shit to do with my operation, but if I can get any information from him, the FBI can launch an investigation into this new potential sex-slave ring. "Yeah… that's good business planning. How are you going to get the girls out of Mexico and over the border?"

"We have a guy with the U.S. Border Patrol at the Antelope-Wells crossing who will turn a blind eye for a cut of the action. Again, eats into our overall profit, but we can move many more girls so we'll be rolling in the dough."

"You have enough buyers lined up?" I ask curiously.

"Simon's working on it… it's mainly word of mouth from our prior buyers. There's an entire underworld clique of these freaks that like to own sex slaves. But he's going to be really busy… doing a lot of travel to set this all up. That means more responsibility on your shoulders here at the club."

"Not a problem," I tell him. "I've got it all under

control here."

Lance reaches over and claps me on the back. "Come on. Let's get back to work."

We both stand up and head toward the door. Just as Lance reaches out for the knob, he casually says, "I think I'm going to have to take advantage of Nikki's skills tonight when she gets off duty. She looked hot as hell when she was crawling. I'll give her knees another workout."

He chuckles over this and starts to pull the door open.

My hand shoots out, connects my palm to the wood, and I slam it shut. Lance turns to look at me in surprise, and I try to keep my voice light... joking.

"No way, man. Already made plans with her for tonight."

"So cancel them," he says dismissively.

"Not gonna happen. Already itching to fuck her after that blow job," I say calmly.

Lance stares at me... his eyes blinking in almost disbelief that I'd challenge him. I'm in a very precarious position right now. If I push this, I'm rocking the boat with Lance and could make him suspicious. But fuck if I'm going to let him take a crack at her.

Knowing what I know about Andrea... she's all in. She'd submit to him to keep up appearances, a thought that I literally don't think I could live with on my conscience. A small current of fear takes hold as I wait to see what Lance does, and I'm fearful because I know deep in my heart that I will jeopardize this entire operation before I let him touch a hair on Andrea's head.

"Dude... you're seriously trying to trump me?" Lance asks, and I relax a bit when I hear the teasing tone of his voice.

"Just consider it a bonus for the way I handled the Carla situation," I say with a smirk.

"Fucker," he says good-naturedly and punches me on the arm. He opens the door, and I follow him out of Simon's office. "Just don't wear her out. She needs to be in good shape tomorrow night. I'm sure her buyer isn't going to wait long before he taps that pussy."

I force neutrality on my face again and swallow the urge to strangle him for his crude words about Andrea. I know I'm taking this a bit too personally at this point, but fuck... the fact I just came down her throat not all that long ago sort of changes my perspective on things.

"I hear ya," I say, and then turn toward the stock room. "I'm going bring a few cases of beer over to the main bar. I saw they were running a little low earlier."

"Later dude," Lance says, and then he's heading toward the main stage.

Once inside the storeroom with the door firmly shut, I move in deeper past rows of stacked cases of beer and liquor. The music is muffled, and I'm confident I can't be overheard in here. Still, I keep my eye on the door while I quickly pull out my cell to call Mike.

"What's up?" he says when he answers.

"Bad news and good news. What do you want first?"

"Bad," he says.

"No more details on where it's going down. All I've been told is to have her drugged and waiting in Simon's office after closing."

"How about we put a tracker on Andrea?"

"No," I immediately say. "In fact, I'm not even going to have her armed when I put her in the car in the off chance Simon takes precautions and searches her. I'll slip her one of my guns at some point before it happens."

"Sounds like you're doing a lot of this without any formal plan," Mike muses. "Not sure I like that."

"Well, tough shit. I'm in the best position right now to know what will fly and what won't. You're just going to have to lock on my phone's GPS and follow as best you can. Get in as close as you can but don't make any move until I do."

"Got it," he says resolutely. "What's the good news?"

"Lance isn't going to be present, so that's makes it easier on me and Andrea when we make the bust. But you need to be ready to put a tail on him starting now. I don't have a lot of time to talk but Simon is expanding. Going to bring in women up from Mexico that have been kidnapped. Lance is going to iron out the details on that deal tomorrow night."

"You have anything else on that?" he asks, and I can hear him typing notes on his computer as he talks to me.

"Only that Simon will be lining up buyers and that the women will come in at Antelope-Wells in New Mexico. He says they have a border patrol guard on the payroll."

"Got it. Good work. Do you need anything else from us tomorrow night?"

"Just ping my phone GPS and have a team near-by."

"You got it," he says and then after a short hesitation, "Good luck, Wyatt. You've done amazing work so far on this. You're close to bringing it all down, buddy."

"Andrea too," I say quickly, and why I'm wasting my time to make sure he knows this is beyond me.

"Pardon?" Mike asks, confused.

"Andrea has done a great job too, so far. She's a real asset to the FBI."

"I'll pass that on," Mike says genially.

"Alright… I'm out and probably won't call again unless I learn something new that changes things."

"Alright, buddy," Mike says quietly. "See you on the other side."

We disconnect, and I grab a few cases of beer. I

have no clue if we're low or not, but if Lance is watching, I don't want to give him any reason to doubt my trip there just now.

When I walk back into the main area, I take immediate notice of Andrea on the stage doing her last dance of the night. I can tell by the look on her face… that sort of faraway, detached look… that she isn't even present other than in body. In fact, her eyes sweep over me as she looks around and then they keep on going. Not like the other night when our gazes locked and for several tense-filled moments, neither one of us was able to look away.

I wonder what that says about me right now? Is she ashamed of what we did? Is her soul tainted by having to go that far in her undercover work? Has she cut me out of that small part of her she keeps locked up tight so she remains protected?

I don't like any of the possible answers that come to mind, so I move along and turn my back on Andrea's erotic dance. Dumping the cases of beer up on the counter, I get a confused look from the bartender so I tell him, "Thought you might be running low."

Walking behind the bar, I busy myself with stocking the beer in the coolers, an action that is not unknown to me. When we're packed like we are tonight, I want the bartenders pouring liquor, which in turn loosens up the wallets, so I don't mind pitching in to do stuff like this.

Plus, it gives me something to do so I'm not tempted to look back up on the stage at Andrea. It's practically killing me not to, but I don't want to risk the imminent erection I know I'll get, and I don't want to have to be reminded that she's doing something very selfless to help us crack this case, even if it sullies herself in the process.

CHAPTER 10

Andrea

WHEN I DECIDED to become an FBI agent at the tender age of eight, I never really thought much about what that really meant. I was following in my dad's footsteps and because he was dead, I couldn't ask him practical advice on my career choice. Even at the wise-old age of twenty-seven, after two years with the Bureau, it never would have crossed my mind that I would be on my knees, giving my partner a blow job.

It seems absolutely ludicrous that this could be my life right at this moment, yet, here I am. Blow jobs for the greater good.

A new FBI motto.

A maniacal snicker followed by a snort slips out of me as I dress in a pair of sweat pants, my sports bra, and a loose t-shirt. I imagine Wyatt will be here soon to discuss our game plan for tomorrow night, and I'm nervous as hell because I know I didn't imagine his reaction as I was licking my lips after a job well done.

He was pissed at me.

As is my habit, I jumped in the shower as soon as I got to my apartment to scrub off the indecency of my job, making sure the heavy makeup swirled down the drain along with the metaphorical slime I was coated in. My shame in baring my body to strangers is lessening, and maybe that's due solely to the fact that I was willing to do so much more than strip to make sure my cover remained intact.

More shame piles on.

More guilt.

More embarrassment.

More than anything, I wish I were back home… in my little bungalow house in Pittsburgh… snuggled on the couch and watching a marathon of *Criminal Minds*. That show is a little out there, and isn't indicative at all of what it's really like in the BRIU, but it provides me with entertainment that I can relate to somewhat.

I want that very badly right now. I'm homesick, beaten down, and I need some type of familiar comfort.

The knock at the door has me padding softly into my living room. Before I can even detour to the couch for my gun, I hear Wyatt's gruff voice. "It's Raze."

My heart starts a mad thumping, fueled on by anxiety and the need to ease my conscience with him. I open the door to let him in, avoiding eye contact because I'm at an absolute loss as to what to say.

Wyatt walks straight into my kitchen and pulls two Diet Cokes out of my fridge. I follow him in and take the can from his offered hand, popping the top and taking a sip. Wyatt sits down at the table and kicks at the chair opposite of him. "Sit."

I pull the chair out a little further and take a seat, setting my can on the table. I notice that my soda is ice cold, which means I'm having a good fridge day, and that is one good thing that has happened to me.

I wait for him to lay into me for what I did to him, but he merely says, "I've got a tentative plan for how this will go down tomorrow. I want to discuss it with you and then hash it out. You have an excellent mind and while I have a general idea of what we should do, I really want your help in figuring this out."

I raise my eyes to his in surprise, and I see nothing but determination on his face.

No condemnation.

No anger.

Nothing but fortitude to get the job done well.

"Then let's get to work," I say as I scoot my chair forward and rest my arms on the table. This is a temporary reprieve for me, but I feel immediate relief we aren't confronting what happened in Simon's office just yet. "Tell me the basics."

Wyatt scoots forward and leans his arms on the table as well, loosely twining his fingers. "It's only going to be Simon and me taking you to the sale. No clue who the buyer will have with him, so that's an unknown."

"We should plan for there to be several," I pipe in.

Wyatt nods. "Exactly. Gomez wants to put a tracker on you, but I nixed that idea, and we'll just depend on him to follow the GPS on my phone. While I don't think Simon doubts you or me, I don't want to risk it if he chooses to search you."

"I'm fine with that," I tell him. "When will you arm me?"

"Just before the sale. They think I'm drugging you with a dose of Ecstasy and ketamine. That would make you a little loopy. I told Lance I'd drug you right after your last dance and then take you to Simon's office to wait. You should act a little buzzed, totally compliant, and in a really good mood. Our cover is that we're taking you to an after-hours party to dance."

"Sounds good," I say as I nod my head. "And how about this... put me in the car unarmed... backseat. I'll pretend to fall asleep. You make sure you're the one that has to get me out of the car... maybe just positioning yourself near the car. When you reach in to wake me up... pull me out, whatever, have a gun in your waistband for me to grab."

Wyatt gives me a small smile. "That's pretty good. Let's do that."

"So, how do you want the bust to go down?"

"We need the money to change hands. This is where a whole lot of luck will be involved. I expect Simon will want to take the cash, so I'll keep a grip on your arm while that's happening. I imagine Simon will then tell me to hand you over. That's when we need to draw our weapons."

"It would really help if we could make sure they were segregated somewhat," I muse.

"Right... make it easier for us to cover them without getting in each other's way," he finishes. "How about you create a bit of a diversion? Maybe fight with me a little before I hand you over. I'll give you a little push toward the buyer and that's the signal for both of us to draw?"

"That's perfect," I say with a respectful smile. "They'll be caught a little off guard. Only downside is if the buyer brings his own security detail. We're in the dark about this guy... no clue what type of power he has."

"That's the major unknown," Wyatt agrees and leans back in the chair, latching his hands behind his head in contemplation. He stretches his legs out under the table, accidentally kicking me in the foot.

"Sorry," he mutters, pulling his legs back and sitting back up straight in his chair.

That's all it takes... a barely there touch and our business-like groove has been broken.

Our eyes lock across the table, and I can't help but blurt out. "I'm really sorry about what happened this evening."

Wyatt immediately throws a hand up to stop me. "Don't. It's done and we need to just forget about it."

"But I can't," I say quietly, and with my feelings just a bit bruised that he could so easily forget what we did. I mean... I know it was all "in the line of duty," but damn it... it was also an intimate moment for me.

Clearly not to him though.

"Look, Andrea. It happened and while maybe that wasn't the best course of action, it's over and done with. It worked... Lance never suspected us, so consider it a victory."

"A victory?" I say with an almost hysterical bark of a laugh. "I fucking violated you. I feel so damned guilty about it, and I don't—"

"Don't," Wyatt barks at me as he lunges across the table. His hands grab ahold of mine, and he squeezes my fingers so he has my attention. "Don't you dare feel guilty."

"But I took advantage of you... of the situation. The more I think about it, the more I know we should have just faked it. It would have worked. It was so unnecessary for me to do that, and you were so angry at me after that. I knew it was wrong. I knew I had violated you."

"No, Andrea," Wyatt says in a low, reassuring voice. "You can't go back and dissect your decisions. You made a split-second decision to do what you thought was best for us to maintain our covers. I'm not going to second-guess your decision, so you shouldn't either."

Oh, a wave of guilt crashes over me again, because Wyatt doesn't exactly get what's at the crux of my turmoil. Yeah, my mind might have been thinking that it was a good, tactical decision, but only I know that there was a personal element involved as well. I *wanted* to take him in my mouth. I *wanted* to make him come. I *wanted* to have a personal connection with him.

"I could have stopped you," Wyatt says softly, breaking into my thoughts. "But I'm a man, and you are an extremely beautiful woman whom I'm attracted to. I'm being straight up honest with you... the minute your hand wrapped around my cock, I wanted you to do it."

I blink at him in confusion, vaguely thrilled that he thinks I'm beautiful.

"Do you understand me?" Wyatt growls as he leans forward in his chair a bit more, squeezing my hands a bit harder. "I wanted you to suck me off. I enjoyed the fuck out of it, and I came harder and faster than I ever have before."

He wanted it?

He enjoyed it?

He came harder and faster than ever before?

My head starts a slight spin, and my chest swells with some weird sensation that I might say is relief and sexual tension rolled into one. I open my mouth to tell him that I wanted it to… that I enjoyed it very much.

But Wyatt isn't done talking. "Listen… we all do things whether in the line of duty or just life in general that we later find to be regretful and the only thing we can do is learn from the mistake and put it behind you. We have got to put this behind us, Andrea, and focus on this operation. Okay?"

For the first time in my existence, I curse the fact I'm a woman. Because the woman in me feels like crying for some ridiculous reason. I think it may be because he used words like "regret" and "mistake," and my silly woman sensibilities may have taken his prior words a little out of context.

He wanted it.

He enjoyed it.

He came harder and faster than ever before.

Well, of course, he was all those things. He's a man, and what man was not going to enjoy that? None of that has a damn thing to do with how he feels about me as a woman. That was all about physical release and nothing more.

So I square my shoulders and lift my chin, because yes, I am a woman, but I am also tough-as-nails Andrea Somerville and I can do exactly as Wyatt has just told me to do. I can put this behind me, learn from my silly mistake—that is, it meant nothing—and move on.

"Okay," I say firmly and with a confident smile. "It's forgotten and you can trust me... my head is in this operation one-hundred percent. Thank you for clarifying that for me."

Wyatt's eyes narrow at me briefly and his lips flatten... I guess testing the sincerity in my voice. But it was strong and clear, and he has no reason to doubt me when I say it's behind me.

As of this moment... it's done... forgotten.

Well, maybe I'll fantasize about it later after I get home to Pittsburgh, but he's right. In the grand scheme of things, we have more important fish to fry.

"So, what other contingencies do we need to prepare for?" I ask him so we can get the important conversation back on track.

Wyatt blinks... once, twice... almost as if he can't believe that I'm moving on so quickly. I engage in a staring war with him, and then he clears his throat. "We need to consider the other parties may be armed."

"Nothing we can do about it but hope we get a good jump on them before they can draw," I point out.

"And hope that the buyer doesn't have anyone stationed on the perimeter we don't know about. Without Mike being able to set up ahead of time, we're going in blind."

"So this could be the end of us," I say with a grin.

I expect Wyatt to be offended over me joking in

the face of potential death, but his lips curve upward. "It might be indeed. But we'll go out in a blaze of glory, right?"

"Damn... now I have that Bon Jovi song stuck in my head," I quip.

"How in the hell do you even know what that song is? You had to have been a baby when that came out."

"Too true, Mr. Observant," I say as I stand from my kitchen chair and stretch. Walking over to the cupboards, I say, "Bon Jovi was like my parents' favorite band."

Opening a cabinet door, I pull out a bag of barbeque potato chips and return to the table. Sitting down, I open the bag, take a chip, and pop it in my mouth. As I crunch on the salty, tangy goodness, I turn the bag around and Wyatt plunges his hand in to grab a handful.

"What do your parents do?" Wyatt asks, and then tosses a few chips in his mouth.

"They've both passed on," I say with a small smile. I smile because I always remember them with fond memories. "My dad when I was just six months old, and my mom just a few weeks before I graduated high school."

Wyatt swallows the food in his mouth and looks at me with somber eyes. "I'm sorry. That's tough at any age."

Shrugging my shoulders, I pull the potato chips

back toward me and take another. "It was... and while I miss them every day, I'm not sad about it anymore. Time really does heal all wounds to some extent."

"Pericles said 'Time is the wisest counselor of all,'" Wyatt muses as he pulls the potato chip bag back his way.

I blink at him in surprise, because cops just don't normally go around quoting Greek orators. His eyes rise to mine, and his hand stops halfway to his mouth with another potato chip.

"What?" he asks in confusion.

I just stare at him, my mouth slightly open in surprise.

"What?" he asks again with a smirk, but he knows why I'm looking at him this way. "I'm not really a slimy general manager of a strip club, you know that right? It's just an act."

My lips curve upward and I pull the potato chips away from him, shaking my head with a silent laugh. "You definitely have layers."

Reaching into the bag, I pull another one out and then push them away so I don't eat anymore.

"We're cool, right?" Wyatt asks.

By the serious tone of his voice, I quickly raise my eyes to meet his. "Yeah... we're cool," I assure him with a smile.

"Because tomorrow is going to be dangerous, and I want us to both have clear heads... clear consciences. Nothing to hold us down."

"I'm good," I tell him firmly. "I've got your back, and I know you'll have mine. We're going to take these assholes down."

Wyatt reaches his hand across the table, fist clenched and wrist facing down. I do the same and we fist bump in solidarity. "Yeah… these assholes are going down tomorrow."

CHAPTER 11
Wyatt

IT'S ALMOST SHOWTIME. Andrea's last dance on the stage has wrapped up, and a feeling of immense happiness courses through me that she'll never have to do that again. I'm waiting at the bottom of the stage while she picks up her clothes. Part of this tease involved her stripping out of a man's blue, button-down shirt so she quickly slips it on and fastens several of the buttons.

She walks down the steps, giving me a short smile, which is what she would normally do, and I follow her back to the dressing room. As has been her habit, she pulls all the cash out of her garters and hands it to me. I immediately start counting it out while she pulls a liter of Diet Coke out of the small refrigerator Simon had put in for the girls and pours some into a red Solo cup.

"I'm going to get dressed," she says, and I just nod at her, keeping my head on the cash. When she turns her back on me, I reach into my pocket, pull out a small packet of paper, and peel the edges back. Keeping my eyes on her as she slips on a pair of jeans, I pour the powder within the packet in her drink. Turning away quickly, I start counting out the cash again.

Yeah… I just drugged Andrea.

With a Goody's Headache Powder. We decided that we needed to go through every scene of this act we had planned out, as there were cameras all over the club. In the off chance Simon was watching, I "drugged" her drink.

After putting on a loose t-shirt, Andrea pulls her hair up into a ponytail and walks over to her soda. She picks the cup up and drinks it down, pausing only once for a breath.

"Damn… I get so thirsty after dancing," she quips and wipes her mouth.

"I imagine… it's quite the aerobic workout," I say distractedly while I partition the cash before me. Picking up the pile that represents her cut, I hand it to her. "Listen… Simon wants you to dance at a private after-hours party. It will be big money. That cool?"

As per our intended plan, Andrea looks at her watch and puts on her most-tortured look. "Damn, Raze… I'm so tired. Seriously, he wants me to go dance right now?"

"Yeah," I say, and add on. "He'll pay you a thou-sand dollars for a few hours of your time. And you can keep all tips. It's for some important business associates of his."

Andrea has become quite the actress and if anyone is watching on camera, they'd probably catch the greedy sparkle in her eye. "Well, shit… I can't pass that up," she says enthusiastically with a big grin. "I'm in."

"Good deal," I say, leading her back into the main club area. "Simon wants us to wait in his office. He's wrapping up a few things, and then we'll all ride over there together."

Part one of our ruse is underway.

I keep careful watch on the clock once we get to Simon's office, as does Andrea. Just as we discussed last night, she alters her behavior… becoming more casually relaxed, giggling at times, and even dancing around the office a bit with nervous excitement for the after-hours party. She keeps up a running dialogue, sounding slightly tipsy, definitely losing all of her inhibitions.

When Simon walks into the office a little over an hour later, Andrea is in perfect form. She even bounces up to Simon, wraps her arms around his neck, and kisses him on the cheek. "Thank you so much for this opportunity, Simon. You're the best boss ever."

She quickly releases him and trots back over toward me, doing a few dance moves along the way. Simon watches her in bemusement and when her back is turned, he gives me a thumbs-up sign. He's duly impressed I've given her a drug that is having a much better effect than whatever they shot Carla up with.

"Let's go," Simon says.

"Grab my bag," Andrea tells me as she practically skips toward the door. "All my best dance outfits are in there."

I give Simon a little smirk, which he returns, and we both share in a greedy and evil look between us.

Simon tosses me his keys. "You drive."

I nod and walk quickly toward Andrea, taking her by the arm and steering her toward the front passenger seat of Simon's BMW 760i.

"Put her in the back with me," Simon says, and my stomach clenches tight. Simon is on the opposite side of the car, and I give him a short nod before he's disappearing inside. I take the moment to turn and look at Andrea. Her eyes are shining back at me with confidence, and she gives me a tiny smile. She's telling me it's fine. She can handle herself.

I'm not sure if I'll be able to handle this, though. Not if that fucker does anything to her.

I get in the driver's seat as Andrea hops in back with Simon. I start the engine and say, "Where to, boss?"

"Head over to 8th and Devine," he says, and a quick glance in the rearview mirror shows me he's looking down at his smartphone.

Warehouse district, I think to myself. Block after block of abandoned buildings, dirty streets, and dark alleys. Perfect place for a kidnapping to occur.

While I drive, Andrea keeps up a running chatter, sounding perfectly buzzed on the supposed drug I dosed her with.

I'm going to dance my ass of, just wait and see.

Oooh, I hope I make enough in tips to get a small microwave for my apartment.

I'm going to be so tired tomorrow, but this will be worth it.

Simon ignores her, working over his phone, but his lips curve up in a smirk. He thinks this is hilarious. He's taking a woman off to her doom and her running banter amuses him.

Andrea never looks at me once in the mirror, and her chatter starts to die down. Her head lolls back onto the seat and she mutters, "I'm a little tired. I'll nap on the way there."

Simon glances over at her, reaches an arm out, and curls his hand around the back of her neck. Pulling her toward him, he pushes her head down and she's gone from my line of sight. "Just rest your head on my lap, baby."

My fingers curl into the steering wheel so hard, I'm afraid they'll break from the tension. He's got fucking Andrea's head on his lap... probably nestled up against his dick... and there's not a damn thing I can do about it.

Simon goes back to messing with his phone, and I breathe a little easier. Looks like he has more important things to do than fucking around with a drugged stripper.

Another ten minutes and I turn onto Devine Street. Just when I hit the intersection with 8th, Simon reaches over my shoulder and points. "Pull into that alleyway on the right."

I make a slow turn and creep the Beamer down the dark alley that runs back a couple of hundred feet past an old warehouse. At the back corner of the building, it expands into a small parking lot surrounded by the backs of other buildings. There are two tall light posts on opposite corners of the lot, but the lights on one are burned out completely. There's a black Mercedes G500 parked under the burned-out lamp, so I pull the car over there and park a few spaces away. However, I pull the car in perpendicular so the headlights of Simon's car illuminate the area.

When I put the car in park, I turn around to look at Simon in the backseat. "How do you want to play this out?" I ask.

"She's out cold so pop the trunk. Roll the window down. Stay in here until I get the money, then I'll tell you when to bring her out."

Relief courses through me that Simon didn't pull Andrea out with him. It was a brilliant idea of hers to fake being passed out from the drug.

"Sure thing, Simon," I say and roll down the

window.

He gets out of the car and at the same time, I see the driver's side doors open in sync on the Mercedes. A huge, beefy guy gets out from behind the wheel. I don't see any obvious gun on him, but that doesn't mean he's not packing. From the backseat emerges a tall, slender guy of about fifty years old. He has thinning, blond hair, pale skin, and a hawk-like nose. He's dressed in an expensive suit, which he buttons the jacket on as soon as both feet on are on the pavement.

I do a quick scan of the area and hope to hell that Mike has his team setting up right now. There's the alley that leads back out to Devine that's open, and one other alley off the west side of the parking lot. My guess is they'll be coming in from that way, as it's closest to our vehicles and completely dark, but I'd bet money they have undercover cars parked right out on Devine as well.

The buyer reaches into the backseat of the Mercedes and pulls out a small, leather satchel. Simon walks up to them, they do a short handshake, and Simon takes the satchel. I watch as he opens it, counts through the cash that's in there, and then turns to me.

"Bring her out, Raze."

Simon and the buyer talk quietly, the big driver standing with his arms crossed over his chest and leaning back against the front fender. This tells me that they don't expect anything but a nice, easy transfer of goods.

I get out of the car and open the back door. An-drea has rolled to her side and is leaning away from the backseat a bit. I notice she's tucked her baggy t-shirt into the back of her jeans. Her eyes are open, and I give her a short nod of my head.

Leaning my entire upper body into the car, I say, "Come on, Nikki. Time to get up."

Andrea deftly slips her hand under the front of my own t-shirt and pulls her Glock out of my waistband. My own gun is tucked securely in the back of my jeans.

My body is completely shielding Andrea from their sight, so I say a bit louder while leaning further into the car. "Come on, Nikki. Wake the fuck up."

As I'm leaning in, further hiding Andrea from their line of site, she tucks her Glock into the back waistband of her own jeans. The minute it's secure, I slide my hands under her armpits and start pulling her out of the car. She looks like dead weight in my arms, and her head lolls to the side. When I pull her free, I loop a forearm under her breasts to hold her up… her back is to my front, hiding the gun, and when I pull her free of the door, I turn her toward the men. Reaching up with my other hand, I lightly slap at her face.

"Wake up, Nikki. Time to dance, darlin'." I turn, giving a smirk and a wink to the men, and they grin back cheesily at me. I think I see the buyer lick his lips as his eyes run down Andrea's body, who is now coming awake. She lifts her head, blinks with bleary eyes, and then stands uneasily. I release my hold around her ribcage and take her by the arm. Standing beside her, I look down at her, and say, "You good? You awake now?"

Andrea looks up at me, blinks her eyes again, and then rubs them with her free hand. She then turns slowly, looks at Simon, then the buyer and his driver, continuing to blink away the sleep.

"What's going on? Where's the party?"

"This is the party, baby," I say as I tug her toward the men.

"She's fucking gorgeous," the buyer says, and I notice his voice is nasally. "I might have to fuck her right here in this parking lot... don't think I can wait."

He punctuates this sentiment by reaching down and rubbing his dick through his pants.

While this is a disgusting move, I don't have time to be affronted on Andrea's behalf, and besides, that was the perfect opening for Nikki to start rebelling a little.

She pulls against my arm and digs her heels into the concrete. "What the fuck is going on here?" she asks hysterically, while pointing at the buyer. "He is not fucking me."

"Feisty," the buyer sneers. "I like a good fight."

Andrea starts struggling hard against me, and just

as we reach the group of men, she breaks free of my grip. Things happen fast but I manage to freeze everything in my mind, noticing several important things at once.

Simon is surprised Andrea broke free, but he's prepared to protect the product, so he throws his arms and legs wide in case she tries to dart past him. His eyes are pinned on Andrea.

The buyer is completely turned on by her spirit, his erection tenting his pants, and he turns his head lazily to the driver and says, "Get her under control."

Neither of those men are looking at Andrea or me.

It's the perfect time.

I reach behind me, grab my gun, and because I got the jump and I'm standing closer to them, I decide to take on the driver and buyer. Pointing it at them, I yell, "Police."

Exactly point-three seconds after I draw my gun, Andrea has hers out... pointed at Simon. "FBI, asshole. Surprise!"

"Hands in the air," I shout loudly to the two men before me. "Down on your knees... *now*. Down, *now*."

My yelling tactics work, as they are so stunned that their hands immediately go up and they're lowering to their knees. If Mike's team is nearby as I expect, they will have heard that as well.

I see a flash of movement from the corner of my

eye, and I hear Andrea grunt. I can't take my eyes off my quarry, but I hear the clatter of her gun skittering across the pavement and the receding sound of running feet.

Before I can even tell Andrea to let him go, I hear her curse and then the sound of her feet are pounding... in pursuit of Simon, who is now on the run.

I risk a quick glance, see him tearing up the alley that we came in on toward Devine. Andrea is after him, her long legs pumping hard, and within seconds, they are both out of sight.

Fuck, fuck, fuck.

I itch to put a bullet in both men's legs before me... hobble them good enough that I can go after Andrea and Simon.

Luckily, I hear more feet... several pairs, and then Mike and his tactical team are swarming the parking lot from the dark alley, just as I'd predicted.

"Cover them," I yell, turning to start running after Andrea.

I vaguely hear Mike saying, "FBI... you're under arrest for the..." and then he's fading away as I enter the alley. Bursting out onto Devine, I see an undercover cruiser with lights flying toward me and a flash of golden-blonde hair disappearing down the alley across the street. I burst into another run, crossing Devine, and dodging one car that slams its brakes on. I slap at the hood with my free hand and keep running.

The cruiser pulls into the alley behind me as I run, but there's not enough room for it to pass me and I'm not giving up the chase. I can see the shadowy form of Andrea ahead, and she's closing in on Simon.

Fuck, she's in great shape.

She's within an arm's length of him and in one stride, she pushes off her right leg and leaps at his back. She misses and I watch her start to fall, thinking she's going to be picking her teeth up off the pavement, but then she manages to latch her arms around one of his legs.

Simons goes down in a tangled mess with her, both of them hitting the concrete hard and rolling. Their lack of momentum causes me to bridge the gap quickly, and just as Simon rolls to his knees, preparing to lunge back into a run, I take three more strides and kick him in the rib cage with a steel-toed boot.

He lets out a huge *oomph* and rolls to his back, groaning and holding his ribs with his hands. The cruiser slams to a halt, and two FBI agents jump out. I know they can handle Simon so I immediately tuck my gun in the back of my jeans again and turn to Andrea.

CHAPTER 12

Andrea

I'M PRETTY SURE the crackling I heard when Wyatt's boot connected with Simon's rib cage was several bones breaking.

I roll... come up to my knees, and lay my palms on my thighs as Simon writhes on the ground in agony. My chest is heaving with exertion, and I suck in lungfuls of oxygen.

"Fuck, I'm out of shape," I gasp to no one in particular.

"Out of shape?" Wyatt says, and when my eyes slide over to his, I see him smiling down at me. "You ran him down... tackled him hard enough the NFL would want to recruit you. I think you're in excellent shape."

Reaching out, he holds his hand out to me and because I doubt I have the strength to stand on my own just yet, I accept. "Yeah... but a few years ago, I wouldn't have been winded by that."

His smile turns into a grin, and then my smile

turns into a grin. He tugs on my hand, and I start to stand up. Acid-like pain flares around my left hip, and I can't stop the gasp that wheezes out of me. "Damn… that hurts," I grit out as I wince hard.

"What hurts?" Wyatt asks as he lets my hand go.

Holding out my left arm, I crane my neck and look down at my hip. My jeans are completely shredded starting just below the waistband, which I guess is a damnable consequence of tackling someone on cold, hard pavement. I can see through the material down to my skin, which is shredded as well and seeping blood.

"Christ," Wyatt says as he takes ahold of my arm, just above my elbow, and turns me toward him. "You're bleeding."

The same acid-like fire now sweeps over my elbow where he's holding me, and Wyatt immediately jerks his hand away. It's covered in blood. "Fuck, you're bleeding everywhere."

"Just two places," I say drily as I pick at the material of my jeans and try to pull it away from the massive scrape on my hip.

I hear pounding feet and see Mike Gomez is running toward us.

"Call an ambulance," Wyatt says. "Andrea's hurt."

"I am not hurt. Just scraped up," I say firmly, giving Mike a hard glare. "No ambulance for me."

"Just to let them clean you up," Wyatt starts to argue, but I hold up my hand and wave him off.

"I'm fine. I'll clean up at the field office," I tell him.

He lets out a grunt of frustration, but then nods his head at me in capitulation.

"Come on," Mike says as he turns and starts heading to one of the many cruisers that are now parked in the alley. "I'll take you back to the field office. You'll need to give me a quick statement so I can use it to question the suspects, and then you two need to get some rest. I'll need more detailed interviews with you tomorrow, and you'll have to work up your reports."

I glance back, seeing that Simon is already in handcuffs and is being led to one of the police cars. His eyes go to Wyatt and then slide to mine. I touch the pads of my fingers to my lips and then blow him a kiss. A short wave of my hand, and I say, "Bye-bye, Simon. Enjoy your time in prison."

Wyatt snickers, and Mike grumbles. "Don't mock the prisoner, Somerville. It's poor form."

I look over at Wyatt, and he's grinning down at me. I lean in toward him and whisper, "Yeah, but it's so much fun."

Hazel eyes crinkle up briefly in amusement, then Wyatt throws his entire head back and starts laughing. He's not paying attention to me, so I take the short opportunity to look at his handsome face, the peek of white teeth, and the strong jaw line.

Damn, he's beautiful… inside and out.

And I don't feel the slightest bit guilty about

acknowledging that to myself either.

♦

I GIVE A lusty yawn as I finish drying myself off and note the clock hanging on the locker room wall says 4 AM. True to his word, Mike took very abbreviated statements from Wyatt and me to get the basic rundown of what happened tonight, and then headed out to the Raleigh Police Department where Simon, the buyer, and his driver were being held for questioning. Lance had also been picked up and was en route to the station. They would be going at them for hours if they didn't lawyer up, and Mike had quite the gleam in his eye over the prospect.

Luckily, my suitcase with my clothes and real ID is here at the FBI field office so I decided to take a quick shower, which was the best way to clean my wounds. Wyatt told me he'd wait for me and give me a ride back to my apartment.

I graciously accepted the ride, but there was no way I was going back to that crappy apartment to sleep. Nope. I was treating myself to a nice hotel, and since we didn't have to be back for detailed statements for another eight hours, I was going to make the most of that time by sleeping the sleep of the dead in a comfortable bed without the ring of gunshots nearby.

I had found some hydrogen peroxide, cotton balls, and large bandages in the supply room, and have them all laid out on the bench that sits in front of the lockers. I take a moment to dry off my body. I didn't wash my hair because I didn't have anything to dry it with here, but rather pulled it up into a messy knot at the top of my head.

I slip on a pair of panties, careful to pull the elastic out and away from the scrape on my hip, and then sit down on the bench to tend to my elbow first. That cut is actually small and looks pretty clean from the shower, so I skip straight toward bandaging. One regular size Band-Aid later, that wound is handled.

Turning my attention to my hip, that one is a little bigger, a little deeper, and I figure that needs a good splash of peroxide. Holding the towel under the wound, I douse it good with the foaming liquid and grit my teeth through the burn. I pat it dry as best I can but the towel hurts too much, so I settle for blowing air over my sensitive skin for a bit.

A knock sounds at the locker room door, and there's only one person it can be.

The field office is cleared for the night except for the agent on duty, so I call out. "Just a minute, Wyatt."

Grabbing a white, button-down shirt—an important piece to any basic, FBI ensemble—I slip it on over my shoulders and button it up. I don't bother with pants... because, well... I can't put them on until I bandage my wound, and besides... Wyatt's seen way more of my body than is showing right now.

"Alright… I'm decent," I call out, and Wyatt is immediately striding through the door.

He looks around in interest… cream-colored walls and shiny tiled flooring, one row of wooden lockers, stained and polished a nice walnut coloring, and a long, padded bench.

"Damn… your digs are much nicer than our police department back home," he says as he looks at me.

I bend over, pick up a large bandage and some tape, and walk to the end of the locker where a full-length mirror is mounted. "Yeah, that's federal dollars hard at work for you," I quip.

Turning to face the mirror, I pull up the hem of my shirt so I can see my hip clearly, which also exposes my panties. They aren't sexy by any means… plain white cotton, but they sit high on my hips and low on my belly, so they aren't horrible by any means.

"Damn… that looks like it hurts," Wyatt says, and I give him a brief glance while I tuck the bandage under my arm and attempt to pull off a strip of medical tape. His eyes are on my hip, and they are warm with sympathy.

"Not so bad," I say, and his eyes come to mine. I smile and then turn my attention to my wound. Holding the bandage out in front of me, I apply the strip of tape along the top. Stepping closer to the mirror, I turn slightly so I can get a better angle on what I'm doing.

There's not an ounce of self-conscious feeling that Wyatt is standing here while I'm half dressed, staring at me. In fact, he leans lazily against the corner of the wooden locker with his arms crossed over his chest.

The hem of my shirt starts sliding down so I make haste to get the wound dressed. Lining the bandage up with the scrape, I start to press it on when Wyatt says, "You did an amazing job tonight, Andrea. You are one hell of a partner."

I make the mistake of looking up at him in surprise, while trying to press the bandage on my wound, and miss by about a mile. The tape goes right onto my raw flesh, and I curse, "Fuck... fuck... fuck."

Wyatt grins and pushes off the locker. "Here... let me do that for you."

My hand falls away from the bandage, and I breathe out. "Okay... sure, that would be good."

Kneeling on the floor, Wyatt crouches a bit lower to bring his face eye level with my hip. He pushes the hem of my shirt up again. His knuckles drag against my skin until he reaches the bottom of my rib cage, and he says gruffly. "Here... hold your shirt up."

My hand clutches onto the material, and I look down at him while he carefully pulls the tape off me. I grit my teeth but don't say a word.

Wyatt efficiently pulls the tape away from the gauze, balls it up, and drops it to the floor. "You should have put the bandage on first, then the tape," he says idly, and then does just that.

CRICRITICAL

From above him, I watch as he works... gently pressing the gauze back to the actual wound, which sticks because it's still weeping with a little blood. He pulls off strip after strip of tape, pressing it to bandage and skin, and then runs his forefinger along the edge to make sure it sticks.

He takes his time... his breath fanning out over my thigh, and while there's nothing sexual at all in his ministrations, I cannot help the goose bumps that break out all over me every time his skin touches mine. I hope to God he doesn't notice that, and I most certainly hope he doesn't notice how hard my nipples have become and—yup, glancing down— poking hard against my shirt.

Shit.

Wyatt smoothes the last piece of tape over my skin as he looks up at me.

"There. All better," he murmurs.

The tone of his voice... husky.

His eyes... warm. No, hot. Definitely hot.

I am spellbound by the intensity of his gaze, and I wait for it to be broken any moment now when he pulls his hands away from me.

But he doesn't... just stares at me, and with just his look... I start to get damp between my legs.

I feel like I'm in a totally dreamlike state when I watch as Wyatt... slowly... ever so slowly, leans in toward me and his lips graze my skin, right beside the elastic of my panty line where leg meets hip.

I jerk slightly from the contact as warm lips part and his tongue flicks out briefly to touch me.

A slight whimper pops out of me, and Wyatt's eyes snap to mine. He looks hesitant for a moment, but whatever he sees on my face causes that to dissolve and then his eyes go practically nuclear.

Raising one hand, Wyatt takes his fingertip and traces it along the edge of my panties… starting just under my hipbone and traveling downward. His eyes slide from mine and turn to watch his own hand as it gently strokes my skin.

I hold my breath and watch, mesmerized, as he touches me languidly, his eyelids heavy and his lips slightly parted. Just before his finger reaches that spot that will put him just an inch away from my core, he stops his progress and looks back up at me.

He doesn't say anything, and I couldn't if I wanted to. Words would break the spell. Words could bring reason back into the equation.

Instead, Wyatt's hands are suddenly behind me, spread wide and cupping my ass. He gives a sharp tug… turns my hips, and suddenly, I'm directly in front of him. He never hesitates a second, and my knees almost buckle when he pulls on my body… causing my hips to flex forward just as he leans in toward me.

His nose goes right into the center of me and he presses me hard against his face, only the thin material of my panties separating our skin. Then he breathes in hard… his fingers clenching into the muscles of my ass.

He inhales so very deeply… sucking my scent deep into his lungs, and then letting out a hot breath that seeps into the cotton, heating my skin below it.

"Oh God," I moan, my hands flying up to fist in his hair.

"Want my mouth on this," Wyatt mutters into me, and I pull him in harder… biting my tongue so I don't start grinding against him.

He doesn't wait for me to respond, and I don't think he was waiting for my assent anyway. Instead, his hands are pulling at my underwear, roughly on one side, but gently on the side with the wound. When he gets them down my legs, he grabs one of my ankles, raising it to pull my panties free. He doesn't bother with the other leg, preferring to leave them pooled around that ankle.

He doesn't lower my one leg either, instead pushing it up higher and draping it right over his shoulder. Hands back at my ass, he gives me a sharp pull and then his mouth is fastened on me. He first gives me one long swipe with his tongue, straight up my center, and a warbled sound bubbles up from my throat.

"So fucking sweet," he says with his lips fluttering over my skin. "Fantasized about this."

Then he's pulling me back to his face. He's diving in… his lips and tongue pushing straight through to my center.

Wyatt doesn't just eat me... he devours me.

I'm mashed against him so hard that he doesn't even need his fingers to help find the way. He uses pure pressure of hot tongue against skin to burrow his way in.

My eyes slide down to look at him. His golden-brown hair with my fists clenching it tight. His back rising and falling with hot and heavy breathing. I let my eyes continue to wander, straight to the floor-length mirror that is behind Wyatt, and my eyes flare wide at the sensual image projected back at me.

Wyatt on his knees in front of me.

One strong, tanned arm wrapped around the leg that is supporting me, the other bicep supporting my leg up on his shoulder with his hand wrapped over the top of my thigh. One hand flexes his fingers into the muscles of my ass and the other into the top of my leg.

The back of his head moving... tilting... plunging in and out as he consumes me.

I raise my gaze up and look at how my leg is hanging over his shoulder, my knuckles white as they grip his head and my own chest laboring along with this.

It's the most erotic thing I've ever seen or done in my entire life.

Wyatt plunges his tongue deep inside me, pulls it out, and then flutters it hard against me. Out of nowhere, my orgasm crashes over me, and the one leg I'm standing on buckles in weakness as I start to collapse. Wyatt never misses a heartbeat, merely shifts his face under me for support, and lets me sag against his mouth while he continues to draw my climax out with continued assault.

The spasms of pleasure go on and on and on.

"Fuck yeah," Wyatt groans against me, continuing to lick and suck. My standing leg finds a bit of strength, locks, and then I'm grinding against him to draw every bit of ecstasy out of this experience.

Then I'm drifting away.

Eyes closed, my fingers now gently rub at Wyatt's scalp.

He pulls my leg off his shoulder... gives a soft kiss to the inside of my thigh.

My eyes open slowly. I gaze down as Wyatt maneuvers my one foot back into my underwear and pulls them up my legs, careful to avoid the bandage. Just before he covers me completely, he leans in, plants a sweet kiss on my bare mound, and then pulls my panties all the way up.

His lifts his face to look at me, and his eyes are dark... thoughtful.

I reach a shaky hand out to cup his cheek. He leans into me for just a second, lets his eyes close so I can see the long lashes for a brief moment against his skin, and then they open.

With a resolute look, he stands from the floor,

which causes my hand to fall away from him. He takes a step back from me, glances down at the floor once, and then back up to me.

"I'll wait outside while you finished getting dressed," he says.

I open my mouth to say… to say… what? I have no clue. What do I say to something that was taboo, erotic, fulfilling, dirty, and absolutely mind blowing?

He gives me a short nod and turns on his boot, giving me his back and leaving me behind.

CHAPTER 13

Wyatt

One week later...

"THIS IS HOW you're spending your last day of vacation?" Hunter asks from behind me. I push up from the deck... lean back on my haunches.

Wiping the sweat off my forehead with the back of my glove-covered hand, I shrug my shoulders. "Sure, why not? Not like I have anything else better to do."

Hunter makes a sound deep in his throat and squats down. Running his fingertips over the wood boards of my deck, he gives a nod of approval. "Very smooth. Gabby would be impressed."

Of course, she would. Gabby lived, ate, and breathed all things wood.

I look around at the back deck of my cottage, which sits on stilts just thirty feet off of the beach. I had been meaning to re-stain my deck for going on oh... about four years now, and I finally decided to do it. Didn't matter that I was undertaking this backbreaking chore at the end of July when temperatures cruised in the nineties. I had a week off from work following my return from Raleigh, and I was bound and determined to be productive.

I was bound and determined to be productive, because I learned very quickly that my idle mind over the last week kept turning over and over again to Andrea. Living in the Outer Banks, it's almost an art form to learn how to sit on the beach with a cooler of beer and bake away your stress under the sun. I've had twenty-eight years of practice doing it.

I figured it would be easy… like riding a bike.

Except, when I was down on the beach… my feet sunk deep into the wet sand and a cold Budweiser in my hands, I found that I just couldn't fucking relax.

Because I kept thinking of Andrea.

Andrea dancing.

Andrea smiling.

Andrea's mouth on my cock.

Andrea tackling Simon.

Andrea's pussy in my mouth.

Andrea, Andrea, Andrea.

After three days of torture, I gave up and started sanding my deck by hand. The muscles in my back and neck were on constant fire and my skin had turned dark brown from the hot sun. I went to bed each night exhausted and slept dreamlessly.

Throwing the block of wood with sandpaper

wrapped around it, I take off my gloves and drop them to the deck. Standing up, I swivel my head and arch my back to work out the kinks.

"Want a beer?" I ask Hunter as I head into the house.

"Sure," he says as he follows me in.

The icy blast of air conditioning is a welcome relief, the coolness of the beer bottle in my hand even better. After our bottles are opened, Hunter cocks a hip against my kitchen counter and levels his gaze at me. "So, what's wrong?"

My eyebrows rise in surprise. "What do you mean 'what's wrong'?"

He just stares at me, not saying a word. He holds his beer casually in his hand, but I can tell he's on high alert.

High alert to call bullshit on me if I choose to dick him around.

Snorting in frustration, I take a long pull on my beer, and then point it at him as I swallow. "I hate it you know me so well."

Hunter shrugs and takes a sip of his beer. "There's no one I know better than you, except for Brody, of course, and that's to be expected since we're identical twins. But I know you very well, my friend, so tell me what's eatin' at you."

"Nothing really," I say evasively. "It was just a really tough undercover operation. I'm a little drained from it."

"No," Hunter says firmly. "There's more to it than that."

"What do you know?" I fire back.

"Well, outside of coming to Last Call your first night back—for just one beer, I might remind you—you've basically been avoiding everyone since you returned."

"I've been working," I say as I point out of the kitchen window to my back deck.

"What the fuck ever, dude. Quit pussy-footin' around and just tell me what the problem is," Hunter growls. He punctuates that by walking over to my kitchen table, kicking one of the chairs back, and dropping down into it. "I'm not leaving until you lay it all out."

"Asshole," I mutter, but I decide it's easier to get this over with than fight with him. I know this man as well as he knows me. He'll sit at that table and won't move until I unload.

I guess that's what best friends are for.

Sitting down in the chair, I pick at the label on the beer. "I guess I better fill you in on the operation first."

This I needed to do before I unloaded about Andrea, because Hunter needed to understand the dynamics of our relationship.

"I can't tell you everything because the case is still open, but I went undercover to work at a strip club in Raleigh. The owner was suspected of selling off his dancers as sex slaves."

"That is sick," Hunter says under his breath.

"Yeah, and you don't even want to know the depths to which I had to sink to work there. But anyway... I got in good with the owner and eventually he brought me in on the operation."

Hunter sits a little straighter in his chair. "You helped to sell women to slavers?"

"No, by the time the first sale went down that I was in on, we had an undercover FBI agent posing as one of the dancers."

"Seriously?" Hunter asks, his face awash in suspicion. "FBI agents know how to strip?"

"This one did," I said, images of Andrea's naked and gyrating body filtering through my mind. "Her name's Andrea."

"So how did it all work out?" Hunter asks cautiously.

"Worked out great. Andrea and I made the bust after money changed hands and the ring has been taken down."

Hunter heaves a sigh of relief, and I'm sure he was thinking something dire happened to Andrea, which was causing my funk. "So, what's the problem?"

I hesitate a moment, wondering just how much I should share, then I decide to just lay it out. Hunter won't judge and he may have some good advice. "The problem is that we sort of crossed a line with each other... twice."

I let that sort of float out there and watch as understanding creeps over Hunter's face. "Sexual line, you mean?"

"Good deduction, Einstein," I say drily and take another sip of beer. "The first time... it was part of the undercover act. At least, I think it was. The second time... was after the bust had been made. No act."

"So, what's the problem?" Hunter asks with utter gullibility.

"The problem is that regardless of what happened or when, we were law enforcement partners. You don't fuck around with your coworkers."

"You most certainly *do* fuck around with your coworkers," Hunter says adamantly. "Gabby was working at my bar. I fucked her. Brody was working with Alyssa at The Haven. He fucked her. Savannah was working for Gavin as his housekeeper. He fucked her. I'm sensing a pattern here," he ends with a grin. "Aren't you?"

"Not the same," I grumble, but it kind of is.

"How did you leave it with her?" Hunter asks.

How *did* I leave it with her?

Not very well, I'll have to admit.

After I lost myself to eating out her sweet pussy, I took my aching dick and stepped away from her. When she finished getting dressed and got in the unmarked car that had been loaned to me, I didn't even know what to say. The taste of her was still thick on my tongue and my balls throbbed.

"Can you take me to the closest hotel?" she asked quietly.

"Sure," I said and proceeded to do just that. Luckily, there was a nice one just a few blocks down.

I pulled up to the curb and then because it was just fucking awkward, I turned to look at her. "Listen… about what just happened—"

"It was amazing," she said as she stared at me with those clear, blue eyes.

"It shouldn't have happened," I told her as I scrubbed a hand through my hair. "I crossed a line… couldn't fucking help myself, and I'm sorry."

"Sorry for what?" she demanded as her eyes narrowed, and I could tell by the tone of her voice she was pissed. "For giving me an orgasm? Well, gee, Wyatt… guess that makes us even now."

She lunged for the door handle, but I grabbed her arm and turned her back toward me. "I didn't do that to make us even," I gritted out. "I did that because I wanted to… because I fucking needed it. But Christ, Andrea… you were injured, worn out… I took advantage of the situation. Didn't give you a chance to say 'no'—"

"I wouldn't have said 'no'," she blurted out.

"Maybe you would have under different circumstances," I said gently and then released her arm. "Look… go get checked in and get some sleep. We can talk about this more tomorrow, okay?"

She stared back at me and tentatively said, "Do you… um… want to come up with me?"

A sharp pain stabbed me in the center of my chest while my balls started tingling just thinking about going up to her room. But I shook my head and gently let her down. "Probably not a good idea. I'll see you tomorrow."

Her smile was sad, but she nodded her head and opened the door. "Goodnight, Wyatt."

She was out and closing the door on me before I could tell her goodnight in return.

The next day at the station, we never did talk about it. We were both busy being interviewed by Mike Gomez and then typing our statements. It was around 4 PM when Andrea glanced down at her watch, stood from the table we were working at, and said, "Damn… I didn't realize it's so late. I need to get to the airport."

I looked up in surprise from the report I was reading over for the second time, completely taken aback that she was leaving. She hadn't mentioned to me once throughout the day that she was flying back to Pittsburgh that night.

Andrea bent over and hastily scrawled her signature on her report. Throwing the pen down, she gave a quick glance at Mike, who had also stood from the table and was putting on his suit jacket. "I'm going to go get my suitcase. Meet you outside."

Mike nodded and said, "I'll go get the car and

pull it up to the front door."

Andrea never looked at me once... just turned and headed back to the female locker room as Mike walked out. I sat there dumbly for a minute, my mind trying to process that she was actually leaving and there were probably things that should have been said between us.

When she returned, pulling her rolling carry-on behind her, I stood up from the table and our eyes locked. She gave me the tiniest of smiles.

"I'll walk you out," I said, motioning with my hand for her to precede me down the hallway to the front lobby.

When we stepped outside into the hot, Carolina afternoon, I immediately reached into the breast pocket of my dress shirt and pulled my sunglasses out. Affixing them to my face, I turned toward her even as I saw Mike pulling up in the car.

"So, are you heading back to Nags Head this evening?" Andrea asked with a warm, interested smile on her face. Clearly, she had no hurt feelings over my refusal to come to her room last night.

A move which may go down as one of the stupidest things I've ever done in my life.

"Yeah... I guess so."

She gave a warm chuckle. "Well, relax. Sit on that beach and drink a few cold beers. You deserve it."

"I will," I said lamely. "Nothing like the Outer Banks in the summertime."

"It sounds lovely."

"It's a great place to visit," I muttered... even more lamely.

"I'm sure it is," she responded quietly... distantly. Then... because Mike was waiting, she said, "Well, good luck to you, Wyatt. It was an honor to work with you on this case."

Her eyes were cool, and she fucking stuck her hand out for me to shake.

She couldn't see the movement of my eyes behind my dark shades, but they glanced down and narrowed at her proffered hand. Fuck no, I wasn't shaking her hand.

Couldn't kiss her either... not the deep and personally invading way I wanted to.

Instead, I ignored her hand and bent down to kiss her on the cheek.

"Take care of yourself," I murmured.

She gasped slightly and gave a small sigh. When I pulled away, her eyes were closed but they immediately fluttered open.

Her face was awash with confused sadness, but she put on a firm smile. "You take care, too."

And that was that.

She left Raleigh and so did I, and here I sit now with Hunter in my kitchen, baring my soul about this woman that I can't get out of my mind.

"So, that's how it ended, and now it's driving me crazy," I mutter. "I feel like there's unfinished business or something. It's hard to describe."

"So get on a plane and go see her," Hunter says with a proud smile on his face, like he just solved the problem of world peace or something.

Oh, poor schmuck. If it were only that easy.

"And do what?" I exclaim as I slam my bottle down on the table. A splash of beer and foam shoots out the top. "What exactly would I be going there for? To fuck her? To start a relationship? Christ, Hunter... you know a long-distance relationship couldn't work. She's not leaving the FBI to move here, and I'm sure as hell not leaving my home. So why would I go see her?"

Hunter looks amused over my outburst. He merely tilts his beer back and takes four long swallows to finish it off. Standing from my table, he stares down at me. "You go and see her because you can't stop thinking about her. What other reason do you need?"

I snort in frustration. "But we could never have—"

"Oh, stop with the fucking excuses," Hunter says as he leans over me and pokes me in the chest. "Just go see her... fuck her. Start there and decide where to go after that. Maybe that's all you need... a closure fuck."

Yeah... I so don't need a closure fuck. I know, without a doubt, that if I fuck Andrea, things are going to get way more complicated and sticky. She and I were intimately acquainted orally, and the things that we did to each other usually come later in a relationship. The mere fact that she had no problem latching onto my dick with that mouth, and I was starved to eat her out, tells me that we had forged some type of connection prior to that all occurring. That meant to me that fucking her was not going to cure the problem—it was going to increase it.

"Sound like a plan?" Hunter asks as he turns away from me and sets the empty bottle down in my recycle bin.

"Yeah, maybe," I say distractedly, but deep down in my heart, I know I'm not going to pursue her. Just like time healed the wounds of her parents' death, and just as I told her that time was the wisest counselor of all, I decided to let things be and hoped that as the days wore on, her memory would just fade away from me, and I could move on with my life in peace.

CHAPTER 14

Andrea

Two days later...

O H, THIS WAS such a bad idea.
        Bad, bad idea.

I glance down at my watch for the fourth time in about four minutes, and admit to myself that every minute that goes by, worry and self-doubt are taking over my psyche.

I tap my foot against the wood flooring of Wyatt's front porch, thankful he has two comfortable wicker chairs with plush cushions decorated in blue and yellow stripes. My ass has been parked in one of them for the last hour and a half.

I'm sitting on Wyatt's front porch because I had made the split-second decision yesterday to fly to North Carolina so I could see him. This came on the heels of me deciding to take a vacation.

When I had flown back to Pittsburgh last week, I was back at work the following day, much to my

SAC's surprise. He tried to talk me into taking some time off, as he had read my report and knew just what I had been through during this operation. I declined, telling him that I wanted to get back into the thick of things.

He didn't argue and much to my surprised delight, even amended his written recommendation to my application at the BRIU, updating them with everything I did on this operation. I couldn't help but get my hopes renewed all over again that I might get accepted into that division of the FBI.

I went straight back to work because I needed to keep my mind busy. Busy with important stuff like catching criminals and doing federal background checks. As always, some of it scintillating and some of it downright boring.

Regardless, being back to work didn't help occupy my mind at all. Several times throughout the day, my mind would drift off and I would think about Wyatt. I'd think mostly about what he did to me in the locker room the evening before I left Raleigh, but that would lead me to think about him saying it was a mistake, and him declining to take it further. Honestly, it was a bit of a blow to my self-esteem, which had already been knocked down a few pegs when David broke off our engagement. I got down and low, wondering what was wrong with me. Why did men kept leaving me?

I had a pity party one night with two pints of Ben

& Jerry's Chocolate Fudge Brownie ice cream, drank four beers, then made the mistake of calling my brother Kyle and unloading on him.

In typical Kyle fashion, he told me I was a dumbass. I had told him all about the operation, and while I did not tell him specifically that there was anything sexual between Wyatt and me, I did tell him that I had some feelings involved that felt unresolved.

The most important thing he reminded me of is that I am one badass chick and that I was not one to piss and moan over my fate. He reminded me that yes... while it was sad that David broke off our engagement, I had actually bounced back pretty well. He reminded me that I helped to take down a sex-slave ring. He reminded me that once, while I was in the FBI Academy, I took one of my sparring partners down to the mat, and he outweighed me by almost eighty pounds.

He didn't need to remind me that I had tackled and brought down a fleeing Simon Keyes, a memory that had me puffing my chest out a bit and demanding my bruised ego to get its act together.

The next morning at work, I asked Dale Lambert if I could have that vacation he had suggested to me a few days prior, and he gladly granted my request.

And so, here I am... sitting on Wyatt's front porch, waiting for him to get home.

Bad idea, I tell myself again.

And for so many reasons.

SAWYER BENNETT

First, Wyatt has done nothing to ever lead me to believe he would want to see me again. He flat out refused to come to my room that last night, knowing I was offering sex. Yes, that bruised my ego a bit, but since Kyle bucked me back up, I choose to believe it's not because I'm not attractive to Wyatt, but rather that he has some misplaced sense of duty or morals that he believed were conflicting.

Fine... good enough reason I should stay away, but another very important reason why this is a bad idea swarms me with unease.

What if Wyatt is involved with someone? I'm sitting on his porch, waiting for him to get home from wherever he is—work, I assume—but the next person to pull into his driveway could be his girl-friend. Or worse yet, his wife.

While my gut tells me that Wyatt isn't the type of guy that would have made me come with his mouth in the locker room of the Raleigh FBI field office if he was involved with someone, I can't discount that it's a slight possibility.

Finally... and probably the best reason of all, is that I'm not even sure what I'm hoping to accomplish by being here. Is he my rebound from David? Is this just sexual tension at its finest that needs to be popped and then we go our separate ways? Or are the feelings and connection I've imagined with this man real and need to be explored?

Yes, this is a bad, bad, bad idea and finally, my

cowardice breaks through.

I stand up from the wicker chair and take one step away from it when I hear the crunch of car tires on gravel. My eyes raise and I see a champagne-colored Chevrolet Suburban pulling into the driveway. The windows are slightly tinted, but I can see through them clear enough to make out Wyatt's handsome face semi-covered by his mirrored aviators.

This is it… do or die. No running now.

Wyatt pulls his vehicle up to the base of the long staircase that leads up to his front porch, which sits up high on the stilts that are typical of the beach cottages here on the Atlantic. He puts it in park and the engine shuts off, and for several painfully long moments, he just stares up at me.

I can't see his eyes, but I feel the weight of his gaze on me behind those sunglasses. Nervously shoving my hands into the side pockets of the pale, blue sundress I'm wearing, I carefully rub them on the material at my thighs because they are nervously sweating.

Wyatt finally opens the driver's door and steps out. He removes his sunglasses and tosses them on the front seat, now staring up at me with those clear, hazel eyes. I can't read a damn thing on his face, but then again, he's always been skilled at masking his emotions. He's dressed in a pair of khaki pants and a light blue, button-down shirt with the sleeves rolled halfway up his forearms. He's more tan than when I saw him last, and he clearly just got off work as he's still wearing his gun holster over his shoulders and his police badge is pinned to his hip.

So. Fucking. Gorgeous.

My mind starts spinning on what will be the first thing I should say. I can't believe I've been sitting on his freakin' porch for this long and don't even have my speech planned out.

Panic flows through me as Wyatt starts walking to the staircase.

No, wait... stalking toward the staircase. Well... more of a prowl.

The minute his foot hits the bottom step, he starts bounding up them two at a time, his eyes pinning me in place.

He nears the top, and I take a step backward, but he keeps barreling at me. I try to take another step back when he reaches the porch, but then his hands are on my face. I catch the briefest glimpse of his eyes, which are blazing with heat, and then his mouth is on me.

Pushing me back, slamming his lips harder against me, he walks me right back into his front door. My momentum is halted, but his isn't as he presses in closer to me and his tongue shoves its way into my mouth.

A feral groan tears out of his chest, and my arms go around his back in an unnecessary attempt to pull him closer to me.

Unnecessary because he pushes me hard into the door, while his hands continue to grip onto the sides of my head. His hips flex in and then grind against me... his cock already hard in his pants, and hot, molten lust almost brings me to my knees.

A guttural moan rumbles out of me as I tear my lips away from his. This only causes him to fist my hair and tug my head to the side so his mouth can move down my neck.

I moan again... harder, and one hand drops to the front of his pants so I can rub his erection.

Wyatt hisses against the skin on my neck and grinds his cock against my hand.

Then he's kissing me again... one hand gone from my hair and fumbling inside the pocket of his pants for his keys. He never misses a beat, his tongue working me hard, his hips moving against me, and yet he still manages to unlock his door.

A quick twist of his knob and we're practically falling through the door. Wyatt pushes me a few steps in, wraps his arm around my waist, kicks the door closed with his foot, and then lowers me right to carpeted living room floor.

I realize I have no clue what his cottage looks like because my eyes have been closed, and they flutter open during our downward descent. I briefly see the back of a navy blue couch with beige throw pillows and taupe paneled walls.

Then my back is resting against plush, cream-colored carpet, and Wyatt's body is covering me with his mouth, still working mine hard. My hands yank at his shirt, trying to get it pulled free of his pants, but I can't work my way around his leather shoulder holster so I start clawing at.

Pushing up off me slightly and balancing on one forearm, Wyatt starts rolling his shoulder to help me work the holster loose. All the while, he continues to feast on my mouth. It's the hottest, longest, most desperate kiss I've ever had in my life.

Once the holster comes free of one shoulder, I do nothing more than toss it over his back, where it still hangs from the opposite shoulder. I don't care though… it's out of my way, and it reminds me much of the same way he left my panties dangling around one ankle the last time we were together.

Tugging hard, I get Wyatt's shirt up, only to be met with a white t-shirt underneath, so I just plunge my hands up underneath of it until I'm able to run my hands over his skin. My entire body spasms when Wyatt drags the hem of my dress up and plunges his hand down the front of my panties.

Then it's really on.

Both of us claw and battle our way to try to touch each other. We're both fueled by lust and desperation, and an almost terror that we may come to our senses at any moment. My hands fumble at his belt and Wyatt thrusts two fingers up inside of me, which causes my back to arch up, my head to throw back, and his lips to leave mine as I groan over the contact.

Wyatt pumps his fingers in and out of me, hitting something inside that makes tremors race up and down my spine, and causing my hips rotate viciously against him. His mouth goes to my neck, where he sucks and bites at me and finally... finally I get his belt undone, his zipper down, and his underwear and pants pushed down. His erection is hot and silky in my hands, wet around the tip, and I squeeze and pump at him, causing his hips to thrust against me.

Our breathing is heavy and hot, and oxygen feels like a precious commodity. I ache... I can't stand the tension he's creating within me.

Wyatt feels it too, overwhelmed with the same desperation that I'm feeling. The same raw need.

Batting my hands away from his shaft, he rears up, pulls my panties to the side so I'm bare to him, and with one hand, guides his cock to my entrance. He brushes through my wetness once... twice... then he lunges forward and slams his way inside, and oh, God... that feels fucking amazing.

His entire body stills for just a second, his head dropping to my shoulder where his breath comes out in large bursts against my collarbone. My arms wrap around him, and I dig my fingers into the muscles at his back.

Wyatt lifts his head... stares down at me with the most intense, wild look I've ever seen on a man's face before. It's at this moment I realize we've haven't said a word to each other, instead choosing to communicate through touch and action.

We stare at each other for the briefest of moments, and then he's moving within me. Sliding an arm under one leg, he pushes it up and out, causing the elastic of my underwear that's stretched to the side to bite into my opposite hip. It's a good sting though because it reminds me that we are succumbing to our baser instincts right now, and I wouldn't want it any other way.

Long, hard thrusts as Wyatt hovers over me while he supports himself with his other arm. He stares down at me, and I stare back at him as I keep my bottom lip clenched between my teeth so as not to scream out.

I can feel him deep… everywhere, while he tunnels into me.

Through the pores of my skin, into the marrow of my bones.

Our eyes stay locked, yet pure ecstasy is etched all over Wyatt's face. I know this feels as wonderful to him as it does to me, because for the first time since I've known him, he's letting go completely on his emotions.

We race… climb higher and higher. Wyatt slams into me; I arch my hips in counter-force. Grunts, moans, whispered curses… I'm not sure if they are coming from him or me, but it just adds to the overall urgency to our fucking.

Racing, racing… can't get enough yet wanting that ultimate crash of pleasure to overtake us.

It starts with me first… after one particularly hard thrust and follow-up grind of his pelvis against mine. Tightening in my lower back, heat spreading between my legs, and then a ripple of the purest bliss rushing up my spine before exploding outward.

"Wyatt," I cry out as I arch my back and dig my nails into his skin.

I can feel my walls rippling all around him. He feels it too because he leans his head down, clamps his teeth into my shoulder, and slams hard into me one more time. His body stills, and then he lets out a singular groan of release as he empties inside of me.

My fingers release their tight purchase into his back, and instead start a soothing motion over his sweaty skin. His chest heaves from the exertion and he lets my leg down, settling on top of me while we both come down.

His cock still buried deep, I feel it twitch a few times, and I clamp down my muscles on him. This causes him to flex his hips again with another moan while the last spasms of pleasure drain away from our bodies.

I'm not sure how long we lay there, but long enough that my breathing evens back out again. Wyatt lifts his head from my shoulder and looks down at me. His eyes flicker back and forth between my own, as if he's trying to figure out what's going through my head right now.

If he asks, I'll tell him the truth.

That was the most insane, intense sexual encounter of my entire life... topping what he did to me in the locker room by just a hair.

He doesn't say anything though, instead pushing his upper body up off me while he dips his shoulder to get the holster completely off him. He pushes it across the carpet and then pulls his hips back so he slides out of my body. With one hand, he pulls my underwear gently back into place and then rolls off me so that we are now lying side by side on his carpet.

I'm boneless... have no desire to move. Maybe I'll get up next year.

"How long can you stay?" Wyatt asks quietly, and I turn my head to look at him. His head is turned toward me and his eyes are warm... satiated.

"You want me to stay?" I ask with surprise.

Wyatt rolls onto his side and pushes up on one elbow so he can look down at me, one eyebrow cocked high. "You fly here to see me, we just fucked like rabid animals, I had an orgasm that almost made me pass out, and you wonder if I want you to stay?"

"It was a legitimate question," I gripe at him.

Leaning over, he kisses me softly on my jaw. When he pulls away, he's smiling at me. "Yes, I want you to stay."

Pushing up on both of my elbows, I angle my head toward him. "I actually have ten days of vacation. Well, a workweek plus this weekend and next. I need to go find a hotel, but yes... I can stay ten days."

"Fuck the hotel. You're staying here with me," he grumbles, and then jumps up agilely to his feet. He pulls his pants up a bit, tucks himself in, and then lowers his hand to me. I grab ahold and he pulls me to my feet, and even once I'm standing, continues to pull until I'm wrapped up in his arms.

"I'm really glad you're here," he murmurs with his lips against my hair.

"Me too," I say with a smile, and then feel a gush of wetness seeping into my underwear, which causes me to jerk. "Oh, shit... we just had sex without protection."

Raising my face, I see Wyatt has a sheepish look on his face, and he scrapes his fingers back and forth across his scalp. "Yeah, well... got a little carried away. You on the Pill?"

"Yeah, but—"

"But nothing... I know you're clean just as you know I am," he says matter-of-factly, and I realize... I *do* know he's clean. Wyatt isn't the type of person that would put me in jeopardy... of that I'm absolutely sure of. He trusts the same about me.

"Well, okay then," I say breathlessly with a smile of my own. "It's settled then."

"Good," he says as his hands come up under my ass and he lifts me up into his arms. My legs go around his hips, locking my feet behind his back, and then he's carrying me through his house. "Because I plan on coming inside of you a lot over the next ten days."

God, I hope that's true, is all I can think.

CHAPTER 15

Wyatt

I UNLOCK MY front door, about to jump out of my own skin over the excitement I have over seeing Andrea. I left her this morning curled up on her side... in *my* bed... naked and exhausted. I was exhausted too after the night we had, but in a damn good way.

This day at work dragged on. It was mostly paperwork followed by one call out to a domestic dispute, but the entire time, I kept thinking of Andrea naked in my bed. To say I was surprised is an understatement when I pulled into my driveway yesterday and saw her standing on my porch. With that blue sundress showcasing her beautiful legs, her golden hair spilling all around her shoulders, I thought I was having a hallucination for a moment.

Lust bolted through me followed by an insane desire to instantly possess her. She came... to see me... and it was almost beyond my comprehension. She clearly had the same feelings I was having, yet this woman was far braver than I ever was. She got her ass on a plane to come see me, while I was still negotiating with myself about how to handle it all. This thought causes me some shame, but there's no use in crying over spilled milk. She's here now, and I am going to use every bit of my free time to make something of this.

My free time just got a little bit freer, because even though I was just on vacation last week, my captain didn't have a problem with me asking for Monday and Tuesday off next week. That meant I had the next four days with Andrea, and I wasn't going to waste a moment.

Do I still have uncertainty as to what this is?

Fuck yeah.

But one thing is certain… last night was not a closure fuck for either one of us. There's some type of tether between us that isn't built on just insane chemical attraction and mind-blowing orgasms. We have a connection that was forged through a stressful undercover operation and mutual respect of each other's abilities. We went through something that was dangerous together, and I recognize now that this overwhelming need to protect Andrea during our time undercover was born not of a law enforcement partner's duty, but by that personal connection that was developing throughout it all.

So hell yes… I'm going to pull and poke at that tether, see how strong it is… if it's worth keeping tied to.

I suspect it is.

Opening the door, I step in and set my keys on the little table just inside the small foyer. I pull my wallet and cell phone out, dropping them there as well. My house is quiet... settled... and I know instantly that Andrea must be outside.

Stepping through the living room, I make my way to the sliding glass door. I immediately see her laying on one of my deck chairs. She's on her back with large, white-framed sunglasses on her face and the tiniest white bikini imaginable. One leg is straightened but the other is cocked up, foot firmly planted on the chair. It's swaying gently back and forth and by the serene smile on her lips, I can tell she's in full relaxation mode.

I quickly head to my bedroom, undress, and put on a pair of shorts and an old Ron Jon t-shirt. The sun is full and hanging low over the sound side of the island to the west, but it's still quite hot outside. I grab two beers from the fridge and walk out onto my back deck.

At the sound of the sliding door swishing in its tracks, Andrea angles her head back and to the side to look at me. Those full lips purse briefly, and then break out into a grin as she props herself up by the elbows on her chair.

This, of course, pushes her breasts out, which, of course, causes my eyes to go to said breasts. I spent a lot of time on them last night, and my mouth was watering to get another taste.

"Eyes up," Andrea teases, and I don't bother doing anything but a lazy slide of my gaze upward.

"Can't help it. They're spectacular," I say with a grin and then hand her a beer.

She sits all the way up in the lounge chair, spreading her legs wide and planting a foot down on either side. And, of course, my eyes flick briefly down but then back up again. She doesn't notice as she's taking a long pull on the beer.

"Damn, that's good," she says. "It's so hot out here."

"Been out here all day?" I ask as I take a seat on the padded bench opposite her chair.

"On and off. Spent quite a bit of time down on the beach... in the water. I don't know the last time I had a vacation where I just relaxed and did nothing."

"Nice, right?"

"So very nice," she agrees. "How was work today?"

"Same old, same old," I tell her with a shrug. "Honestly... it's been a bit hard to get back into the routine."

"I know what you mean," she says and then pulls her legs up to sit Indian-style. "It's hard to go from working the pole, flashing my goods to strangers, to sitting back at a desk in a polyester suit."

I snicker at her imagery. "You don't wear polyester."

"Close enough. The FBI-standard attire isn't all that flattering."

"You'd be beautiful in a burlap sack," I tell her truthfully as I lean forward with my elbows on my knees, and looking deeply into her eyes.

I'm surprised when Andrea's cheeks pinken, and she lowers her face shyly. Her fingers play at the bottle, and she has a tiny smile on her face.

"What's this?" I ask as I reach out with a hand and lift her chin up so she looks at me.

Andrea gives me an embarrassed smile. "It's just… I didn't know you thought of me as beautiful. All those weeks we worked together… me dancing around naked, you being so impassive about it… I just didn't know you thought that about me."

Leaning over, I set my bottle of beer on the deck—which while smoothly sanded has remained unstained—and then reach over to take her beer away from her, where it finds rest next to mine. I snag her hand, pulling her up from the chair. Her long legs uncurl, and then I'm tugging her forward as I lean back on the bench.

Hands to her waist, I encourage her onto my lap and she straddles me beautifully, her arms naturally coming up to rest on my shoulders.

Leaning forward, I place a soft kiss over the sun-warmed skin of her chest.

"You are immensely beautiful, but I couldn't

show that to you while we were undercover," I tell her softly, moving my lips upward to her collarbone. Her head falls back, and I can feel her long hair floating around my arms that are wrapped tight around her waist. "You have the body of a centerfold, the face of an angel, and the heart of a lion. Add in the fact that you are, without a doubt, the sexiest woman I've ever known—and I swear this has absolutely nothing to do with the way you can dance—and you can rest assured that your beauty is absolutely dazzling."

Andrea's eyes go soft, even as she blushes again. One of her hands slides over, fingers inching into my hair and then gliding over my scalp. She leans in and brushes her lips against mine. "That may be the nicest thing a man has ever said to me before."

I kiss her back, softly and sweetly. When our lips part, I say with a grin, "You must not have known many nice men."

Immediately, I know it's the wrong thing to have said because it's like a shutter comes down over her eyes, and she pulls back from me slightly. I don't let her withdraw though, tightening my hold around her waist.

"What's wrong?" I ask quietly. "Why did that bother you?"

She shakes her head, gives me a tremulous smile, and warmth is back in her eyes again. "It's nothing. Just a bad experience with a man. Silly, really."

Andrea leans back in to kiss me again, but I pull

my head back to avoid her lips. Bringing up one hand, I encircle it around her throat and stroke her skin with my thumb. "Not silly. What happened?"

She doesn't respond, choosing instead to dip her ear toward her shoulder before leaning in to kiss me on my neck. Her tongue flicks out, then her teeth scrape along my skin, which causes my dick to start getting hard. I try to mentally demand my erection to stand down, but then Andrea dips her pelvis and grinds herself against me.

Full. Fucking. Hard-on.

Just like that.

"Christ, woman," I growl and move the hand around her throat to the back of her head so I can grab a fistful of hair. Tugging, her head falls back and her breasts push outward. It's all I the invitation I need before I'm leaning down and closing my mouth over one bikini-clad globe. Her nipple pebbles hard and I latch my teeth on it, giving a slight tug.

Andrea's arms clamp tight around my head, pinning me to her breast as she moans, "Oh."

I surge to my feet, bringing her with me. Her legs lock around me tight and my hands come up to squeeze and hold onto her ass. Spinning toward the sliding glass door, I'm there in two strides.

My hand falters at the handle to the sliding glass door when Andrea leans in and bites my earlobe, then sucks on it. I make another grab and pull it open hard, surging through. In three more strides, I'm in my bedroom where I toss her down onto the bed.

Following her down, I cover her body with my own and love how her arms automatically wrap around me, and she lifts her mouth... ready for mine.

Our kiss is deep and languid. I swallow the soft moan she places on my tongue, but I need to hear more of that.

It's an absolute need.

I pull my mouth away from her lips, moving across her jaw, down the slope of her throat. I kiss and softly bite my way to her collarbone, her fingers loosely sift through my hair then hold on to my head. Over the curve of her breast, over to the side and down her ribcage. While I lick at her hipbones, I untie the strings of her bikini bottoms and pull them free.

With just a soft push of my hands, she spreads her legs for me and I put my mouth to work on her. I don't devour her like I did in the FBI locker room but rather gently feast. Soft licks, tiny flutters of my tongue, gentle strokes of my fingers. Her moans are breathy, sometimes purring low in her throat. It's fucking sexy as hell to build her up slowly.

When her breathing becomes more shallow... when I know she's close and just needs a tiny push over the edge, I suck at her hard and feel immensely triumphant when her body spasms as she comes for me.

Then I feel immensely fulfilled when she calls my

name softly while her fingers tighten on my head and tremors continue to ripple through her.

Christ... she's fucking beautiful.

Planting a soft kiss just above her pubic bone, I kiss my way back up her body. Her eyes are closed but when she feels me settle over her, they slowly open and she gives me a satisfied, lazy smile.

"Damn," she says as she scrapes the nails of one hand down the side of my neck, bringing it down to rest over my thumping heart.

"Like?" I ask with a grin.

She nods coyly at me, and then her hand slides down lower. "Time for me to return the favor."

I reach down, loosely grab her around the wrist, and tug her hand away. "Not yet. I want to hear more about this man that wasn't nice to you."

She blinks at me in surprise, and then her eyes shutter down again. "Not an interesting story."

"And yet, I'm interested," I tell her firmly as I prop myself above her on my elbows.

"Seriously, Wyatt," she says in exasperation and pushes at my chest. I don't budge an inch. "It's stupid really. Nothing to even waste my breath over."

Leaning down, I push back against her and drag my lips over hers. She opens her mouth, and I stroke my tongue against hers before pulling back. "Andrea... you taste yourself on my tongue just now? I had my mouth on your pussy and you came hard for me. Nothing you could say to me would ever be stupid or a waste of breath."

I wish I had a camera to take a picture of her face at this moment because her eyes flare wide... disbelieving, and then they immediately melt into warmth as she realizes what I just said to her.

Her hand comes up. Touching her palm to my face, she whispers, "You seriously want to hear my sad tale?"

I nod with a smile. "Yes. And why wouldn't you want me to hear it?"

"Because I don't want you to think I'm weak... or stupid... or pathetic."

I grin at her big, lean down again, give her a swift kiss, and then roll to my back pulling her with me. When she settles on top, her arms crossed over my chest, I tell her, "You're fucking adorable when you get all soft and vulnerable. But I could never think you're weak, stupid, or pathetic. So lay it on me."

Blowing out a breath and raking her hand through her long hair, she huffs, "Fine."

Pushing against my chest for leverage, Andrea sits across my lower stomach and places her palms on her thighs. She looks down at me with clear eyes and determination. I lace my fingers with her and give her a squeeze.

"I'll give you the short version. I was engaged to a guy... in Pittsburgh. I thought he was it. *The one*. He broke off the engagement about three weeks prior to me going undercover with you."

I tense slightly that just a few months ago, she belonged to another man, but I give her hands another encouraging squeeze because I want to hear all of it.

"Why did he break it off?" I ask.

She looks at me directly... her chin tilted up and defiance in her eyes. "Because I had applied to the Behavioral Research and Instruction Unit of the FBI. They're based in Quantico and he didn't want to leave Pittsburgh. He asked me to pull the application and when I refused, he called off the engagement. Left me. I haven't heard from him since."

"So why does that make you pathetic?" I ask in confusion, because this douche seems to be the pathetic one.

"Because... I considered it. I actually thought about giving up my dreams to keep him."

"But clearly you didn't," I point out. "So what's the problem? Seems to me you made a strong move. Seems to me his lack of compromise makes him the weak one."

She shrugs her shoulders and pulls her hands free of mine, placing them on my chest so she can lean over me a bit. Her face hovers over mine. "Because for the longest time after... I kept doubting myself. That maybe I made a mistake. Maybe I should have agreed to stay in Pittsburgh. Shouldn't I have been willing to sacrifice something for love?"

Her face is troubled but not pained. I find this

interesting, so I prod some more. Reaching up, I take her face in my hands. "I still don't see how having those doubts makes you weak? What's really going on?"

She gives me a shy smile, and then blasts me with utter honesty that takes me aback. "I feel a bit foolish... because the times you and I were together... the things you made me feel. Hell, the way you told me how beautiful I am just a few minutes ago. The way you made me feel beautiful just a few minutes after that. And the way you want to know about my feelings... I realize I didn't have any of that with him. In hindsight, I find myself to have been stupid for even thinking of giving up my dreams for someone that didn't truly touch me. You know what I mean?"

I lean up, kiss her, and then pull her down to my chest. She rests her head there for a minute, and I stroke the back of her head. Finally, I have the words to say.

"Andrea... you may have had moments of self-doubt, but in the end... you are where you are. You made the strong choice... the right choice. Everyone's always so focused on their destination that we forget to appreciate the things we learn along the journey. You did nothing more than have a few bumps along the way. That's all that is. Nothing more."

She pulls her head up off my chest and looks at me as if I'm a living miracle. It makes my chest warm to receive it.

"How is it you can spout a few philosophical words of wisdom and have me turning my perspective around?"

"I'm just brilliant that way." I grin at her.

"You are kind of brilliant," she says with a laugh and then looks at me mischievously. "And kind of sexy."

"Oh, yeah?" I ask, smiling back at her.

Andrea pushes up off me and scoots backward, down between my legs. Her hands work at the button and zipper of my shorts and then she has me in her grasp, stroking and squeezing me with beautiful torment.

"Definitely sexy," she breathes out and lowers her mouth down. Her eyes rise up to me for a brief moment before she makes contact and my lungs freeze in anticipation. "Let me show you how sexy and brilliant you are."

CHAPTER 16

Andrea

I FINISH GIVING the pancake batter a few more brisk strokes as I stare out Wyatt's kitchen window to the Atlantic Ocean. I woke up early, happy to be in Wyatt's bed... his home... sharing my free time with him. I decided to let him sleep, made a cup of coffee, and watched the sun rise over the steel-gray waters.

Last night with Wyatt altered something within me. After he told me I was beautiful, went down on me, and then made me realize that maybe I was too hard on myself over my self-doubts about David, I did, in fact, return the oral favor. It was completely different from the last time I had my mouth on him in Simon Keyes' office.

While I enjoyed *that* encounter, I still suffered guilt over it. It wasn't something we've discussed since then, and in fact, we haven't really discussed the operation at all. I'm not sure if that's good or bad.

This time, however, with my mouth on Wyatt's cock and his hands in my hair urging me on, it was an entirely different experience. Still hot as all get out, but infinitely so much better because of this new personal connection we had acknowledged. My goal to pleasure him last night came from deep inside... a raw need to give him something of myself. This wasn't curiosity and hormones surging high like the last time.

No, last night was about me giving him an ultimate and pure gift of intimacy that I haven't really shared with anyone else. Oh, I've shared the act with someone before, but never gave it as a gift, and that made all the difference in the world to me.

Afterward, we lay in bed, cuddled, and talked a bit, then we decided we needed nutrition. Wyatt whipped up a quick pasta with a red sauce, and we ate side by side on his couch while we watched a movie. Then we watched another movie, and I fell asleep with my head on his lap and his hand stroking my hair. He woke me up close to midnight, carried me to bed, made love to me, and then tucked me in tight against his body. I slept like a log and woke feeling amazingly refreshed and riding high on happy endorphins.

Putting the bowl of batter down, I flip on the electric griddle that I had found tucked in the back of his tiny pantry. While it heats up, I pull out a stick of butter from the fridge. I cut a few pats off, throw them on the griddle, and once they are melted, I pour out enough batter to make four small pancakes.

As I wait for the cakes to start to bubble on top, I let my mind drift a bit. I have eight days left here with Wyatt, and I'm not sure what I'm hoping to accomplish. I knew there was a very distinct possibility when I came to visit that we would have sex. But that's not why I came.

I came because he stirred feelings up inside of me that wouldn't let my mind have any rest. Too much emotion was churning within me, and Wyatt and I had been through something together that forges a bond. I simply had to come and try to figure out what it was.

I have no more clarity on the matter other than to know, without a doubt, that Wyatt is a much finer man than I ever gave him credit for. I mean... I knew he was a good and decent man from the start. He went out of his way to protect me, and I know deep down in my gut, he probably would have sacrificed the mission to keep me from harm. I know, without a shadow of a doubt, that he would have died protecting me if it came down to it that night during the bust. But just these last two nights with him, talking to him, seeing how he gets me to open up... his easy charm, his humor and his kindness.

Well... it seems I may have found what may be a genuine soul, and the thought of leaving that in eight days is already sitting heavy with me. Sitting heavier is the fact that I have no clue if he feels anything remotely near what I feel, and worse yet... maybe my feelings are seemingly strong because I'm rebounding off David and the way he jilted me.

Tiny bubbles rise up from the pancakes, spurring me into action. I grab the spatula and slide it deftly under the first one.

"Jesus Christ, Andrea… are you trying to give me a heart attack first thing in the morning?" Wyatt barks at me from behind.

I yelp and jerk upward, causing the pancake to flip up and right off the back of the griddle, where it lands with a splat on the counter.

Turning to Wyatt with the spatula in one hand and my other slapped over my chest, I gasp, "Oh my God. You gave *me* a heart attack sneaking up behind me like that."

Wyatt stands there in a pair of pajama bottoms made of blue cotton, his hair sticking up all around his head and his eyes roving over me. His gaze finally comes to meet mine and his eyes are sleepy… yet totally hot with lust.

He prowls toward me, again raking his eyes from head to toe.

"What's all this?" he says as he waves his hand up and down, pointing at my body.

I look down, and then back up with a sly grin. "Oh, this?" I ask coyly as I twirl around once in front of him. "I'm making naked pancakes for you."

He grins and grabs ahold of my waist, pulling me in tight to him. I can feel his erection pushing up against my stomach. His face goes into the crook of my neck and he murmurs, "Naked pancakes, huh? Never had those before."

Scraping his teeth along my neck, I giggle and wrap my arms around him, the spatula still in my grip. "It was supposed to be surprise. Now go get back in bed so I can bring them to you."

"No fucking way," he growls, and then pulls back to look at me with a grin. "I'm too hungry to wait. Need something right now."

Before I can even comprehend what's going on, he spins me around, latches an arm around my stomach, and pulls me back tight to him. His hand shoots out, grabs the syrup I had previously pulled out, and turns it upside down. A hard flex of his hand on the bottle and he squirts syrup on my chest, right in the center, moving it to the right to cover one of my breasts.

"What the hell—?" I yelp as the spatula clatters to the floor from my hand, but then Wyatt spins me again.

One of his hands goes around my back, the other to my hair, and he tugs hard on it so I bow backward, thrusting my breasts up. His head bends, his tongue starts working on the syrup, and in two swipes, he has a nipple in his mouth.

My hands go to his hair, and I give a purr of contentment while he laps at me. This is what I want to wake up to every morning. Wyatt licks, sucks, and bites at my sticky skin. It makes me ache... My skin tingles and my blood heats so hot, I swear I can smell it burning.

Burning?

Wait... what?

"Oh shit," I yell out as the acrid smell of burnt pancakes penetrates the fog of lust Wyatt put me in. I shove out of his arms, turn to the griddle, and slap the switch off. Thick smoke filters up into the air, and I wave my hand through it to help it dissipate.

"First attempt at naked pancakes," Wyatt says sadly as he looks at the smoking mess. "Epic fail."

I turn to him with my mouth open. He looks so serious... so forlorn. I start to say something... a commiseration maybe, but he starts snickering. Then he bends over and starts laughing.

"Damn, baby... I thought for a moment you were going up in flames in my arms," he chortles. "Turns out it was just burned pancakes. I'm losing my touch."

Spontaneous giggles pour out of my own mouth and I slap him on the shoulder. "Great job. You made me burn our breakfast."

Wyatt straightens and pulls me back in his arms, wrapping his arms loosely around my waist. Grinning down at me, he says, "Big, bad, FBI agent Somerville... who would have known... she's a giggler."

I suck in a breath and hitch my shoulders back, leveling my most stern look at him. "I most certainly do not giggle."

But then I break down in a fit of hilarity again when Wyatt snorts at me.

Giving me a quick kiss and skimming his hands up my ribs, he murmurs, "Why don't you go get cleaned up and I'll take you out to breakfast? I'll clean up this mess."

I stare at him a moment. He stares back at me with the happiest, most carefree look on his face. It makes him look boyish and charming, and I feel my heart sigh. "Okay. Sounds like a deal."

One more soft kiss, then he's turning me around, slapping me on my naked butt, and pushing me back toward the bedroom. When I get to the hallway entrance, I sneak a peek back over my shoulder. He's scooping up pancakes from the griddle and throwing them in the garbage. The early morning sunlight is pouring in through the window, lighting up his golden-brown skin and making the natural highlights in his hair sparkle.

I think about the man that was Raze Hawkins.

Cold, hard, detached. Prostitution peddler and lap dog to a slave trader. I'm amazed that someone as easygoing and down to earth as Wyatt was able to pull off that role. When I first met him as "Raze," I had no clue he was in character. I just assumed that was Wyatt's natural personality.

As I came to know him over the course of the operation, it started to become clear to me that he was putting on just as much of a performance as I was. The memory that guts me… the one that I think forged a personal connection between us, was that night in Simon's office when Lance forced me on Wyatt.

As I crawled toward him… put my hand on his knee to ease my way in between his legs, he had a look of such sorrow on his face that I saw the real man behind the facade. I knew that he was also sacrificing a part of his soul to see this mission through, just as I was. No one that was involved in this entire scheme would ever know the immoral stains that Wyatt and I would need to scrub off us when this was finished. It gave us a common experience that no one would ever share or understand.

It is amazing to me that we've yet to talk about that, but I think that has more to do with the fact that we have been immersed in a fog of lust since I arrived. I do think we should probably talk about everything that went down, if only for each of us to have an outlet.

I head directly into Wyatt's bathroom that is part of the master suite. It's small with only a corner shower, small sink, and toilet, but I expect a bachelor doesn't really need much else. Wetting a washcloth, I wipe the rest of the syrup off my chest, although I have to admit, Wyatt did a good job of licking most of it away.

After rinsing the cloth out, I hang it up and give my teeth a quick brush. Quick swish of mouthwash and I'm ready to get dressed to go out to breakfast.

I pad back into the bedroom and kneel down on his carpeted floor where my suitcase is lying. I rifle through, grabbing panties and a bra, and a pair of jean shorts and a tank top. One thing I've learned since coming to the Outer Banks is that casual is the mode of dress around here.

Before I can stand to put my clothes on, I hear a "ding" on my phone, which is charging on the dresser right next to me. I reach up, disconnect it from the cord, and see a text from Kyle.

Just checking in. Hope you're having a good time on vacation.

My smile burns bright over his thoughtfulness. I should have taken some time and gone out to visit him, and I feel slightly guilty choosing Wyatt over Kyle. But I think he'd understand.

Oh, not that I'm having hot and wild sex with my undercover partner, but that I'm happy and having fun, and mostly… that I'm not pining over David.

I quickly text him back. *Having a great time. Call you later.*

Before putting my phone back and getting dressed, I do a quick check of my email and don't see anything important. I switch over to my Facebook app and give a quick perusal. I don't post a lot of personal stuff on my wall, but that's only because I sadly don't have a lot of personal stuff to share. My life had been filled with nothing but my career and David. My FBI work was private so I couldn't post about that, and David wasn't on Facebook. I used it mainly to keep in contact with old high school and college friends but sometimes, I'll go weeks without getting on.

In fact, I haven't been on since before I left for Raleigh to go undercover.

When the app opens, the first thing I notice is several notifications at the bottom and one friend request. Ignoring the notifications, I click on the "Requests" icon. My jaw drops when I see who is asking to be friends with me.

David Lovitt… my ex-fiancé.

What in the hell?

I have no clue when he sent this friend request, and I'm absolutely perplexed as to why he would bother to want to be friends with me as our break up was not pretty.

There was lots of crying and pleading on my part—which sort of shames me now—and a lot of hurtful words on his part.

"I don't understand where this is coming from, David?" I had said with tears pooling in my eyes. He had just broken my heart by telling me that he wanted to call the engagement off.

"Seriously, Andrea?" he had sneered. "I told you I

am not moving from Pittsburgh. You refuse to pull your application. A husband and wife can't live in different states, so there's no fucking reason to stay engaged. I'm sure as hell not marrying someone that can't respect my decision on that."

"But I might not even get accepted," I pointed out as I wiped the back of my hand over my eyes. "Everything could just stay the same, and you're willing to throw everything away over the possibility I might have to move?"

David sneered at me. "It's more than that. It's the fact you're choosing your career over me. I don't want to be with someone like that."

"David, please—" I had implored, but he cut me off.

"Just forget it," he said and turned toward my door. "We're done unless you pull that application. And even if you did... I'm not even sure we can fix this."

He left me standing there. Only after the door closed behind him did I let the tears really flow.

I could have pulled my application. Those first few days I was so lonely... so desperate to have his love back... I came very close to doing just what he wanted. But I never could seem to actually make myself do it. Instead, I kept hoping he'd come to his senses. I called him... sent him texts... a few emails. He never responded, and I eventually gave up.

In hindsight, and especially with Wyatt's words of

wisdom still ringing in my ears, it's easy to see that I made the right choice—even if it hurt like hell to do it. I'm better off without him.

Still… my curiosity is killing me, and while I truly don't believe that we are meant for each other, there is a large part of me that wants to know what he's thinking. Why is he contacting me? Especially because he has my phone number and my email. He could have contacted me if he wanted.

What if… what if he's found someone else, and he's just friending me on Facebook to rub my face in it?

Now my curiosity is through the roof—morbid as hell—and before I can stop myself, I accept his friend request. Then I exit out of Facebook and put my phone aside. I'll check back in a few days and see what he does.

Until then… I suddenly decide that I'm not interested in going out for breakfast. I think Wyatt was on to something when he poured the syrup on me, and I think I'd like to revisit that idea with him right now.

CHAPTER 17

Wyatt

MMM... WAKING UP to Andrea making naked pancakes.

That is something I could definitely get used to.

Laughing over burnt, naked pancakes? Yeah, I could get used to that too.

I scrape the charred, little discs off the griddle, depositing them into the garbage. After filling the sink up with soapy water, I make a quick cup of coffee while I wait for the griddle to cool just a little more. I think after breakfast I'll take Andrea on a drive and show her around the Outer Banks. Maybe a nice seafood lunch somewhere, then back to my cottage where I will insist we spend the rest of the day in bed.

Good plan.

As I take my first sip of coffee, I hear a knocking at my front door. Leaning back against the counter, I ignore it and enjoy another sip of coffee... the nectar of the gods.

The knocking continues and I just stare at my door, willing whoever is on the other side to just go away. I only have Andrea for another eight days, the next four of which I want her all to myself since I don't have to work. I'm not sharing a single minute of my time with anyone else.

BAM, BAM, BAM!

The door practically rattles with someone pounding at it now.

"Wyatt... open the damn door. I know you're in there, and I'm not leaving until you do."

Gabby? What the fuck is she doing here?

Immediately, my thoughts go to Hunter and worry that something has happened to him, but then I dismiss that. She would have called... not wasted a trip over here. So I continue to ignore her.

Until she yells, "If you don't open the door right now, I'm going to call your mother."

Okay, now that is something I can't ignore. The girl is crazy enough to do just that and while my mother is the sweetest, most genteel southern lady you can imagine, it's a known fact that southern women can be quite scary when provoked. Seeing as how I haven't seen my parents yet since I've been back, a call from Gabby that she was worried about me would set into motion a cataclysmic mothering event that I would like to avoid.

Don't get me wrong. I love my mother to the ends of the earth. We're tight, as I am with my father, my three sisters, and the passel of nieces and nephews they all have birthed. But I don't have it in me to be "mothered" right now, particularly when I want to do nothing but hide away from everyone so I can enjoy every minute of my free time with Andrea.

I set my coffee cup down on the counter and stomp toward the door. Flinging it open, I glare down at Gabby as her fist is raised up to strike again.

"I can't believe you'd threaten me with calling my mother," I snarl at her. "That's low, Gabs... way low."

She gives me a grin and pushes her way past me, actually lowering her shoulder and ramming it into my ribs so I move out of her way. "Can it, Wyatt. It's time for you to stop hiding."

I shut the door and turn toward her. She walks right into my kitchen, pulls a cup out of the cabinet, and then pours coffee into it. Never glancing back at me, she says, "I have no clue what's up your butt or why you're ignoring your friends, but Hunter's worried, which makes me worried, so I'm here to get your head out of your ass."

Strolling casually back into the kitchen, I grab my cup and resume my leaning position against the counter. Taking a sip, I eyeball Gabby over the rim of the mug and have to admit to myself... she's cute when she's all worked up. Hunter landed himself a winner with her and while I've known her all my life seeing as how Hunter was my best friend, and Gabby was Hunter's sister, Casey's best friend, I've come to know her pretty damn well. Her being here... in my home and reading me the riot act, is not surprising.

It is however, annoying, particularly when I have breakfast plans with Andrea, so I figure the best way to pacify her and get her out of the door is to play her game.

"Listen... I just needed a little time to myself," I assure her quietly, and maybe a little dramatically. "Just taking a much-needed break after that under-cover operation... trying to get back in the swing of things. It was really draining, Gabs. But I swear there is absolutely nothing for you to be worried about. I just need some solitude for a few days."

Gabby tilts her head to the side and her eyes swim in sympathy. I can tell she buys my story... that I need some "alone time" because this undercover operation has me beaten down a bit. She opens her mouth... I'm betting to give me some commiseration and then hopefully, to tell me goodbye with an apology for barging in, but before she can say a word, I hear coming down the hallway from my bedroom, "I changed my mind, Wyatt... I decided we should stay in for breakfast and if you're a good boy, I'll let you have me for starters."

Wincing, I lower my head and rub the bridge of my nose. I didn't miss the high arch of one of Gabby's eyebrows and her lips pursing in surprise.

Andrea walks around the corner and into the

kitchen. I swivel my head and take in her appearance... fucking gorgeous in nothing but one of my white, button-down shirts, which she is currently holding closed with her hands and not the buttons. She has a sensuous look on her face as she comes into the kitchen.

Her eyes pin to me for just a moment... full of wanton promise... but just as quickly, she registers that Gabby is here. Her gaze goes quickly to Gabby, who only arches an eyebrow higher, and then looks back to me.

Face flushing red, Andrea immediately starts stammering, "Oh, my God. I am so sorry. I didn't realize you have company. This is so embarrassing."

She says all of this while clutching my shirt around her tighter and backing away from Gabby and me.

"So, you need some solitude, huh, Wyatt?" Gabby says with a light sneer. "This operation really wore you out, didn't it?"

"It's not what it looks like," I say as I scrub my hand through my hair in frustration.

"Really?" Gabby says sarcastically as she sets her coffee down and crosses her arms over her chest. "Because it looks to me like you're blowing off your friends... in particular, your best friend... under the guise of needing alone time, and yet... you don't look to be alone, do you? Looks like you are very occupied."

"Um… I think I'm going to go get dressed," Andrea says and starts to turn away from us.

I lunge off the counter, grab her by the shoulders, and haul her back around to face Gabby.

"I assume Hunter told you about our talk the other day?" I ask Gabby.

She nods her head. "Of course he did. He shares everything with me, which is a warning to you that you shouldn't ever tell him a secret you don't want me to know."

"Duly noted," I say curtly. "Then I assume he told you about Andrea, right?"

She rolls her eyes but comes around full circle, pinning me with a direct stare. "He sure did. Said you were all stuck on her but didn't have the balls to go after her, which is sort of lame, Wyatt. I thought you had more gumption than that, but anyway… now I know why you didn't bother going after her," she says as she gives a nod toward Andrea. "You clearly found something to occupy your time."

Then, as an afterthought, she actually looks at Andrea with a soft smile, "No offense."

"None taken," Andrea says with a smile, fully enjoying this now.

I can't believe Gabby just fucking outed me in front of Andrea… that I had feelings for her. Not that I would hide something like that, but it would have been nice for me to tell Andrea that, rather than her hearing it secondhand.

SAWYER BENNETT

Gripping Andrea firmly by the shoulders, I give her a little push toward Gabby and in two steps, we are right in front of her.

"Gabby... I'd like you to meet Andrea," I tell her. Angling my head down toward Andrea, I say, "Andrea, this pain in my ass is Gabby... a longtime friend and fiancée to my best friend, Hunter."

Andrea's hand shoots out toward Gabby. "Pleased to meet you."

Gabby's face is filled with utter confusion, and I have to restrain myself from laughing at her. She slowly reaches out and shakes Andrea's hand, her eyes flicking back and forth between the two of us.

"This is Andrea?" she asks me dumbly. "Your Andrea... the one that was undercover with you?"

"Yup," I say.

She releases Andrea's hand and shoves her hands in the pockets of her shorts. "I don't understand... when did you go out to visit her?"

Slipping an arm around Andrea's waist, I pull her in close to me. "I didn't. Luckily, she had balls big enough for the both of us and took it upon herself to come visit me. Showed up on my porch step day before yesterday."

Understanding dawns bright on Gabby's face... the light bulb has clicked on. "Okay, now I understand."

"Glad you get it," I say as I release Andrea and reach out to take Gabby by the arm. Tugging her, I start leading her back to the front door. "And now… if you don't mind, you're ruining our breakfast plans."

Gabby turns on her heel, easily pulling out of my grasp, and heads back toward Andrea. Taking ahold of her elbow, she leads her over to the counter and pours her a cup of coffee. "So, Andrea… this is awesome you came to see Wyatt. What made you do it? Were you stuck on him the way he was—?"

"Oh-kay," I drawl as I stalk toward Gabby and take her by the elbow, this time latching onto her hard. Turning her toward the door, I hear Andrea let out a giggle. "That's it. I'm throwing you out. It was nice seeing you and all, but I'd like some time alone with Andrea. I'll see you and Hunter next week after she's gone, and we'll get all caught up."

Just as I succeed in practically dragging her to the front door, she digs her heels into the carpet and pulls away again. Not as easily this time, but she still slips free.

Turning to glare at me with her hands at her hips, she says, "Yeah… that's not going to work. You both are coming to Last Call tonight, and you are going to hang out with your friends. It's long overdue and besides… we want to get to know Andrea."

"Sorry… no can do," I say with an apologetic shrug to my shoulders but with finality in my voice. "Andrea and I already have plans."

It's not that I am ashamed of Andrea, and it's not

that I don't think we'd have fun hanging out with them, but I sure as hell am not sharing her when my time is limited. If this works out... and she comes back to visit, then sure... she'll slip right into my crowd of friends as if she always belonged there. But I'm feeling too proprietary toward her right now.

Rather than capitulate, Gabby takes a step nearer to me and rises on tiptoes. "Tough shit. Cancel your plans. You're hanging out with your friends tonight."

"I am not—" I start to say, but she runs right over me.

"We missed you, haven't seen you in months."

"I get that but—"

"And on top of that," she says while poking me in the chest, "Gavin and Savannah are leaving day after next to spend a few weeks in England visiting his parents. This is the only time they can go out."

I take in a breath to argue with her, but then I feel Andrea's hand press into my back. She takes a step around me, and Gabby's gaze goes over to her.

"We'd love to come," Andrea says. Then turning to look at me, she gives me a steely look... daring me to argue with her. "Wouldn't we?"

Grimacing, I huff out an offended breath and lean down until I'm nose to nose with Andrea.

"You're not as cute as I used to think you were," I grumble, but she just smirks at me before turning back toward Gabby.

"What time should we be there?" she asks.

"Around 9 PM," Gabby says and then leans over and spontaneously hugs Andrea. "Yay. This is going to be so much fun."

"Not so much," I mutter, but Gabby pays me no mind.

"See you two later," she calls out as she opens my door, and then she's gone.

Andrea and I stand side by side for a moment, silently staring at the door. I faintly hear Gabby's car start up outside.

Slowly turning my head toward Andrea, I growl at her. "You are in so much trouble."

Her own head turns toward me, and her eyes widen in surprise. Our gazes lock... bodies tense.

I lunge at her, dropping my shoulder down low and catching her right below her sternum. She half-shrieks, half-laughs as my arms wrap around the backs of her legs and I haul her up and over my shoulder.

"Put me down," she cries out as her hands slap at my lower back.

"Quiet," I bark at her as I walk back toward my bedroom. I raise a palm up and bring it down with a sharp crack on her naked ass—because my shirt has fortuitously bunched up nicely around her waist.

She yelps, then starts laughing at me, and I'm grinning big by the time I toss her on the bed. She immediately rolls to the side and starts to scramble off, but I jump on her, easily grabbing her wrists and forcing her on her back. I straddle her at her waist and then pull her arms down, pinning them under my shins.

Andrea struggles, her face red from laughing and the effort to get away from me, so I decide to really make her suffer. Fingers to her ribs, I start tickling her.

A piercing shriek comes out of her mouth, and she bucks up hard against me, laughing hysterically. "Don't, Wyatt. I can't stand to be tickled."

"Should have thought about that before you committed us to going out tonight," I growl at her and double up my efforts on her ribs.

"Stop," she yells while gasping for breath and trying to wriggle away. "I'm going to pee."

Laughing, I slow my fingers and then lift my legs up to free her arms. Sitting back on my haunches, I look down at her. "Okay, that's a level of kink I'm not into."

She giggles and takes a few deep breaths. We grin at each other a moment, but then her eyes turn a bit serious.

Reaching one hand out, she grasps the elastic waistband of my pajama bottoms between her forefinger and thumb, pulling it away from my skin. Releasing it just as quickly, it snaps back.

Raising her eyes to mine, she asks, "So... you were kind of stuck on me, huh? Thinking about coming to visit me?"

My face flushes, but I don't look away. Staring

down at her, I reach out and take the edges of my shirt she's wearing and peel it back, exposing her breasts.

"Just a little," I tell her quietly, dropping my gaze to her chest. I place my palms over the swells and rub my thumbs in circles over her nipples. Her breath catches, and she arches her back.

"Do you think you would have ever come to see me in Pittsburgh?" she asks.

My eyes rise back up to hers. I consider her question, and I'm not sure if my answer is based on what I'm feeling here and now, or what I was feeling then, but it's completely honest when I say, "Yeah... I would have."

"I'm glad," she says with a soft look.

"Me too," I tell her. "Same page and all."

"Same page," she agrees, but I do have to wonder what page we'll be on when it's time for her to return home.

CHAPTER 18

Andrea

WYATT TURNS OFF the ignition to his Suburban, and I stare through the window at Last Call. It's a one-story, moderately sized building with gray siding that sits oceanside on the Atlantic. From our angle, I can see a large deck on the back strung with white lights and loaded with people. A large, wooden sign that says, "Last Call" hangs over the tinted-glass door at the front. Based on the amount of cars in the parking lot, I'd say this place does quite well for itself.

We both exit his vehicle, and Wyatt meets me at the front where he takes my hand. He's wearing a pair of dark jeans, a gray V-necked t-shirt that's semi-tucked into his pants, which is paired with a brown, leather belt. As I've discovered most people on the beach wear flip-flops, I'm not surprised that's what Wyatt decided to wear on his feet.

I myself chose to wear a maxi-dress with a lime-green, white-and-black geometric design that was cut low in front and even lower in the back. It was tied halter-style around my neck and although you couldn't see them because the dress was so long, the cutest pair of white, gladiator-style sandals.

"So, let me make sure I have this all straight," I say conversationally as we walk toward the building, our clasped hands swinging in between us.

"Hunter is your best friend. He owns this place and is a retired, pro surfer. Gabby is his fiancée and a building contractor."

"Right," he confirms.

"Brody is Hunter's identical twin. You're friends with him as well, but not best. He spent time in prison for a crime he didn't commit and his wife, Alyssa, is an heiress. Both of them work at The Haven, which is a non-profit, no-kill animal shelter that Alyssa started, and they have a little baby boy named Trey."

I have to admit… Brody's story fascinates me. In the field of law enforcement, you just accept that if someone was convicted, they were guilty. Brody sadly took the fall for someone else in a drunk driving accident that killed a person, and I would assume he must have tremendous depth of character to do something like that.

"Excellent," he praises me. "You were really listening to me earlier, weren't you?"

I tap a finger on my free hand against my temple. "Mind like a steel trap."

Wyatt laughs and squeezes my hand. "So let's hear

the rest."

"Okay... Casey is Hunter and Brody's little sister and Gabby's best friend... They grew up together and are a few years younger than you, Hunter, and Brody. Casey isn't involved with anyone and in your words, 'Everyone despairs of her ever settling down'... or something to that extent."

"You're three for four," he says. "Let's hear the last one."

Taking a deep breath, I blow it out. "Okay... last to round out your posse is Savannah, who is a photographer, but was actually cleaning houses for a famous author named Gavin, who is originally from England. Savannah doesn't have long ties to all of you, but was a friend of the girls and Casey's roommate at some point. She and Gavin are the newest to your bunch, and they aren't married... not even engaged, but they have a little girl named Clare."

Wyatt stops our progress and turns to me, wrapping his hands around my waist. Pulling me in tight, he says, "That's impressive you remembered all of that."

"It's the FBI in me... paying attention to details," I say with a grin before planting a quick kiss on his chin.

"The biggest thing you have to remember is that despite the fact they can be loud, sometimes obnoxious, and completely nosy in an overbearing sort of way, they really are the greatest. You're going to love them."

"I can't wait," I tell him, attempting to step out of his grasp so we can go in.

He doesn't let me go though, his arms banding around me tighter. Wyatt pulls me in close until our bodies are flush with each other. "And, as much as I adore my friends and want you to meet them... have a good time... whatever, I don't plan on sharing you the entire night. We'll stay for a few drinks, and then we're leaving."

"Yes sir, Officer," I tease with a snappy salute... and then he kisses me.

Hard.

Deep.

Possessively.

When he pulls back, I hum low in my throat. "Mmmm... what was that for?"

"Because I can't seem to fucking help myself around you," he mutters as he grabs my hand and starts stalking to the entrance door.

I lower my head so he can't see the grin on my face and keep it tilted down until we step inside.

And wow... this place is so cool. There's a large bar to my right that runs down the length of the wall done in a rich, dark stain with a brass foot railing along the bottom. The floors are done in what looks to be reclaimed wood, also polished to a dark sheen. The walls, however, are painted in texturized blues of about three shades and swirled to resemble large ocean waves. The decor is simple but speaks to the owner's history... a variety of framed prints showcasing various surfers, along with an eclectic mix of surfing memorabilia. A digital jukebox sits in the far corner, but that's all I can see as Wyatt is turning left and headed down a short hallway that intersects with another that seems to lead back to the bathrooms.

We emerge out into an even larger area than where we entered with a bar that's easily twice as big as the one out front. It too, is done in dark stained wood with the brass foot railing. Mirrored glass with accent lighting reflects the various bottles of liquor and glasses on the shelving, and five keg taps are mounted at the very center of the bar. Three bartenders move efficiently, fulfilling orders to customers that are standing two deep. I can hear muffled music coming from the back of the room where there is a door, which I can tell must lead to the rear deck.

"There's a live band tonight on the back deck... actually every Saturday night during the summer months," Wyatt says and starts leading that way.

I look around as I follow along behind him. The place is packed, but I don't fail to notice numerous women checking Wyatt out as he walks by.

Yeah, girls... I get it. He's pretty damn hot.

I squeeze his hand, and he reflexively squeezes me back.

When he reaches the back of the bar, he pushes

open the glass door and we step out onto the deck. Even though the temperature is hovering around the low eighties, the breeze off the Atlantic immediately feels refreshing. It's a cloudy night but the cover isn't complete, and I can see part of the silver moon peeking out. It makes the edges of the clouds glow, and the water sparkles from the cast off.

Wyatt winds us through several tables until we reach the back of the decking where a group of people stands, holding drinks. I immediately recognize Gabby as she stands next to a tall, gorgeous man with golden-blond hair just a little longer than Wyatt's. A quick slide of my gaze over a few feet and I immediately see another man that is his identical twin talking to a dark-haired man, so I know deductively this must be Hunter and Brody Markham. I'm going to guess that Hunter is the one talking to Gabby since he seems to be eating her up with his eyes while they converse. Three other women stand talking togeth-er... completing the group. The first one I notice is a leggy blonde who could be a model for Victoria's Secret. Based on her coloring and height, I'm going to guess that's Brody and Hunter's sister, Casey. One woman is classically beautiful in the face and has a short, pixie haircut, while the last woman has long, dark hair past her shoulders. I don't know enough about who these are, so I'll have to wait for Wyatt to make the introductions.

When we reach the group, Brody is the first to see

us, and he approaches Wyatt with his arms open wide. Hand falling away from mine, Wyatt steps into Brody's embrace… endures some manly backslapping, and I hear, "Welcome back, dude. We missed you."

I watch as Wyatt shakes the dark-haired man's hand, and then alternately gives hugs to the other women. He fist bumps Hunter and leans down to kiss Gabby's cheek.

Then, as if planned in unison, the entire group turns to look at me, and I feel the spotlight burning down on me brightly. Wyatt holds his hand out to me, and I reach out for it. He pulls me into his side, turning me toward his friends.

He has to talk a little loud to be heard over the band, but it's not too bad since we're outdoors and much of the music filters away from us on the breeze. "Everyone… this is Andrea Somerville."

Everyone beams at me.

Wyatt then starts pointing out introductions, left to right. "You know Gabby… that's her fiancé, Hunter. Next to him is Gavin, then Brody, Alyssa, Casey, and Savannah."

I smile and nod at each person. I know now the woman with the short pixie cut is Alyssa, the dark-haired beauty is Savannah, and the very dark and sexy-looking man is the Brit, Gavin.

It's a gorgeous group of people, and my hand comes up to self-consciously fluff my hair out at the side.

Leaning down, Wyatt asks, "What do you want to drink?"

"I'll take a draft… something seasonal if they have it," I respond.

He kisses me on the temple and then says to the group before he leaves, "Don't scare her away."

Gabby grins large and as Wyatt walks away, the group sort of collapses inward and forms a circle so we can talk. For a split second, I feel like I'm under the microscope, and a moment of panic courses through me. What if they all hate me? What if they don't see something redeeming within me and don't think I'm good enough for their guy?

And then I have to wonder… does it really matter? Is this going to go any further than the next several days I have with him?

I would hope it would, because while the sex has been phenomenal, it certainly isn't all there is to us. In fact, I'd go so far as to say that I'm not sure the sex would be as phenomenal if we didn't have an intense bond formed first through dire circumstances.

One could even say that maybe what we have is stronger than most people just starting out, because we survived a dangerous situation together… helped each other along the way. We had to count on each other… we had to trust. All important foundations for any relationship.

I look around… they all stare at me with open

faces, warm smiles. They're nice people… that's what Wyatt said. They'll like me because Wyatt likes me. I have nothing to prove.

Taking a deep breath, I let it out and say, "So… it's really great to meet Wyatt's friends. He's told me a lot about you."

♦

THE BAND IS playing Van Morrison's *Brown-Eyed Girl* and while I don't really know all the lyrics, I follow along as best as I can.

With my new buds… Alyssa, Gabby, Savannah, and Casey.

It's getting late, I'm pretty buzzed, and all the tables on the deck have been pushed back to make an area for people to dance. My new buds and me stand in a circle with our arms all thrown around each other's shoulders, bouncing in place to the music and singing at the top of our lungs. Well, I'm singing about every fourth word that I might know, but the other girls have mastered this song. It must be a popular one around here.

Casey's arm around my neck tightens and she pulls me in closer, giving me a resounding kiss on my cheek. I think she's a little bit more than buzzed.

"I'm so glad you're here," she shouts above the music. "Wyatt looks so happy."

My chest constricts, and I shoot a glance over at him. He's sitting on the deck railing… Brody perched beside him. Hunter and Gavin are standing, and they are all deep in discussion. But maybe he feels the weight of my stare because his eyes slide over to mine and his lips curve up in a smile.

I smile back because yeah... he does look happy. Turning back to Casey, I yell, "He makes me happy too."

"Are you drunk enough yet to tell us the details of how you two hooked up?" Alyssa yells, just before releasing her grip around Gabby's shoulders and doing a nice spin move.

I smile, lower my gaze, and shake my head. When I look back up, the girls have all stopped bopping to the music and look at me expectantly.

"Come on," Savannah implores. "We're all in committed relationships... we've forgotten what it's like to be in the game."

"Speak for yourself," Casey scoffs.

"Except for Casey," Savannah acknowledges. "She swears she's never falling in love. But come on... tell us something."

"Yeah... just one tiny hint," Gabby begs with hopeful eyes.

I look around at their expectant faces... silly, buzzed grins shining at me. I've known them for going on about three hours, and yet... they all seem trustworthy... nonjudgmental.

Sneaking a glance back at Wyatt, I see he's not watching me and seems immersed in something that Gavin's saying. But still... I can't be shouting this stuff over the music.

I lean in to the girls conspiratorially. They lean in toward me eagerly. "Let's all go to the bathroom. This requires a quieter atmosphere."

They all grin and nod, then we are pushing our way through the crowd to head back into the bar.

When we get to the ladies' restroom, there is only one woman in there washing her hands. Everyone waits patiently for her to finish and once she's gone, Gabby locks the door behind her.

Turning toward me, she says, "Okay… dish."

"Well, you already know I met him on our undercover operation," I say with a silly grin. "What you don't know is that I was posing as a stripper in the club where Wyatt was working as the General Manager."

Four sets of jaws drop open… four sets of eyes blink at me in astonishment.

For a brief moment, I think maybe I made a mistake in revealing that. Maybe this wasn't something I should have shared. Maybe they are all four looking down at me right now, silently digesting that Wyatt's new flame knows how to work a stripper pole.

My mind whirls, trying to figure a way to sugarcoat this, when Alyssa slaps her hand on her thigh and says, "That is so freaking cool."

Casey gives a dreamy sigh. "I'd love to know how to strip… you know, do it right for a man. Get him all hot and bothered."

"Best story ever," Savannah exclaims.

I look over at Gabby, and she has a knowing smile on her face.

She knew already!

Which means Wyatt must have told Hunter, and as I've figured out... he shares everything with Gabby. But apparently, that little gem didn't go any further as the other girls were clearly not privy to this.

Placing her hands on my shoulders, Gabby says, "Whether you stripped or not... I don't think Wyatt ever stood a chance with you."

Tilting my head to the side, I give a slight nod of appreciation over her words before Casey is pulling me away from Gabby. "Okay... I want more details. Like specifics... did you just strip on stage, or was there a pole? Because there's this place over on the mainland that offers stripping lessons, but maybe you could teach me instead."

Before I can respond, someone starts banging on the door.

"Come on," Savannah says as she heads toward the door to unlock it. "People need to get in here. We'll get details later."

Casey gives a long-suffering look but heads out with Alyssa and Gabby trailing.

I, on the other hand, actually have to pee so I call out, "I'll catch up with you."

I hurriedly take an open stall as women pour into the restroom once Savannah opens the door. I do my business, wash my hands, and take stock of myself in the mirror. My face is flushed but even though I'm a bit buzzed, my eyes are still clear. I want to make sure I don't get too drunk tonight, because I really, really can't wait to get back to Wyatt's place.

Moving away from the sink, I finish drying my hands and head out of the bathroom. As soon as I open the door, I see him standing there.

Six plus feet of male glory.

Wyatt leans back against the wall of the short hallway that houses the bathrooms. His arms are folded across his chest, and it's clear he was waiting for me.

I walk right up to him. His arms unfold, his legs part, and I press in close. He pulls me tight and nuzzles my neck. "Everything okay?"

I nod against him, my fingers digging into the muscles at his back. Pulling back slightly, I look up at him. "Your friends are a blast. And so nice."

He smiles down at me. "They're pretty cool, I guess. So I take it you're having fun?"

Winding my arms up around his neck, I lean in and kiss him briefly. It feels so natural... these little signs of affection... attraction. There's no hesitation in giving on my part, and Wyatt likes to receive judging by the look on his face. "I'm having a great time."

"Good," he says, gently pushing me back. Grabbing my hand, he pulls me back toward the bar. "Let's have one more drink and then we'll head out. I'm dying to get you alone."

Hmmmm... I sigh internally. *Me too.*

CHAPTER 19

Wyatt

T HE GIRLS ARE all back on the makeshift dance
floor again, making the most out of their limited
time left with Andrea, as I advised the group we were
leaving soon. I bought Andrea another beer, although
it's sitting here beside me on the deck railing as she
was pulled out by the girls to dance in front of the
band as soon as we got back.

I sip at my bottled water, which I had started
drinking about an hour ago, and just watch Andrea.
She said she's have a great time, but I didn't need
those words. I can see it… she's bonding fast with my
group of peeps, which is a little surprising. Andrea
had told me last night that she really didn't have any
friends, which I found to be sad. She didn't think so,
though. She was pretty matter of fact… she didn't
have much of a life outside of her job and the rest of
the time was spent with her ex-fiancé.

But as I watch her now, happily dancing with the
rest of the girl-crew… her head thrown back,

laughing and bouncing around... I know her lack of friends wasn't from a desire to avoid friendships. I think it was a lack of options for her at that point in her life.

"Your girl has some moves," Hunter says as he nudges my shoulder and cocks his heard toward the dance floor.

Oh, if only he really knew the extent of her moves.

"She's having a great time," I agree.

"Things going well with her?" Hunter asks, and this catches Brody and Gavin's attention for some reason, and they step in closer to hear my answer.

Looking at my buds, I can't help but give them a little sneer. "What is this... a girlie-gossip session?"

"Hey man," Brody says with a punch to my shoulder... that sort of hurts, "we've all fallen hard. We're just waiting for you to do the same."

"So... what's the deal with her?" Gavin asks as he twirls the Scotch in his tumbler. The entire gang drinks beer except for Gavin.

"She's amazing," I say as I cut my eyes between them and the girls dancing on the floor. The last strains of *Animal* by Maroon 5 fades, and then the band launches into a classic, Warrant's *Cherry Pie*. "Sucks she lives so far away."

My words are simple and short, but they pretty much sum up the situation, and all three of the guys sort of nod their head in agreement.

We all fall silent, because when men do decide to gossip, we are emphatically short about it. Sipping at our drinks and watching the women dance, I realize that I am really, really happy to be back home. I knew that being immersed undercover is always a drain on one's psyche, but I didn't realize how much of my personal happiness comes from the mere fact that I live in a beautiful place where I grew up, work at a fulfilling career, and I'm surrounded by friends and a loving family. I didn't realize how much I actually need that in my life... not until I came out tonight and truly reconnected with my friends.

"Damn, your girl can seriously dance," Brody says, clasping onto my shoulder and ogling Andrea on the dance floor.

Yup... Andrea's putting a bit of sexy into her dancing. Grasping the material of her long dress, she pulls it up a bit higher. Nothing indecent but enough to see just above her knees. Her hips gyrate fluidly, her hands release her dress to come up into her hair, and she looks like a goddess out there.

And what the fuck... Casey and Gabby are now lined up beside her, watching Andrea's movements. They're talking... asking for pointers, and Andrea is now apparently giving them dance lessons.

I wonder if I let Brody and Gavin in on the secret that Andrea knows how to strip if they'd want her to give the girls lessons. I'm betting the answer would be a resounding *YES*!

While it doesn't bother me that my friends are ogling how sexy Andrea is, because I know they would never make a move on her, I don't particularly like how she's gotten the attention of many of the other male patrons. A few men make their way onto the dance floor and start dancing closer to the girls. They hang back a bit, content for the moment to keep their eyes pinned on Andrea's ass and the way her hips are moving.

She's oblivious to it all, rather concentrating on showing Alyssa, Gabby, Casey, and Savannah some dance moves.

Two men, who I can tell are quite drunk, move in a bit closer. They keep looking at each other with leering grins before staring back at Andrea's body.

"Dude… you going to do something about that?" Hunter says as he nods out toward the guys inching in.

"They make one step closer to Andrea and I am," I growl.

I'm not sure Andrea would like me stepping in to defend her honor. I know if one of those guys touches her inappropriately, she'll lay them out flat. I've come to quickly know that she's tough as nails and actually takes pride in the fact she could handle this type of situation.

"Maybe I should just go have a word with them… in a gentlemanly way," Gavin suggests with a grin, just to goad me.

"I'd totally go pound those guys into the ground," Brody says wistfully. "But that would break my probation."

One of the guys now moves in directly behind Andrea and is grinding air just inches away from her. Reaching out, I slap my water bottle into Hunter's chest and he takes it from me. In three strides, I've reached my destination and with perfect timing as the dude's hands reach out to grab Andrea by the hips.

Striking fast, I grab him by one wrist, bringing my other hand up and capturing his fingers, and then I bend them back toward his forearm.

I know, from training, that this causes immense pain and is an easy way to subdue someone.

The guy drops like a sack of bricks to his knees and shrieks. From the corner of my eye, I see Andrea whirl around to us, but I don't take my attention off this guy. The band keeps playing, but the dancing all around us has stopped while everyone watches in interest.

Hunter's bouncers on duty don't make a move toward us. They know who I am and they won't interfere.

Leaning down so I don't have to shout above the music, I tell the guy who now has tears leaking out of the corners of his eyes, "You're fucking lucky you didn't touch her or I'd be breaking this wrist right now."

"Fuck," the guy wails. "You *are* breaking it."

"Nah man," I say as I get right in his face, pulling his fingers back just a hair more. "You're just a pussy. Now I suggest you get up and move far away from these ladies. Understood?"

"Yes," he practically sobs, and I immediately release him. The guy rolls and stands up, cradling his wrist against his chest. He refuses to meet my eye and scurries off the dance floor with his friend.

Delicate hands touch me on my lower back, and I turn around to see Andrea there with her lips curved upward appreciatively. I note the other girls have left the dance floor.

Stepping in closer, her arms wrap around me and she tilts her head up. Her hips are swaying softly to the music, and while I don't dance, I sure as hell don't have a problem encircling her in my arms so she can sway against me.

"That was kind of hot," she says with a grin.

"Yeah? I was a little worried you would take offense to me stepping in," I tease her.

She tilts her head and purses her lips as if in contemplation. "No. I definitely think I liked you protecting my virtue."

Leaning down, I scrape my cheek along hers, which puts my lips near her ear. "I'm not going to protect your virtue tonight when we get back to my house."

Her laugh echoes like music to me. "I'm also okay with that."

♦

THIS IS DIFFERENT.

So very different.

I'm making love to Andrea slowly.

Tenderly.

Sleepily.

From behind, as we lay on our sides.

After we had come home last night, fueled on by her residual buzz, some sexy dancing on her part and a vague awareness that one more day was gone and our time was getting shorter, we went at it like horny animals.

Clothes were torn off, skin was bitten, and I'm pretty sure the neighbors heard us.

We collapsed onto my bed, sweaty and exhausted, and fell into a deep sleep with her face in my chest and my arms around her tight.

At some point in the night, she must have turned over and we assumed the classic spooning position.

At some point after that, I woke up and decided to take advantage of said spooning position. How could I not with a warm, soft body pressed intimately against me?

And now I have one of her legs bent with my palm at the back of her thigh and my breath hot on her neck. I move in and out of her from behind, the only noise in the room the sound of our sliding flesh and panting.

Angling my upper body down a tad, I hook her leg within the crook of my elbow, pulling it up higher to give me better access.

Fucking perfect.

I slam hard into her.

She lets out a tiny *ooph* followed by a moan as I do it again.

I get a deeper moan as I do it again.

"You okay?" I breathe in her ear.

"Yes."

"Feels good, doesn't it?"

"Mmmm. Hmmm."

I flex my hips hard, go extra deep, and then grind myself against her ass. "Andrea?"

"Hmmm?" she vaguely answers, and I can tell she's on the precipice… getting ready to fall over. Just one more push… maybe two, and we'll both go together.

"Ever felt this good before?" I ask with my lips against her shoulder.

I pull out… thrust hard and deep again. "God, no," she groans as she starts to spasm around my cock.

The tortured pleasure in her voice is my undoing.

"Me either, baby," I grit out as I slam into her one last time and let loose inside her body.

I seem to fucking come inside of her forever. Burying my face into the back of the neck, I let go of my hold on her leg and wrap my arms around her waist. Then I just close my eyes and concentrate on the spasms coursing through me, giving tiny, shallow thrusts inside of her body.

Letting her milk me dry.

Fuck, that's good.

So fucking good.

Her body is pressed up nicely against mine, and I can tell when it settles down... finishes trembling from her own orgasm. I float down with her as her fingers stroke along the skin of my forearm.

After a minute or so, I start to get drowsy, and I can feel Andrea's breathing getting deeper. We're on the verge of slipping back under.

"Wyatt?" whispers to me in the darkness.

"Yeah?"

"That was different, right?"

She's not talking about the sexual position we were in. She's talking about the way that just felt.

"Yeah... that was different," I confirm as I squeeze her with my arms.

She gives a tiny chuckle. "I have no clue what has gotten into you tonight, but I like it."

Grinning from behind her, I press my lips to the back of her head. "I think it was the way you were dancing... so damn sexy. Reminded me of watching you up on that stage at The Platinum Club... having a perpetual hard-on for you."

Andrea immediately flips in my arms, and I can tell she's nowhere close to being ready to go back to sleep now.

"You did not have a perpetual hard-on around me," she accuses, pushing at my chest playfully.

"Yeah, I fucking did," I assure her. "And you wouldn't know because when you danced, you always had that far away, dreamy look on your face. I came to understand that look… you'd checked out… your mind a million miles away. I was able to always adjust myself without you even noticing."

I can't see her face, but I can actually feel her smile. "You're very observant. And clearly, I'm not."

"All I know is that whenever you got up on that stage and your clothes came off… and I got to look at that amazing body of yours, all sleek and soft… completely bare… I wanted to do nothing more than to drag you off and jam my face between your legs."

Andrea purrs low in her throat over my proclamation. "Well… if we're being truthful… the only person I wanted to affect with my dancing was you. You just seemed… so far removed. Totally into your character, which wasn't really all that interested in the girls there."

"I was totally playacting," I tell her. "And speaking of affecting with your dancing, I never asked… but where in the fuck did you learn to dance like that? Does the FBI have a course on it or something?"

Andrea giggles… the best sound ever. "Actually… I have some personal experience with it."

I go absolutely still… process what she just said,

and then flip to my back so I can reach over to turn on the beside lamp. Turning back to her, I lean over and take in the shy smile on her face.

"You danced... stripped... before?"

She nods. "College and law school. It was the only way I could afford it."

I study her face. No embarrassment... no battered ego. In fact, she stares at me with clear eyes and waits for me to make comment.

"I don't know how I feel about that," I tell her truthfully. "I hate you had to do that, but I also admire you for doing whatever it took to accomplish your goals."

"I don't regret it," she says. "It's part of my past and while I was never comfortable with it, it really helped to build me into what I am today."

"Strength," I say as I bend down to kiss her softly on the lips.

"Determination," I say as I kiss her jaw.

"Fearlessness," I murmur, grazing my lips along her neck.

"You're fucking amazing," I tell her as I pull back.

She blinks repeatedly, and then her brows furrow inward. Her bottom lip is pulled in between her teeth, and I know something is pressing on her mind.

I wait for it.

"It's weird... I've been here with you less than three days, and you see those things about me, and yet... if I had to ask what I think some of my most important characteristics are... that's what I'd say about myself."

I give a nod of understanding, flip back over to turn out the light, and then gather her in my arms. When she's got her head to my chest and our legs are intertwined, my hand rubbing her lower back, I tell her, "I've had more than three days with you, Andrea. I knew you were all three of those things the minute you took on that undercover job. It was validated when you stepped onto that stage, and completely hoodwinked a suspected slave trader. If it weren't for you... none of that would have gone down the way it did. Like I said... you're pretty fucking amazing."

She doesn't say anything, but I can feel her body relax into mine. Her own fingers play across the skin on my stomach.

I start to get drowsy, but then she says my name softly.

"Wyatt?"

"Yeah?"

"I think you're pretty fucking amazing too."

CHAPTER 20

Andrea

I WAKE UP before Wyatt again and so the pattern has been set. I'm a morning person, whereas he is definitely not. I think about my attempt at naked pancakes and quickly put that thought right back out of my head. We had gone out to the grocery store yesterday and stocked up with a variety of staples. I'm thinking it's going to be naked bagels instead, but I'll wait a bit before I wake him up. I'm sure he's pretty worn out after our impromptu bout of sex we had followed by some pretty awesome pillow talk.

I loved his reaction about me dancing. I loved how it pained him that I had to stoop to that, but I was also grateful for how he admired me. It's sort of how I view myself, and while a lot of people could never understand baring your body for money, I guess the only one I really need to answer to is myself. I've never had a problem looking at myself in the mirror since that time in my past, and knowing that Wyatt still respects me is just icing on the cake.

Rolling out of bed, I quietly slip on my underwear, a pair of shorts, and a t-shirt. Grabbing my phone off the dresser, I head out to the kitchen and make a pot of coffee. After it's brewed, I pour a cup, doctor it up with an obscene amount of cream and sugar—Wyatt's characterization, not mine—and head out to the back deck.

As always, the beauty of the Atlantic always catches me by surprise. I'd never been to the beach growing up, and got my first look at the Atlantic while in undergrad when a bunch of friends and me road tripped to Virginia Beach one weekend. I've since seen the Pacific while on an assignment with the FBI, and the Gulf of Mexico, but for some reason... the Atlantic is what calls to me. I'm not sure if it's the blue-green waters, the low-breaking waves that make the best sound to sleep to, or the way the sun slowly emerges from the horizon each morning. I just know it resonates with me, and I eagerly make my way down the steps of Wyatt's back deck down to the cool sand below.

The sun's edge hasn't even made appearance yet, and the sky is tinged gray. I walk a few feet away from the steps and sink slowly down into the soft sand so as not to spill my coffee, only to have a small shell poke me in the butt. After wedging my mug into the sand, I lean over, remove the offender, and sink back down, burying my toes in the coolness that the evening has brought to the sand. I know by midday, it will be blistering hot.

While I wait on the sunrise to make its appear-ance, I turn on my phone. I need to call Kyle and check in with him, but it's far too early in Wyoming and he'd never answer. I had successfully avoided my phone all day yesterday and hadn't even brought it out with us to Hunter's bar last night.

But it's a new day... I've got my coffee, a gor-geous guy sleeping just up those stairs to my back, the promise of another spectacular sunrise... and yet, for some idiotic reason, I'm dying of curiosity to see if David has reached out through Facebook since I accepted his friend request.

My curiosity is completely upstanding. I don't have any desire to get back with him, and I certainly don't want to reconnect. But it's killing me not knowing why he is reaching out, especially when he drew a very deep line in the proverbial sand with me. It stunned me then and continues to flummox me now how he could have thrown away everything we had on almost a whim. I want to know if I did something wrong... did I miss something? Was I not attentive enough to him, was I not that great in the sack, or maybe he really just didn't love me the way I thought he did?

I have to know. He never gave me an opportunity to talk about his reasoning and if there is something that could have saved that relationship, it's imperative I know it. I have to know, because if it's truly my fault... I don't want to make that mistake again.

I'm not sure if it's because of this amazing connection with Wyatt, but I need to know that I have my priorities straight when it comes to balancing me, my career, and my personal life together. This is especially important to know because Wyatt and I are starting something here... something amazing, I can tell, but we are already facing the monumental hurdle of physical distance between us. This was clearly a point of contention with David, something he had no amount of compromise for, and the thought occurs to me... maybe I was the one that was unreasonable.

Again, I don't want to know these answers to fix my issues with David. I'm confident that that ship has sailed right out of my heart. I know this to be true because after that amazing connection we had last night while making love, it's brutally clear that my feelings for Wyatt are immensely stronger and deeper than what I had for David.

And I don't mean that I love him... because how could I? We haven't spent that much time together. But what I mean is that everything between us, broken down into component parts, is almost electrifying.

The way he kisses.

His touch.

His voice.

The way in which he listens to me.

Everything seems amplified... almost tangible. It's

so strong.

Wyatt is quickly becoming very important to me and while I'm not sure exactly how he feels, my gut says he's feeling something too. Therefore, I want to make sure I don't fuck up.

Pulling up the Facebook app, I immediately see I have a message waiting for me. I have no clue if it's from David or not, but I don't waste any time opening it up.

And sure enough… he wrote to me.

Andrea,

I know you're surprised to hear from me and through Facebook no less. My sister finally convinced me to sign up so I could see all the photos she always posts of her kids, so I gave in.

I wanted to check in to see how you were doing. I didn't feel comfortable emailing you at work, and I was honestly afraid of reaching out through the phone. I know I left things badly between us, and I also know I didn't handle it in the best way. I hurt you, and I really am sorry.

So, how are you? Work going okay? Any word on the BRIU? I'd really like to talk if you're open to it. I think there are some things that maybe I should have explained to you. I know, for sure, we should have definitely had more of a discussion rather than me unilaterally throwing everything away. All I can say is I was operating out of a place of fear and anger, which usually always leads to poor decision making.

You have my number. Call me if you want to

talk, or maybe even better yet... meet for coffee? Next few days?

Love,
David

I stare at the words on my screen, scroll up, and read through it one more time. I'm not sure what I should be feeling at this moment, but I can tell you how I'm not feeling.

I'm not feeling overly grateful he's reached out. No fluttering in my stomach, no thumping beat of hope within my chest.

I'm not angry or annoyed that he's now realizing he was so very wrong to do that to me.

In fact, the most overwhelming feeling I have right now is wondering if I should really make naked bagels for Wyatt or make another attempt at pancakes.

The most I feel about David, at this moment, is a vague curiosity as to why he wouldn't at least talk this out with me. Why didn't he afford me that respect?

I don't bother responding. I will, of course, but I want to wait until I can get on my laptop so I can type out my thoughts. I also want to think carefully about what to say to him. I am curious enough that I want to know the "why" of what he did, but I'm not overly eager to actually talk to him. I'll have to think on that, and bagels or pancakes seem like a more important thing to ponder.

The sound of feet trotting down the deck steps penetrates, and I turn to see Wyatt coming out to join me. He's got on just his jeans that he wore last night, and he looks absolutely edible and completely huggable the way his hair is sticking up all over the place. He's not a calm sleeper, that's for sure.

Sitting down beside me, he says, "Good morning," and then leans over to kiss me on my temple.

"Morning," I say and then scoot in closer to him. His arm comes around me, pulling me into his warmth and security.

"Waiting on the sunrise?" he asks.

I nod, lean over to grab my mug, and bring it up for a sip.

"Usually a pod of porpoises will be swimming along the coast around this time. If we're lucky, we'll catch sight of them."

"I saw them yesterday morning when I got up. They were spectacular."

"They used to give me the willies when I was younger. I used to surf with Brody and Hunter. Usually, the waves are always better in the early morning. That first flash of fin breaking the water while we were out there made me always first think it was a shark."

I laugh as he actually shudders when he says the word "shark". "Do you still surf?"

"No way. Didn't you just hear me? There are sharks out there. I got older and wiser."

My belly rumbles with laughter, particularly at the thought of this very brave man being scared to surf because of sharks. "So… what you're saying, is that if I was out in the water and needed saving, you wouldn't come in and get me?"

"Not if there was a shark out there I could see," he says emphatically. "But I'd run up, grab my gun, and then run back and try to shoot it for you."

"You're a true hero," I say drily while I pat him on the leg in acknowledgment.

We sit quietly together, and the sun finally starts to peek up over the horizon. I knew it was coming because over the last few minutes, the lower part of the sky started turning light blue, and the clouds hanging low started glowing with various shades of orange and pink.

When the first rounded edge looked to seemingly break the surface of the water, it was a brilliant neon of yellow glow that was still low enough that I could look straight at it.

Just as Wyatt had predicted, a pod of porpoises came swimming by, and I alternated my gaze going from them to the emerging sun.

The full, spectacular show doesn't take very long and within moments, it had broken free of its prison and was hanging in the newly minted sky. It was lovely… just sitting here quietly with Wyatt and sharing something so beautiful.

"My ex-fiancé—David—reached out to me

through Facebook," I say suddenly, succumbing to the impulse to share this with Wyatt.

He turns his head to look at me, his eyes wide and curious. "What's he want?"

"I have no clue. Said he was checking on me to see how I was. Said he wanted to talk... explain a little more about what happened between us."

Wyatt turns his face back out toward the beach, staring thoughtfully at the water. "I guess I don't understand what more he needs to explain. I know you only gave me the short version of what happened, but you applied to the BRIU... he said he wouldn't move, asked you to pull the application, and when you didn't, he broke things off."

"That's the gist of it," I say quietly.

"Then he has nothing to explain," Wyatt says as he turns to look back at me. His blue eyes are so light in the morning sun, his dark lashes making them pop even more brilliantly.

Seriously, I could get lost in those eyes.

"Yes, his position was clear," I admit as I turn to look back out at the water. "I guess... I guess I just wanted to know why he didn't bother to talk to me about it. Just gave me a unilateral decision without giving me a chance to make things work."

Wyatt leans back in the sand, punching his elbows down deep and then bending his legs.

"Let me ask you something," he starts out. "Could you have fixed it? Were you ever going to pull that application? Were you going to stunt your FBI career and agree to live out said career in Pittsburgh?"

I don't even have to give serious thought to those questions. "No. I was not going to pull that application. It's been my dream to work in the BRIU since I was a little girl."

Wyatt jerks up from his position and turns to me with a shocked look. "Really? I don't know many little girls that aspire to be in a particular unit of the FBI."

I smile at him and push up from the sand until I'm standing. As I look down at him, I say, "Well, my dad was a member of the BRIU. He was killed in the line of duty when I was six months old, so I didn't even remember him, but I wanted to follow in his footsteps. Became obsessed with it actually."

Wyatt stands up from the sand, brushing his jeans off. He holds his hand out to me, and I take it.

As we stroll down toward the water, and then angle south, he says, "That's tough about losing your dad so young. At any age really. But I can see how that would totally drive your goals."

"Or maybe it was a silly pipe dream for me to be chasing after a career my father had. I mean... he's virtually unknown to me. Maybe I sacrificed a relationship over something that shouldn't have been important to me to begin with."

Wyatt squeezes my hand. "And yet... it seems to me that the fact you didn't know your father at all makes you getting in with the BRIU all that more important. It's the only way you can connect with him."

I turn to look at him... surprised that he would make that leap. I mean... I know deep down inside that's what's driving me, but I didn't expect Wyatt to get it because David clearly didn't. I had started doubting myself, figuring my reasoning was stupid.

"Thank you," I say as I stop our walk and turn to him. "For validating my feelings."

Wyatt's hands go to my waist... With a tug, I'm pressed up against him. I wrap my arms around his back and hold him tight.

"Listen," he says with his chin resting on the top of my head. "There is nothing your ex can say that will explain his actions away. He had his reasoning. You had yours. He disrespected you by not giving you the chance to talk about it... to at least see if it could be worked out. You following me?"

I nod against him and press in closer, because he feels so good to me.

"He knows he fucked up. I suspect the reason he wants to talk to you is not to check in on you and give you an explanation. I suspect he's back in touch with you because he's missing you. I'd bet my last dollar that if you were to call him right now, he'd want to get back together. I'm even betting that he will be more than willing to move away with you."

Pulling back, I arch a skeptical eyebrow at Wyatt.

"No way. You don't know David. He was adamant about not leaving Pittsburgh. That's his home. He loves it a lot… clearly more than me."

"Maybe that was his initial reaction to your refusal to pull the application, but Andrea… I've only spent a few days with you, and I sure as hell don't want you to leave. That's because I've come to understand what an amazing, beautiful, and talented woman you are. Trust me… this dude is seeing the error of his ways. I can almost guarantee you that he's wanting back in with you."

My hands drop away from Wyatt's waist and I turn away from him, rubbing my finger against my chin in thought. Could that be it? Does David want to just forget about what happened and try to start over?

Turning back to Wyatt, my face flushes red with anger and I grit my teeth hard.

"Um… I'm guessing by that look on your face, that's not something you're interested in?" he says with a smirk.

"That really pisses me off," I say indignantly. "If that's what he's thinking… that he could just break my heart… dump me… cast me aside, and then when he's a bit lonely or probably not getting any pussy, he comes crawling back to me."

Wyatt's eyebrows raise sky high, and he starts laughing about the time the word "pussy" comes out of my mouth. He reaches out and pulls me back into his arms, his shoulders shaking with humor.

"My girl has a dirty mouth when she gets mad," he observes.

"You're fucking right I do," I grouse, and because that makes Wyatt laugh even harder, I can't stop the chuckles that come out.

We resume our walk and the laughter dies down. Then Wyatt says something that makes my heart melt just a little bit more for him.

"Seriously though… if you need to explore this with him, you should. I wouldn't hold you back from that."

I turn to look at him. "I don't want to."

He rewards me with a bright grin and loops his arm around my shoulder, pulling me in so our hips bump as we walk along the shore. "Good. I don't want you to either, but I thought I'd be a gentleman."

And that right there sort of sealed my fate where Wyatt Banks was concerned.

CHAPTER 21

Wyatt

I PULL INTO the parking lot of the Last Call and see Hunter's car. Figured he'd be here and he's just the person I need to rant to. There are three other cars in the lot, but it's too early for any of his employees to be here so I'm assuming those were from patrons of last night's crowd too drunk to drive home.

Still bristling with anger, I shut the car off and get out. I stalk up to the entrance door and pull on it, but it's locked. That's easily fixed by a swift banging on the tinted, Plexiglas door and in less than fifteen seconds, Hunter's there opening up to me.

"What the hell are you doing here?" Hunter asks with surprise as I stomp past him.

"I'm here because of your annoying and completely frustrating fiancée. Dude, you have to get her under control," I grit out.

Hunter starts chuckling and walks past me. I follow him back to his office. "She must have done something really annoying then. I seem to recall you warning each and every one of us before you left the bar Saturday night that you would rain—what were the words—hellfire and destruction down on any of us if we disturbed you and Andrea for the next four days. The fact you'd leave your woman to come here to complain to me about Gabby means that she's really on your shit list."

He walks around his desk and sits down, leaning back in his chair. I flop down in a chair opposite his desk and kick my legs out. "Yeah… I didn't leave my woman to come complain about Gabby. Gabby stole my woman out of my house this morning."

"What?" Hunter asks, trying desperately to hide the amusement on his face.

"That brat showed up half an hour ago, banging on my door again. I wouldn't let her in, of course, but she stood on my porch and demanded that Andrea had to come out to breakfast with her."

"Wait?" Hunter exclaims, sitting up straight in his chair. "You mean she invited Andrea to the exclusive girls' club breakfast every Monday at The Sand Shark?"

I nod… painfully.

"You mean… that hallowed establishment that has seen Gabby, Casey, and Alyssa meet exclusively for breakfast every Monday morning for like a millennium?"

"They did let Savannah into the club," I mutter.

"Yeah… but like only because she had to sign

some sort of blood pact or something," Hunter says, shaking his head in amazement. "This is huge, dude. You know that right?"

"Fuck yeah, it's huge," I agree and sit forward angrily. "I now have to figure out how to rain hellfire and destruction down on your fiancée without ruining our friendship."

Hunter laughs and leans back in his chair again. "Seriously, Wyatt… this is huge in another way. She's been accepted."

"To breakfast," I add on.

"No… she's been accepted into our circle. No woman you've ever dated before has been afforded that. That means they're keeping her. I suggest you figure out a way to do the same."

And that is the source of my true frustration.

Not only have I decided that Andrea needs to remain a fixture in my life, but my friends have equally done so. This is big… a huge endorsement, and on the one hand, it helps to validate that my feelings for her are strong and true. They would never accept her so easily if they didn't think she was the right one for me.

I think she is… the right one, that is.

And now, apparently, the girls do too, and of course, the men will follow right along, because fuck… every one of my bros are heart whipped.

The frustration comes from knowing that Andrea is leaving on Saturday morning, and I don't need

Gabby kidnapping her from my house to know that there is something special going on between us.

I have no clue what it means for the long haul, but I do know that it won't be over when she gets on that plane to fly back to Pittsburgh.

"Listen, man," Hunter says confidently. "Long-distance relationships suck, but they are workable. Y'all will find your groove."

"Oh yeah?" I ask skeptically, because the real reason I'm here is because Hunter actually has some experience with this concept. "You chose to give up your surfing career so you could stay here with Gabby."

"That's true enough. But I didn't give up my career to stay here with Gabby because I was afraid the long-distance thing wouldn't work. I know it would have worked, because when you love someone, you simply find a way to make it work."

"So then why give up the career? If you're so sure it would have worked," I ask, and this is a really important question, so I listen raptly for his answer.

"Because I just didn't want to deal with the hurt of being away from her. And besides… I was ready to give up my career. I had already retired if you'll remember and came back home to open up Last Call. I had already walked away from surfing before I fell in love with Gabby. I just chose not to go back after."

Well, shit… that doesn't really help me at all. I'm unfortunately very tied to an active and satisfying career. I'm also very tied to this community. While Andrea isn't tied to Pittsburgh, she's tied to the FBI, and that includes a very sought-after position in Quantico, Virginia. Even if she doesn't get into the BRIU, the closest she could ever be reassigned—if she did want to be reassigned—is the Raleigh field office. That's still three hours away, which would still make this a long-distance relationship.

And shit... for all I know, feelings here are one sided. Here I am, thinking of potential ways to keep this relationship alive, and Andrea may not feel that way at all.

Sighing with more frustration, because Hunter didn't really provide me with anything helpful, I stand up from the chair. It seems to me that what I really need is a frank conversation with Andrea. I just have to figure out how to broach it with her.

"Where are you going? Want to help me do inventory and stocking?" Hunter asks as he stands up from behind his desk.

"Um... that would be a big fat, fuck no," I tell him with a grin. "Besides... I'm hungry. Going to go get some breakfast."

"You are not going to The Sand Shark?" he asks with a mock gasp and his hand over his heart. "You'll get shanked by those girls if you show up. Men are not allowed."

"Brody ate with them one time," I counter confidently as I walk out of his office and head for the front door.

"Yeah... but I heard a rumor they put poison in his food or something. Maybe it was a laxative, I'm not sure. Just be careful, dude... those girls are dangerous when you encroach on their territory," he says in all seriousness.

"Want to come?" I ask as I step out into the parking lot.

"No fucking way," Hunter says as he prepares to close the door and lock it behind me. "I like my balls intact."

♦

I STEP INTO The Sand Shark, do a quick sweep of my eyes, see about ten different people I know, and then pin my gaze at the far back of the restaurant.

Gabby and her kidnapping posse are sitting at a round table that seats five. Her back is to me with Alyssa to her left and Casey to her right. Andrea and Savannah round out the table and are facing my way. As if she can sense me standing there, Andrea's eyes cut over Gabby's shoulder to meet mine.

Her eyes light up in happiness—over seeing me—and it's like a homing beacon. I start walking toward her, nodding distractedly as a few people call out "Good Morning" to me.

It's inevitable, really, that Gabby notices Andrea's attention has gone elsewhere because she's turning in her chair to look my way. Then she's out of her chair and by the time I reach them, her hands are out in front of her and she's saying, "No, Wyatt. Absolutely not. You are not invited, so go away."

I ignore her, step to the right, and start rounding the table, never taking my eyes off Andrea. Her smile lights up and then turns into a big grin.

"Petey," Gabby yells to the short-order cook behind the counter. "Get me your rolling pin. I need to bash this guy on the head."

I hear Babs, the senior waitress and person you do not want to piss off, hiss back at Gabby. "Pipe down, Gabby Ward, or I'm going to tan your hide."

Glancing across the table, I see Gabby sit down in a huff but she still tries to hold me off. "You can't stay, Wyatt. Say hello, give her a kiss, whatever... but then get gone."

I give her a lazy smile and then turn to the table beside theirs. "Hey Mac... Carl," I say to the two men sitting at a four-seater table. "Mind if I borrow a chair?"

"Help yourself," Mac says with a grin, completely enjoying the show.

I slide the chair out and over, pushing it right in between Andrea and Savannah. "Scoot over a bit, Savannah. Give a man a little room to sit next to his girl."

Savannah sighs, because she's definitely a romantic at heart, and dutifully moves over.

When I'm ensconced at the table, I wrap my hand around the back of Andrea's head and pull her to me for a slow, long kiss. I do this mainly to piss Gabby off, but also to hear that little breathy sigh that I know Andrea will give me.

She does, and I release her.

With a bright smile, I turn back and give the women a big smile. Leaning my elbows on the table, I say, "So what are we talking about today?"

Gabby crosses her arms over her chest and gripes, "Men aren't allowed in on our conversation here."

"You let Brody eat with you one time," I shoot back, and I see Alyssa lower her face, covering her mouth with her hand to suppress a laugh.

"He paid for it," Gabby shoots back.

"Yeah... I heard you put laxative in his food or something," I say as I reach over to Andrea's glass of water and pull it toward me for a sip.

"It was poison," Gabby snaps.

"Whatever," I say dismissively. "The point is... I'm staying so I can spend as much time with my girl as possible. Deal with it."

"That's so romantic," Savannah breathes out.

I turn a grateful smile toward her. "Thank you," I say sincerely. "I think so too."

I know this is pissing Gabby off royally, and I know I shouldn't take such immense pleasure from that... but damn it... this is fun.

"Well, you know I think romance is generally for

the birds," Casey butts in, "but I spent all day and night yesterday with this man that really tried to woo me with romance. He brought me to his yacht... and there was champagne, flowers, and a personal masseuse. He went all out."

"Wow," Alyssa says in surprise. "I didn't think you'd ever be romanced, Casey."

"Oh, I wasn't," she says dismissively. "I mean, it was a nice effort... bonus points and all that. And sure... I gave him a stellar blow job in appreciation, but—"

"Okay," I blurt out, repressing the urge to slap my hands over my ears. "I do not want to hear that. You're like my little sister, for God's sake."

I hear Andrea giggle beside me, and Gabby's arms uncross as she looks like this could start to get interesting.

Casey just stares straight at me, completely disregarding my request. "Well, we didn't invite you here, Wyatt, and sorry... but this is what girls talk about. If you can't handle the fact that I like sex with wealthy men, and I like it a lot, and I also like to share the deets with my bestie girls, then you need to just leave."

I snap my mouth shut, because I know my jaw had sunk almost down level with my collarbone over her proclamation. I look around the table, and each woman stares back at me with resolve. I am encroaching on their girl time, and if I'm going to be a

WITH A TWIST

temporary member of their little gang this morning, I need to accept the things they talk about.

Turning to Andrea briefly, I narrow my eyes at her. "What exactly have you shared with the girls about us?"

She smiles at me sweetly and pats me on the knee. "Nothing other than how we met."

I let out a breath of relief because the way we met was highly unconventional and the ways in which we "explored" our attraction to each other before we left Raleigh still causes me to feel guilty. It's not something we've talked about but that will get rectified before she leaves.

Rewarding her with a relieved smile, I turn back to Casey and sweep my hand out in a grand gesture. "Then by all means... continue on with your story."

And she does.

For the next five minutes, I listen to Casey give the details about some young, rich playboy who is yachting down the coast and who she apparently had a very raunchy time with last night. According to Casey, he's the perfect man because he's rich, hung like a racehorse—which fuck... that caused me to blush—and most importantly to her, he was leaving town today.

I always knew Casey shunned relationships, preferring men to come and go out of her life like a revolving door. I have no clue where that stems from because she has a wonderful home life with devoted, loving parents and two brothers that have fallen deeply in love. She has a lot to offer, but I have to wonder… what is it keeping her from settling down?

It's slightly disconcerting to hear that she slept with this guy without even really knowing him, but then I feel like a neon sign with a big arrow that says, "Hypocrite" is pointed down at me. I know I've certainly had my share of one-night stands, as has Hunter. Brody… not so much as he spent five years in prison and then fell in love with Alyssa, but still… I know it's generally acceptable for men to be able to sleep around, and they're just considered studs. Women do it, and they're called whores.

But that doesn't set right… not when I'm looking across the table at Casey. I don't see her as that. Instead, I just see her as an incredibly strong, mature, and liberated woman who believes that whatever is good for the goose is good for the gander.

It's hard to argue with that line of thinking.

Luckily, this group of women now includes Alyssa and Savannah, who have babies, and the talk eventually turns to that. That's definitely more along the lines of what I prefer the women discuss, but even that turns boring to me.

Not because I have anything against kids. On the contrary, I love them to distraction and dote on my nieces and nephews. I want at least two myself, but my limit would be four.

But this is boring me because as Andrea sits next

to me, her hand casually resting on my thigh, all I can think about is getting her alone again.

To fuck, to talk, to cuddle, to walk along the beach, to laugh.

All the things we have been doing oh so damn well since she arrived.

I want more of it, and time is ticking.

But I don't drag her out, and I continue to add into the conversation when I can. I do that because she's having a good time with the girls, and I'm not about to take that away from her.

Besides, I like knowing she's so accepted into our crowd. I like that she likes that as well. It means that our foundation keeps building steadily.

Breakfast is ordered... it's served, and I eat it quickly and without taking my eyes off my plate so that poison and/or laxatives are not placed on my food. I laugh when appropriate, and I watch Andrea start to make new friends, grateful that it's another way to cement her to me.

CHAPTER 22

Andrea

WYATT WALKS OUT on the back deck, a bottle of wine tucked under his arm and two glasses held tight by the stems in one hand. With the other, he pulls the sliding door closed.

"Ready?"

I pat the blanket folded over my arm. "Ready."

But not really. I'm not ready for us to take one more step forward in time, because it's our last night together and I'm sure as hell not ready to leave tomorrow. I'm not excited about returning to Pittsburgh or even returning to my job. I'm only vaguely excited about the prospect of getting into the BRIU.

All of that... my life... just seems so far removed at this moment. It seems like a dull dream. It's like the gray of Kansas before Dorothy landed in the brilliance of Oz.

I follow Wyatt down the deck stairs, and we only walk a few feet away before he motions for me to spread out the blanket. After both of us have our butts firmly planted, side by side, facing the moonlit ocean, Wyatt cracks open the wine—twisting the cap actually—and pours us each a glass.

He holds his glass angled toward me, and I tap mine against it.

Clink.

"So… are we celebrating your last night here?" he asks softly.

"Not something I think I want to celebrate," I murmur.

"Me either."

"This sucks."

"Big time."

"This is deep conversation."

"The deepest."

We both start laughing, and he bumps his shoulder against mine. I push back gently against his and then take a sip of my wine.

After I swallow, I tell him, "So… I sent a message back to David."

"Yeah?"

"Mmmm. Hmmm," is all I say before I take another sip of my wine. The ocean is lovely… a pure cloudless night with a bright moon, causing the water to look like it's covered in floating, crushed diamonds.

"Are you going to tell me what you said to him?"

"Sure. Why not."

His head swivels to me, and I can see the moon

glittering in his light blue eyes filled with serious interest. He patiently waits for me to divulge.

"I just told him that I wasn't interested in talking. That it was best that we just both keep moving forward with our lives, but I appreciated his concern. I assured him I was fine."

"Did he respond?"

"No," I say while rubbing my finger around the edge of my glass. "But I expect him to. David was never one of those types that let me have the last word."

Wyatt snorts. "Maybe I need to step in and play the jealous boyfriend role."

I reach out and lace my free hand with his. Leaning my head on his shoulder, I ask in a teasing tone, "Is that what you are? My boyfriend."

His hand reflexively squeezes mine but his tone isn't teasing when he says, "Boyfriend sounds so juvenile. All I know is that you're mine and I'm yours."

My smile comes immediately... the warmth in my chest right behind. Lifting my head up, I reach over and push my wineglass into the sand. Coming up to my knees, I turn to face him and take his wineglass away. It finds a resting spot next to mine.

I scoot in closer to him, maneuvering my way in between his legs. I keep on scooting, and only when his arms are wrapped securely around me do I lean in to kiss him. When his tongue is against mine, I bring my hands up to cup his face. I pour every bit of feeling into my kiss, not so I have to avoid the words, but because I just want this to be a prelude to them.

When I pull away, I tell him as honestly as I can, "We can make this work. I know we can."

He smiles at me... bigger and brighter than the moon. "You think so, huh?"

Dropping my hands from his face to his shoulders, I sit back on my haunches a bit so he can see me clearly. "Wyatt... when we were in Simon's office... when Lance forced us to... you know."

"Yeah, I know, baby," he says softly.

"I wasn't afraid. I wasn't repulsed. I didn't feel like I was doing my duty to save the mission. I didn't give a shit that Lance was standing there, and I sure as hell didn't crawl across the carpet toward you because he was making me."

Wyatt's head tilts to the side... a tiny huff of breath comes out of his lips. "Why did you do it then?"

"Because of the way you were looking at me. The way you were aching for me... the sorrow you held for me, because I was in that position. You were angry with yourself that you couldn't protect me. You blamed yourself because I was on my knees before you. I saw all of that, Wyatt. I saw into your soul in that moment. And I knew... I knew that you were something different... something special, in my life. I may not have pieced all of this together right away. I surely didn't know that I would be sitting here with you in this moment, but I knew you were brought into my life for a reason."

"Andrea," he says softly, almost pleadingly, as his hands now come up to frame my face.

"So, why did I crawl across that carpet toward you? Why did I refuse to fake that act and take you into my mouth instead?" I ask him fervently.

He shakes his head... because he still doesn't understand it.

"I did it because my heart told me to do it. In that moment, my heart was already offering up a piece of itself to you. It had decided that I was going to be yours, and you were going to be mine."

Wyatt's fingers squeeze against my temple slightly. He does this because he's moved by what I've said so far, and I know this by the naked emotion on his face. But there's one more thing I need to say.

"I know this may seem weird... having feelings like that. And I really didn't recognize what was going on at that time until just recently... as I was trying to get a handle on how I felt about you now. All I know is it's really how I felt about you then. Maybe not the same level, but that's where it started taking root. When I took you in my hands... my mouth. Such an intimate act and it was beautiful for me. I didn't feel degraded... only fulfilled."

"Fuck, Andrea," Wyatt growls out, and his arms band around me, jerking me into him, his face going into my neck. "Fuck, baby. I've felt so bad about that. It's weighed on me, you have to know that, or you wouldn't have bothered to give me that speech."

"I know," I murmur as I snuggle in deeper to him. "I know and I want *you* to know that you have nothing to feel bad about. That was our first beautiful moment together. Our second was in that locker room… your face between my legs—"

"So beautiful," he says and squeezes me hard.

"You see why I had to come and see you?" I ask him. "I had to let this continue to play out. We weren't done."

I don't know how he does it, but one minute I'm kneeling before Wyatt and the next I'm in his arms and he's carrying me up the stairs, blanket and wine completely forgotten. My palm lays against his chest and I can feel how hard his heart is pounding.

Straight to his room… his stride never wavers. He sets me gently down on the floor and when I'm standing steadily, we both proceed to remove each other's clothes. We do this taking brief moments to kiss, stroke, or squeeze exposed skin. But there's an urgency riding hard within us so we don't linger too long.

When we're both naked, he turns away from me, crawls onto the bed, turns over, and lies on his back. Reaching a hand out, he says, "Come here, Andrea. I want you straddling my face."

I swallow hard and his words alone have the space

between my legs cramping hard with anticipation. Reaching out… I take his hand and he pulls me toward him. One knee goes up on the bed, then another, and then both his hands are on me and he's pulling me up his body.

"Yeah, baby," he rasps out. His muscles bulge as he lifts me slightly, pulling me right up and over his face. His breath is hot on me, and I shudder when he says, "Yeah… want you on my face so I can show you that you're mine. Then I want you straddling my aching cock. I want you to ride me… show me that I'm yours."

"I can do that," I manage to whisper but then that turns into a gasp… then a moan as his head tilts up and his mouth closes over me.

Oh, God… oh, my freakin' God. Wyatt's mouth and tongue should be licensed weapons, because surely, I'm going to perish from how good this feels. I grab onto the headboard, because if I don't, I will collapse on him due to the weakness in my legs.

Wyatt devours me from below, groaning his own pleasure into me… causing vibrations and skittering impulses to fire off throughout my body. It's seconds only… maybe milliseconds… but I don't hold it back and I come harder than I ever have in my life.

And because I want to show Wyatt that he is indeed mine, I manage to haul my pleasure-flushed body down his and sink onto his hard shaft. I ride him good and long, I fire off one more time, and then he's coming deep inside of me, knifing up into a sitting position, and fusing his mouth with mine.

He pours out the most beautiful moan into my mouth while he shoots into me, and I think to myself… *yeah, we are never going to be done.*

♦

MUCH LATER… AFTER Wyatt is asleep, I grab my laptop and creep out into his living room. In the dark, I boot it up and wait for it to connect to his Wi-Fi. I pull up my browser, which preloads with open tabs for Facebook, Twitter, the FBI secure-server email, and Google.

I ignore the notification that tells me I have a message on Facebook, knowing in my gut it's from David. But I'm not interested in what he has to say. I'll read it at some point, and maybe I'll need to respond, but maybe I'll decide I don't want to. Regardless, he's not a priority to think about.

I quickly check my work email. Two new cases are awaiting me… both involving bank fraud. We'll have to bring in consultants from our White-Collar division. Nothing that causes me concern but certainly doesn't cause excitement. An email from Dale Lambert though has my heart beating a tad faster when I see that his subject line says, "BRIU Application".

Clicking on the email, I try to read it slowly, but

my eyes keep flying forward over the words. I see "received my update," "impressed," and "another interview". Taking a deep breath, I read the email more slowly, and it's good news. The BRIU is interested in another interview with me, in light of my efforts and success with the Simon Keyes bust.

Sitting back into the couch cushions, I just stare at my computer a moment. I feel happy… proud of myself. Finally, I'm one step closer to achieving my goal. And yet, I don't feel exhilarated. No full-blown elation. I would have thought this moment would at least bring a fist pump or a strange shake-your-booty-type dance.

Shrugging my shoulders, I log out of the secure server and flip over to Google, which was my main reason for coming out here. I couldn't sleep… my mind on absolute overdrive fretting over the next time I could see Wyatt again. I know it seems a little obsessive, but I'm already missing him and I haven't even left yet.

I know Wyatt will gladly come and visit me in Pittsburgh. I'm sure he will at some point. But while the weather is still spectacular, I thought maybe I could find a place that was halfway in between our two homes, where we could spend time outdoors. Some place romantic… special.

Annapolis, Maryland came to mind. It's special to me because my dad graduated from the Naval Academy there.

I've been there twice. The first time was after I graduated from UVA. I took a trip there by myself... seeking a connection to my dad, who was still inspiring me from the grave to be an FBI agent. I went after my college graduation because it was the first big milestone I had accomplished on my own, and I wanted him to be proud of me. It seemed fitting to go tour his Alma Mater, a place I know was special to him because he wrapped me in a Navy blanket. My dad had served six years with the U.S. Navy after he graduated, and then he became an FBI agent.

The second time I visited was after my first BRIU interview at Quantico. I took an extra day and went to Annapolis. I didn't walk the Academy's campus on this trip, but rather stayed in a hotel down on the waterfront, completely charmed by the cobblestone streets and eclectic shops. I sat at an outdoor cafe and sipped at a latte while I thought of how my dad made it into the BRIU just three years after he became an agent. I was convinced at that time, more than ever, that I was following correctly in my dad's footsteps.

Now, I'm not so sure, since the prospect of another interview is causing only some mildly happy feelings, and I'm much more concerned with finding a nice place for Wyatt and me to meet.

Yes... Annapolis is the perfect place for us to get together, and I'll have to verify with him in the morning when he can get away so I can get it planned.

I know we can make this work.

CHAPTER 23

Wyatt

I PULL UP to my sister's house in downtown Edenton, North Carolina and parallel park on the street. Aubrey married a small-town attorney by the name of Chester Plum... I kid you not... and they live in a gorgeous, pre-Civil war home just a hundred yards off the Albemarle Sound, and a little over an hour away from Nags Head.

It was mandated that I attend Sunday dinner at her house, and since Andrea and I couldn't get together this weekend because she had to work, I decided not to rock the boat and spend some time with my family.

I've seen my parents a few times since returning to Nags Head after the slave bust went down. They only live about two miles from me so it's easy to get over to visit them. Not so easy to get over to Edenton to see Aubrey though but today's trip was warranted. My parents and my other two sisters, Lacy and Jillian, are going to be there along with Lacy and Jillian's husbands and an entire boatload of kids.

My sisters didn't waste any time getting married. All three of them are older than I am and were fine only to aspire to be a good wife and mother. While Lacy went to college, her arts degree has gathered dust since that time, and now they spend their days shuffling kids to soccer practice and making nice, southern homes.

I know I sound like I have little respect for that, but that's not true at all. In fact, my sisters are all beautiful and loving women. Their husbands adore them, as they should, and their kids are wonderful. They lead damn good lives, and I couldn't be happier for them.

While Lacy and Jillian live in the Outer Banks, I don't get to see them as often as I do my parents. It's just because work keeps me so damned busy, that if I have free time for visiting, it's usually to see my parents. I'm lucky though, as sometimes they'll be over visiting as well.

But today is a day for a Banks family get together and Aubrey is hosting. I step through the white, picket swinging gate that borders around Aubrey and Chester's cream, bricked home. The front of the house faces the street and has a small, covered porch only big enough to walk up to the door. But along each side of the two-story home, they have sprawling, veranda-style porches filled with glossy, black-painted rocking chairs and large ceiling fans to stir the humid

SAWYER BENNETT

air. Baskets of trailing petunias hang over the railing to create a peaceful space to relax in on a warm, summer evening. I head up to the porch on the east side of the house, because the door on that side leads into the large, open-air country kitchen. I know that's where the family will be gathered.

Just as I reach the door, three of my nephews come barreling out, one of whom clocks me in the hip and yells out, "Sorry, Uncle Wyatt," before disappearing around the side of the house.

"Hellions, all of them," I hear from the door, turning to see Chester standing there.

Now, as a small-town attorney, it's apparently mandatory that you wear seersucker suits, straw hats, and silk bow ties when working. Chester does this to perfection. But when the man relaxes, he really relaxes. He greets me in a pair of frayed khaki shorts with a chocolate stain on one thigh and a threadbare Boston Celtics t-shirt that has a large hole under one armpit.

"Hey man," I say as I walk up the steps.

"Welcome to family day," he says drily as we shake hands. "Come on in… I've got beer."

I walk into the kitchen, and I am immediately assaulted with the smell of baked ham and sweet potatoes. A whirlwind of remaining hellions circle around me, grabbing onto my legs and hugging my waist. After all the nieces and nephews are appropriately patted on the head, all except for Jillian's littlest... Annie Lynn... who insists on staying wrapped around my lower leg, I make my way over to greet the rest of the adults.

For the next ten minutes, I shoot the shit, sip on some beer, and lug around Annie Lynn, who remains attached to my leg. We talk about Chester's law practice, Lacy's book club, and Frank—who is married to Jillian—fills me in on his latest business venture... which is apparently an antique store that's for sale.

When dinner is finally served, we all sit around outside at large tables Chester and Aubrey had set out and covered with white tablecloths. The sun starts to set, and although it's on the opposite side of the house, it doesn't stop the Albemarle Sound from turning orange in the dying light.

I look around at my family... healthy, happy, joking, and laughing, and fuck... I want this too.

Almost as if by cue, my phone starts buzzing in my pocket and I pull it out. Andrea's beautiful face stares up at me, and I can't help the smile that comes to my face.

Standing up from my chair, I start walking toward the back of the yard that has a small rose garden and oddly enough... a large, trellised pen covered in chicken wire that houses the pet peacocks my sister raises.

Weird... I know.

"Hey babe," I say as I answer the phone. "Did you

make it back okay?"

"Yeah," she says softly. "Just got in the house and getting unpacked."

The reason Andrea and I couldn't see each other is because she flew to Quantico on Friday for another interview with the BRIU. I didn't begrudge her that, and I'm hoping with all my might that she's offered the position. But damn this weekend fucking sucked without her. It's the first weekend in the last month that we haven't managed to see each other. Our work schedules must have been created from Heaven above, because for the last three weekends, neither one of us had to work.

The first weekend, we met in Annapolis, Maryland. The second weekend, I flew to Pittsburgh. Last weekend, she came back to Nags Head.

All three weekends were spectacular and we made the most of every minute we had together, completely shutting out the world around us. But as each weekend ended, and we were hugging and kissing each other goodbye, it seemed that it was just a little bit harder to let go each time. It was also not lost on us that we wouldn't be able to continue to see each other as often, mainly due to the expense of travel. Our chosen careers unfortunately did not pay enough for us to buy plane tickets every weekend.

I couldn't speak for Andrea, but I know I was getting frustrated. This was only made worse by coming here to Aubrey's and seeing the rest of my family so happy to be with their loved ones.

"How did the interview go?" I ask her, sitting down on a little stone bench that bordered the garden.

"It went fine. They actually seemed interested in me. Talked about the Keyes bust a great deal."

"I'm sure it went more than fine," I tell her. "Because you are the most amazing woman ever, and the most complete, badass FBI chick around, I bet they are going to beg you to join them."

She's silent a moment, and I wonder if I said something wrong. Then she has me smiling.

"Oh, Wyatt," she sighs into the phone. "What did I ever do to deserve you?"

I close my eyes, let her words seep into me, and clear my throat. When I open them, I'm looking at my family sitting at the tables... laughing and eating good food. I want Andrea to sit there.

"I miss you," I tell her.

"And I miss you," she says simply, but those words hold a wealth of emotion in them.

"Listen... I better get going. We're in the middle of dinner."

"Okay," she says wistfully. "Talk tonight?"

"Skype tonight," I correct her. "Want to see that face."

She laughs huskily. "You play your cards right, you'll see more than just my face."

Yeah... didn't need to hear that as my cock jumps

at the thought of Andrea's naked body on Skype. We've done some pretty dirty things the last few weeks over the Internet and while not as satisfying as having my hands on her, there's definitely something to be said about watching each other get ourselves off while we whisper filthy words.

"Thanks, babe," I mutter. "Nothing like attending a family dinner with a hard-on."

She laughs into the phone, makes a purring sort of noise, and then tells me good-bye. I stare at the phone for a moment after she disconnects, immediately feeling the loss of her.

Making a surreptitious adjustment on myself and mentally telling my cock to go back into hiding, I head back over to the group.

"Was that Andrea?" my mom asks in her sweet, southern accent. Glenna Banks is a beautiful woman at sixty-two. She wears her silvering, blonde hair in a sleek bob and her skin still looks as smooth as porcelain. She knows about Andrea because I told her one night when I stopped by her house after work. I just laid it all out to her, knowing that my mom would always be a good sounding board for me.

"Yeah... she just got back to Pittsburgh."

"Where was she?" Aubrey asked, and while I have not talked to my sisters about Andrea, I also know that my mom dutifully filled them in.

"She had an interview with the Behavioral Research and Instruction Unit of the FBI in Quantico.

She's hoping to get a position there."

"Now that sounds impressive," Jillian says.

"I don't know," Frank says. "A woman like that scares me a bit."

Jillian smacks him on the arm. "Why? Because she carries a gun?"

"No, because she's probably way smarter than I am." Frank taps his finger against his temple. "I bet she could probably read minds. Isn't that what they do in that Behavioral unit place?"

We all start laughing, and my father tells Frank he watches too much *Criminal Minds* on TV.

Dessert is served and I have a cup of coffee with mine. After the sun sets, the fireflies come out and the kids start winding down, I know it's time to head back home. I have to get up early for work tomorrow.

My mom walks me out to my car, her arm looped through mine.

"So how are you really doing, sweetheart?" she asks, her voice worried. I know this is a direct question regarding Andrea, because while my mom will always worry over her youngest child and only son who is a police officer, she's also come to accept that part of my life and keeps her worries hidden.

"I'm okay," I tell her as we step through the gate. "Sucks she lives so far away, is all."

"I bet," she says with a squeeze to my arm. We round the front of my Suburban and she releases me so I can get my keys out of my pocket.

"Have you given any thought to maybe moving... to Pittsburgh?" she asks hesitantly.

My head snaps her way, surprise lighting through me. "No... why?"

"No special reason. It's just... when two people love each other, it's not good to be away. It causes hurt and loneliness."

Love? Where did she get love from?

Before I can even ask her that, she goes on. "Wyatt... you've talked about Andrea to me. I watched you just a little bit ago while you were on the phone. This is something special you have with her. Now, I haven't met this girl yet, and that is something you better rectify on her next visit here, but I do know you well, son. The look on your face... the happiness... the peace. All from just talking to her, or talking about her. I don't know if *you* call it love at this point... that's between you and her. But I know what *I* call it."

She looks at me expectantly... as if I should know what to call this.

I'm not sure that I do, so I just tilt my head at her in question.

Standing on her tiptoes, she kisses my cheek. When her feet are planted solidly again, she pats my face with her hand. "I call it destiny, Wyatt."

My mom's words continue to ring inside my head.

Destiny.

It's not a word I'm sure I've ever used in my vo-cabulary before. I certainly never paired that word with what I have with Andrea. But now when I think about how we met... the bond we forged while working together... about reconnecting and the way we seem to be growing closer every day... maybe my mom has it right. Maybe she is my destiny.

What necessarily follows that line of thinking is the concept of love.

If she's my destiny and the future means our paths will merge permanently, that only happens with the added feature of love.

So now I have to consider... is Andrea really my destiny? Do I love her?

I want those answers to be "yes". I don't even have to think about that.

But never having felt love before, I'm just not sure if that's the way to describe this deep, emotional pull I have toward this woman. Is it love when Andrea is the first thing I think of when I wake up in the morning and the last thing I think of when I go to sleep, which doesn't include the million other times I think about her during the day? Is it love that my heart hurts when she's sad, or that I'm fearful of not being able to protect her? When she laughs, I can't help but laugh as well... so is that love? What about that when I'm sunk deep inside of her, and she's staring up at me... completely fulfilled, and my heart squeezes in pleasure. Is that love? Or how about that I ache from loneliness... missing her desperately? Love or not?

I think back to what Hunter told me. About the reason why he gave up his surfing career to be near Gabby.

He said it could have worked... because if you love someone, you make it work. But he said ultimately he just didn't want to deal with the hurt of being away from her.

It was just that simple.

He loved Gabby and being away from her hurt him.

Being away from Andrea hurts me.

Doesn't take a fucking genius to figure out what's going on here.

CHAPTER 24

Andrea

I OPEN THE oven, eyeballing the lasagna I have cooking. I just put it in, and it has a while to go yet. Glancing at my watch, I see I'm running short on time before Wyatt gets here. I still need to get the salad together, pop the wine, light the candles, and um… I need to get naked. He said he would call and give me a heads up when he hit my neighborhood, so I'll at least have a few minutes' notice shed my clothes.

It's been two weeks since we've seen each other, and I think the main priority should be for us to get naked. In fact, I'm loving my grand plan to meet him at the door without a stitch of clothes on, and well… we'll let nature take its course.

But first… the salad.

I open the fridge and pull out the big bag of mixed lettuce. A quick swipe of the knife into the plastic and a hard shake into a wooden bowl, and voila… the salad is complete.

If only life were so easy… if it were like a big bag of salad you could shake out and where it all lands is how it should be.

That would be the easy way, but it leaves too much to chance. And when it comes to Wyatt… I don't want to take any chances.

So, I've been giving my life some serious thought. I've evaluated my goals, and then reevaluated them. I've prioritized what's important to me, and when I weigh all considerations, I've come up with some surprising conclusions.

Surprising and one somewhat crazy conclusion, and yet… what I've decided feels right.

So very right.

I can't wait to talk to Wyatt about it when he gets here, but first things first. We've been apart too long and talk can wait. The sex can't.

I reach into my utility drawer beside the stove and pull out the matches, but before I can take a step into the living room to light the dozen candles I laid out, my phone rings.

Crap… time's almost up. Pulling it out of my pocket, I answer, "Circle around my block twice, babe. I'm not quite ready for you."

"Um… Andrea?" I hear a hesitant voice ask.

"David?" I say with shock and an equal amount of dismay.

"Hey," he says jovially. "It's good to hear your voice."

I glance at my watch again, over to the book of matches in my hand... the bowl of salad on the counter. I don't have time for this.

But I try to be as gentle as I can. "David... hi... um, listen... now is really not a good time—"

"Listen... I know you told me that you've moved on, and I respect that, but I just think if we could sit down and talk, you'd see that we could—"

"I'm sorry, David," I butt in before he can start spilling his guts to me. "But I truly don't have time. I'm expecting company any minute."

"Who is he?" he asks in a dead voice.

"Pardon?"

"When you answered the phone... you said "babe". Unless you started batting for the other team, that means you were expecting a man to call you. So who is he?"

Anger surges through me, not because he's questioning me, but because he's cutting into my precious time to finish getting ready for Wyatt. "David... that's not any of your business."

"Jesus Christ, Andrea. We were engaged, and you've seemed to move on awful easily from me," he sneers.

"Just as easily as you walked out the door on me," I say quietly. "Doesn't that tell you something? This was awful easy for both of us."

David is silent... processing my harsh words, contemplating the next best thing to say to me.

I don't give him the chance. "I'm sorry, David. But I have moved on, and there is someone else. Someone very special. And I only wish for you to find the same thing. So please... move on with your life and be happy. That's what I'm going to do."

The doorbell rings. I look at the book of matches in my hand... over to the bowl of salad on the counter... down to my fully clothed body. Damn... Wyatt didn't call me to give me a heads up.

"Andrea... darling... let's just meet and talk about this before you make any hasty decision—"

I press the disconnect button on my phone and toss it onto the counter... David absolutely forgotten. Instead, I concentrate on my pulse, which has sped up knowing that Wyatt is on the other side of my front door.

There's no time to light the candles or strip down. I do spare three seconds to do an excited, happy jig— right in place—then I run to the front door.

I pull it open, and right there... standing before me... the only truly important thing in my life right now. He takes one step in and I'm in his arms, his mouth is on mine. We kiss as if starved. I pull on him... urging him closer to me. I'd immerse him inside of me if I could.

When Wyatt pulls back, my lips tingling from his onslaught, he looks down at me and says, "Hey baby. I missed you."

"God, I missed you too," I tell him, and then

push my face into his chest for a hug.

One of his hands comes to the back of my head and his lips press into my hair. "I have something important to talk to you about. But first... and I'm sorry, baby... but I need to fuck you. It's all I've been thinking about for the last two weeks."

That's all I needed to hear, and I love how we clearly have the same priority in mind. My hands start working at his belt but I glance up at him briefly. "I have something important to talk to you about too, but it can wait until after we have sex."

His mouth is on mine again, and he's pulling at my clothes.

"Door," I manage to gasp and he kicks his foot back, slamming it shut and sparing the neighbors.

◆

WE'VE GONE FROM fully naked, fully writhing, and fully moaning to semi-dressed and eating lasagna on my couch. The candles never got lit and the salad was ignored. The wine, although a nice touch, was also ignored in favor of two bottles of ice-cold water to quench the thirst we had worked up.

Sighing in contentment because my lust for Wyatt has been satisfied—for now—and my belly is almost filled, I look at him sitting on one end of the couch. He's only wearing his jeans, halfway zipped up, with his legs stretched out and bare feet resting on my coffee table. I chose to sit at the other end, wearing only my t-shirt and underwear, sitting cross-legged and facing him.

"This is really good, baby," he says before stuffing another bite of cheesy mess in his face.

"It did turn out good, didn't it?" I respond, staring overly long at the start of his happy trail peeking out of his unzipped jeans.

"Keep your eyes on your food," he teases, and I glance up to see him smirking at me.

I smile, duck my face, and take another bite of lasagna. I'm so freaking happy he's here, but I'm a little nervous about how he'll react to my idea. Even though we've both been very clear in our feelings so far, which I think are parallel to each other, there is still some doubt in my mind that Wyatt wants the same things I do for the long haul. It's not a subject we've discussed because the physical distance between us presents quite the wall of opposition.

"When do you think you'll hear from the BRIU about the position?" Wyatt asks.

Distractedly, I look over at him. "What? Oh… they made me an offer a few days ago."

Wyatt's body stills, the fork in his hand stopping in mid-scoop. He blinks once at me, and then removes his feet from my coffee table. Leaning forward, he sets his plate down, then leans over and takes mine from my hand, also setting it on the coffee table.

"They offered you a position?" he asks quietly.

"Uh-huh," I say with a sheepish smile on my face.

Wyatt lunges at me, wraps his arms around my waist, and hauls me off the couch. Spinning me around, he yells, "That's fucking amazing, Andrea. Fuck… I'm so happy for you."

My hands come up to grip his shoulders and after two complete circles that make me kind of dizzy, I try to take a moment to appreciate his joy for me. Giving him a sweet smile, I lean in and kiss him. "Thanks. It was a bit of a surprise."

Sitting down on the couch, Wyatt tucks me onto his lap and looks at me with excited eyes. "So… when do you start? Shit… there's so much to do. Get your house on the market, get you packed up, and find a new house. Or maybe it's an apartment you'll need in Quantico? Regardless, I'll take some time off work and help get you moved. And what the fuck… how come you didn't tell me? Were you trying to surprise me?"

I stare at Wyatt, completely amazed over his utter abandon. The simple, yet deep happiness he has for me… that I've accomplished a major goal in my life. I'm not sure anyone in my life has ever felt this type of happiness or pride for me before, and it's humbling.

Before I can even answer those questions, he keeps right on going. "Okay, so this is the perfect time I guess to tell you what I've been thinking about. I hadn't really factored the Quantico job into my thoughts, but that actually works out better."

"Better?" I ask with confusion.

Wyatt takes a deep breath, leans in, and kisses me. "You know I'm crazy about you, right?"

"Yeah," I say hesitantly. Even more confused.

"I mean… you really know that about me? That I'm crazy about you and that I miss you terribly when we're apart?"

"Yes," I say emphatically. Because I do know that.

Wyatt takes my hands in his. "What you probably don't know, though, is that I love you. Have for a while."

"You love me?"

"I do," he says simply. "And I can't stand this long-distance shit. It's eating at me, and I fucking hate it."

I'm still reeling from the fact he told me he loved me, but he doesn't seem to notice. Nor has he given me an opportunity to respond. He just keeps on talking.

"So, I was going to talk to you about me moving here to Pittsburgh… to be closer to you. My plan was to maybe try to get on the police force here, or at the very least, I'm sure I could do some type of private investigative work. Not sure how you feel about moving in together… that would be my preference, of course, but I'd respect you if you wanted to take it a little slower. I wouldn't be able to come right away.

I'd need to give some good notice to Nags Head, and then find a job, but I'd bet within a few months, I could make the move. And now... now you tell me about Quantico, and that's even better because it's a lot closer to the Outer Banks, so I could get back frequently to visit."

At this point, I'm staring at Wyatt with my jaw hanging open, a deluge of emotions filtering through me. He'd be willing to move here... or to Quantico to be with me? He'd give up his career, his family, his home and his friends... to be with me?

"I'm sensing this might not have been the best idea I've ever had," Wyatt says quietly, and I can see disappointment on his face.

"Wyatt," I say softly, squeezing his hands. "I wasn't going to take the job at the BRIU. That's what I wanted to talk to you about."

Brows furrowing inward, his head tilting to the side, he asks, "I don't understand. I thought that was your dream?"

"It is," I say, but then I correct myself. "Or, at least, it was my dream."

"Doesn't matter," he says dismissively. "I was willing to come to Pittsburgh and still am if you want."

Again, I don't say anything because he's thrown me for such a loop. I still can't believe this amazing man is willing to give up everything for me.

"You've got that look, baby," Wyatt says as he

chucks me under the chin so I look at him. "Talk to me."

I sit up on Wyatt's lap, change position, and fling one leg over so I can straddle him. When we're face to face, I place my palms on his cheeks and look right into his eyes.

When I'm sure I have his attention, I say, "You've said a lot. Now I've got some things to say to you, okay?"

He nods, his blue eyes sparkling… his lips curled up in a patient smile.

"I love you," I tell him.

His smile gets bigger.

"And while it was my dream to work at the BRIU, I've recently come to realize that a person's dreams can change."

I take a moment to kiss him lightly and say, "Mine have changed."

"Oh, baby," he breathes softly.

"What I wanted to talk to you about was an idea I had… one that would let us be together. I was thinking about leaving the FBI and taking the North Carolina Bar Exam. Maybe setting up a law practice in Nags Head. I thought I could move there to be with you."

Now Wyatt is the one whose jaw drops and his eyes go dark. I can actually tell that he's going to nix this idea, so I keep on. "It's not something that would happen overnight. I'd need several months to study for it, and the next available exam would be February. I'd have to keep working here until then, but I would think by next spring, I could make the move. So we really wouldn't have that long—"

Wyatt places his fingertips over my lips to shut me up. He gives a slow shake to his head. "You are not giving up the BRIU. You've wanted this since you were a little girl."

Pushing his hand away, I say, "I'm not letting you give up your career and your home. You have family and friends there. I'm the more mobile of the two of us."

"Forget it," he says. "You join the BRIU and I'll move to Quantico. That's only about four hours from Nags Head. We'll keep my house and visit there on the weekends."

"But seriously, Wyatt," I say… maybe with a bit of a whine. "That's not my dream anymore. You're my dream. I want to be with you, and this is the best way."

"Not going to argue with you about it, Andrea," he says gruffly.

"Of course you're not," I snap. "Because there's nothing to argue. I didn't accept the position."

"You didn't turn it down yet either, did you?"

"Well, no," I say in a small voice. "But only because I wanted to make sure that you wanted to be with me."

"I do," he says. "More than anything. So it's

Quantico for both of us."

Jumping up from his lap, I plant my feet on the floor, hands to my hips, and stomp my foot. "No, no, no, no. I'm not going to Quantico. I'm going to study for the Bar and then my ass is moving into your cottage with you, and that's final."

Wyatt stares at me... surprise and amusement on his face. His hands reach out and grab me by the hips, pulling me back down on the couch with him. He maneuvers our bodies until I'm under him and he's planted firmly between my legs, supporting his weight on his elbows.

"We at least agree on one thing, right?" he asks with a grin.

"What's that?" I ask petulantly. "That you're a stubborn mule?"

Wyatt laughs, leaning down to nuzzle my neck. When he pulls back, his face is serious... filled with utter devotion. "No... we both at least agree that we love each other. That little tidbit seemed to get lost in the conversation we just had."

My lips purse and then break out into a grin. "Yeah... that is definitely something we both agree on."

His lips touch mine... whisper soft. I open up, and then he kisses me long and slow. My heart swells with so much love that I feel it might burst within my chest.

Wyatt pulls away from me. His eyes pin me in

place. "I love you, Andrea. I think we'll be able to figure this out."

I raise my hand, bring my fingers to his temple, and then thread my fingers backward through his hair. He arches into my touch and his eyes close.

"I love you beyond measure, Wyatt. You're my destiny, so yes, I know we'll be able to figure this out."

Wyatt jerks slightly and his eyes snap open in surprise. "What did you say?"

"That we'll figure this out."

"No... before that?"

"That you're my destiny. Don't you feel it? With everything we've been through together... how we found each other. It's supposed to be."

"Destiny," he repeats with amazement.

"You and I are supposed to be," I murmur. "It's destiny."

He leans down. Another soft kiss. Another sweet smile. "Yeah, baby. It's destiny."

EPILOGUE

Eight Months Later…

I PLACE THE last screw and, with the electric screwdriver, tighten it in. When I lean back so I can make sure the sign is straight, the ladder wobbles on me a bit but then straightens out. I eyeball my work and yup… it's perfect.

I climb down the ladder, pack up my tools, and then push the toolbox across the concrete until it hits the brick wall. Dusting my hands off my pants, I mentally calculate if there's anything else I need to do before Andrea gets here.

Furniture moved in. Check.

Computers hooked up. Check.

Sign hung up. Check.

A car horn gives a short toot behind me, causing me to practically jump out of my skin, and I turn to see Andrea pulling into the storefront parking space. Her eyes are covered by sunglasses, but her smile is big as she looks up through her windshield at the sign I just hung.

The engine shuts off and she's stepping out of the car. She pushes her sunglasses up her face to rest on top of her head and once her eyes are revealed, my heart thumps when I see them sparkling with happy tears.

"Oh, Wyatt... oh, geez... that looks amazing," she says, her voice quaking.

I look up and over my shoulder at the sign.

Andrea Somerville, Attorney at Law

Turning back to her, I say with a wink, "Some of my best work."

She shuts her car door and steps up onto the curb. Her eyes finally leave the sign and come to me, her face awash with emotion. I open my arms, and she steps into them.

"I can't believe this is actually happening," she mumbles into my chest.

I can't either, really.

It's been a long road.

Eight months ago, Andrea and I declared our love for each other. That weekend was filled with long bouts of lovemaking, followed by longer bouts of arguing about what we were going to do. Obviously, I wanted her to take the job at the BRIU, but she was just as adamant about leaving the FBI and practicing law in Nags Head.

Ultimately, what finally caused me to give in was something that she blindsided me with. I can still remember the conversation, clear as day.

"Andrea," I had implored her. "I don't want you to give up this opportunity."

She was lying next to me in her bed, her head on my chest and her hand lightly stroking the skin over my lower abdomen. She was silent for a long while, and I thought that maybe I had finally reached through to her.

I was wrong.

"Wyatt... let's not look at it in terms of what I'm giving up. I want you to consider the things I'll be getting. A new career... one that I put a lot of effort into getting a law degree. I'd be getting you, which is the biggest prize of all. But there's something else important I'm getting... something I don't have here and I won't have in Quantico either. If I come to Nags Head... I'll be getting your family and your friends. I've never had that before. Not really. Kyle's so far away, and we don't see each other. I've never had friends like Gabby, Casey, Alyssa, and Savannah. So, to me, the sacrifice doesn't seem all that much. What I would be getting is so much more."

And just like that, I rolled.

Her speech was pretty, but she had me when she said that she would be getting my family. Because she would be getting a ready-made family with a new mother and father, sisters, and a ton of nieces and nephews. That was important to her, and when I envisioned our own kids playing with my sister's kids... yeah, well... the decision was made.

She was coming to Nags Head.

The next six months were terrible. She stayed in Pittsburgh to work and studied for the North Carolina Bar. When she took it in February, she passed with flying colors. She tried for a few months to get a job, but the Outer Banks isn't very big and there aren't many law firms, so ultimately, she decided to hang out her own shingle and practice criminal law.

I loved it... she went from catching criminals to defending them. My girl was multi-versatile. And I figured... with me catching the crooks and her defending them, the system would be fairly represented and balanced.

"Come on," I tell her as I pull away, grab her hand, and tug her into her new law offices.

She had rented a small space in downtown Nags Head, ironically just two doors down from Savannah's photography studio. They already had a standing lunch date every Wednesday.

The offices are small with a tiny lobby that had room for just a small desk and two chairs, along with one office that was set up for her, a conference room, a small break room, and a bathroom.

I pull her back through the lobby, down the short hall, and to her office. She had ordered the furniture online, and I took the time to set it up today while she was out shopping for office supplies.

She gasps when she steps into the office and takes note of the cherry L-shaped desk that I outfitted with a green banker's lamp. I also had her degrees framed and hung up on her wall behind her desk, as well as a black-and-white beach landscape on the adjacent wall.

Her eyes sweep the room and then come to mine. "It's beautiful. I can't believe it's really mine. That I'm going to be practicing law here."

"You're going to be fantastic at it too," I tell her. "Now… go sit behind your desk so I can see what you look like. Then maybe I can see how you look on top of your desk."

Andrea rolls her eyes at me but trust me… before we lock up the place for the evening, I'm going to have her on top of that desk. We need to break it in nice.

I follow her around and lean my hip on the edge as she sits in the petite, executive chair covered in cream leather.

Her hands come out and smooth along the edge of the desk, a goofy grin on her face. She's fucking gorgeous and adorable all at once.

"This is so surreal," she whispers.

"I even stocked your drawers with some supplies," I say casually, knowing she'll take the bait because she was just out buying supplies. Her brows draw in and she opens the desk drawer in the middle.

My heart pounds as I watch her face. Confusion to surprise to immediately... tears.

Yup. She's crying.

I can't help but smile.

Her hand shakes slightly as she reaches in and pulls out a black, velvet ring box. Swiveling her head to look at me, her lips tremble into a smile.

I'm not one for tradition, but because I want to be down on her level, I go ahead and drop to both knees on the carpet by her chair and reach out to take the box from her.

I open it up and turn it toward her. Her gaze stays on me for just a moment... so much love in her eyes that my chest aches. Then she drops her face slightly and finally looks at the engagement ring I bought her.

She doesn't move. Just stares at it, silvery tears leaking out of the corners of her eyes.

"Baby," I say softly, and her gaze comes to mine. I reach over with my free hand, cup her chin, and pull her in for a kiss. It's soft, and she sighs into my mouth. "I love you, Andrea."

"I love you," she murmurs.

"So say yes, okay?"

"Okay."

"Say yes," I repeat.

"Yes," she says, her eyes blinking and her smile growing bigger.

"Yes!" I exclaim with a fist pump and pull the ring out of the box. It slides beautifully onto her finger, and she doesn't even bother to look at it.

Instead, she launches out of the chair, smacks into my body, and we go crashing backward onto the plush, burgundy carpeting. Her mouth fuses to mine, and love and lust start an immediate battle within me.

"Going to make you so happy," I say and then growl as her hand comes down to cup me.

"You already have," she says before her lips attack my neck. "Now… should we stay down here on the floor or try the desk?"

"Floor," I mutter as my hips buck against her hand that's squeezing my cock. "It's closer."

"Floor's good," she yelps as I flip her over so she's on her back and I'm in charge now.

Our eyes lock as I hover over her. "It's destiny."

"Destiny," she agrees.

Connect with Sawyer online:

Website: www.sawyerbennett.com
Twitter: www.twitter.com/bennettbooks
Facebook: www.facebook.com/bennettbooks

Other Books By Sawyer Bennett

The Cold Fury Hockey Series
(Random House / Loveswept)

Alex

Garrett (releasing 2/17/15)

The Off Series

Off Sides

Off Limits

Off The Record

Off Course

Off Chance

Off Season

The Last Call Series

On The Rocks

Make It A Double

Sugar On The Edge

With A Twist

Shaken Not Stirred (Coming Soon)

The Legal Affairs Series

Objection

Stipulation

Violation

Mitigation

Reparation

Affirmation

Confessions of a Litigation God

The Forever Land Chronicles

Forever Young

Books of the Stone Veil

The Darkest of Blood Magicks

To Catch a Dark Thief

Stand Alone Titles

If I Return

Uncivilized

About the Author

New York Times and USA Today Bestselling Author, Sawyer Bennett is a snarky southern woman and reformed trial lawyer who decided to finally start putting on paper all of the stories that were floating in her head. Her husband works for a Fortune 100 company which lets him fly all over the world while she stays at home with their daughter and three big, furry dogs who hog the bed. Sawyer would like to report she doesn't have many weaknesses but can be bribed with a nominal amount of milk chocolate.

Made in the USA
Lexington, KY
13 January 2015